Esmée is a dynamic mother of two daughters, originally from Freeport, Long Island. An avid traveller with a love for exploring diverse cultures, she spent four enriching years living in Germany. Fluent in Italian and proficient in French, Spanish and German, Esmee embraces the art of communication. She finds joy in painting, writing poetry and delving into the realms of sci-fi and comics, from Star Wars to Marvel. Now, as a first-time author, she brings her unique experiences and vivid imagination to life on the page.

To my moon and star, Avani and Evie, this book is for you, my guiding lights. Your laughter sparks my soul; your strength inspires my dreams. May these pages echo the possibilities that await you and the love that will always be your compass. With all my love, Mom.

Esmee Geier Carmichael

TERAHAVEEN

AUSTIN MACAULEY PUBLISHERS

LONDON * CAMBRIDGE * NEW YORK * SHARJAH

Copyright © Esmee Geier Carmichael 2025

All rights reserved. No part of this publication may be reproduced, distributed, or transmitted in any form or by any means, including photocopying, recording, or other electronic or mechanical methods, without the prior written permission of the publisher, except in the case of brief quotations embodied in critical reviews and certain other non-commercial uses permitted by copyright law. For permission requests, write to the publisher.

Any person who commits any unauthorised act in relation to this publication may be liable to criminal prosecution and civil claims for damages.

This is a work of fiction. Names, characters, businesses, places, events, locales, and incidents are either the products of the author's imagination or used in a fictitious manner. Any resemblance to actual persons, living or dead, or actual events is purely coincidental.

Ordering Information
Quantity sales: Special discounts are available on quantity purchases by corporations, associations, and others. For details, contact the publisher at the address below.

Publisher's Cataloguing-in-Publication data
Carmichael, Esmee Geier
Terahaveen

ISBN 9798891559455 (Paperback)
ISBN 9798891559462 (ePub e-book)

Library of Congress Control Number: 2025902373

www.austinmacauley.com/us

First Published 2025
Austin Macauley Publishers LLC
40 Wall Street, 33rd Floor, Suite 3302
New York, NY 10005
USA

mail-usa@austinmacauley.com
+1 (646) 5125767

Table of Contents

Foreword	11
Prologue	13
Alpha and Omega	*14*
The Twins	*15*
The Beginning	*17*
T'haeri	*22*
Bhabhi Salaah	*31*
Saala Ganatantr	*39*
Chapter 1	46
Chapter 2	52
Interlude	76
Chapter 3	77
Postlude of Chapter 3	82
Chapter 4	85
Prelude to Chapter 5	92
Chapter 5	93
Chapter 6	103
Prelude to Chapter 7	108
Chapter 7	110
Aashvi	*110*

Arunima	*111*
Baidya Nath	*112*
Budh	*114*
Mangal	*115*
Omaja	*116*
Saanvi	*117*
Postlude of Chapter 7	**119**
Chapter 8	**122**
Postlude of Chapter 8	**127**
Prelude to Chapter 9	**130**
Chapter 9	**132**
Preparations for the Test Voyage	*139*
Postlude of Chapter 9	**142**
Chapter 10	**144**
Postlude of Chapter 10	**150**
Mzaliwa	*150*
Prof Ofeefee	*150*
Chapter 11	**152**
Postlude of Chapter 11	**157**
Chapter 12	**159**
Postlude of Chapter 12	**166**
Terahaveen	**168**
Postlude	**176**
Epilogue	**177**
Srimad-Bhagavatam (Planetary System in Anagha)	**183**
Cetus sector (Quad 1)	*183*
Lynx sector (Quad 2)	*184*

Indus sector (Quad 3)	*185*
Venatici sector (Quad 4)	*186*
T'haerian Gyneocracy	**187**
Political Leadership	*187*
Legal System	*188*
Economic Structure	*189*
Social and Cultural Influence	*190*
Military and Defence	*192*
Family and Social Structure	*193*
Political Representation and Participation	*195*
Religious and Spiritual Practices	*196*
Glossary	**197**
Endnotes	**201**

Foreword

In the quiet corners of my mind, *Terahaveen* was born—an odyssey of my thoughts, dreams, and the kaleidoscope of experiences that have shaped me. As a woman of African descent, living in America after a transformative sojourn in the Alsace/Black Forest region, the canvas of my existence is painted with the hues of cultural diversity and personal revelation.

Living abroad was more than a change of scenery; it was a metamorphosis of the soul. The Alsace/Black Forest region whispered ancient tales, where each cobblestone carried the weight of history. It was amidst those towering pines and whispered legends that my worldview expanded. The subtle dance between tradition and modernity shaped my thoughts, and I became a mosaic of cultures, embracing the harmonies of diversity.

Rooted in Christianity, my upbringing was a complex tapestry. My birth parents wielded religion not as a beacon of faith but as a tool of control. Dogmatic and unwavering, their words resonated with the divine, yet their actions were a stark contradiction—bordering the profane. The dichotomy between their teachings and their deeds was a constant source of perplexity. In the Alsace, I found solace in the whispers of the forest, where spirituality transcended the confines of dogma.

Questions lingered in the air like the scent of pine after rain. Terahaveen became my exploration of one such question—the musings on whether society would have unfolded differently if woman, the bearer of life, had been the genesis. As a woman navigating the intricacies of societal expectations, I wondered if the narratives of power, hierarchy, and balance would have woven a different tale.

Terahaveen is not just a narrative; it is an excavation of my thoughts, an unravelling of the threads that connect the past to the present. It is an offering to those who, like me, have pondered the intersections of identity, faith, and societal constructs. As you embark on this journey with me, may the echoes of

Terahaveen resonate with your own reflections, inviting you to explore the corridors of your mind and the landscapes of possibility.

Furthermore, within the pages of *Terahaveen*, I weave a tapestry of bonds forged not merely by blood but by shared resilience, love, and the quiet, unyielding strength of women standing shoulder to shoulder. The exploration of the mother-child relationship became a cornerstone of *Terahaveen*, a deliberate choice rooted in my own quest for understanding and healing.

My childhood was marked by a scarcity of nurturing warmth, where the cold winds of indifference blew through the halls of my home. In the absence of the gentle embrace of maternal care, I sought solace in the arms of the Alsace's ancient forests and motherly figures who took me under their loving wings.

Through *Terahaveen*, I sought to depict the transformative power of a mother's love—a love that becomes a sanctuary, a source of strength that transcends the mundane. The narrative underscores the significance of creating a nurturing environment, one that was regrettably lacking in my own early years. It is a homage to the resilience of women who, despite the absence of traditional maternal figures, find ways to cultivate love and foster growth.

The decision to position strong female leads at the forefront was intentional, a reflection of my belief in the richness of women's narratives. In *Terahaveen*, the women take centre stage, not as a deviation from reality but as a celebration of the strength, wisdom, and resilience inherent in the feminine spirit. While male characters play vital roles, they primarily exist in the background, allowing the spotlight to illuminate the nuanced stories of the women who navigate the complex tapestry of their lives.

As a storyteller, I am driven by the desire to offer a narrative where women shape their destinies, and where their voices echo with authenticity and strength. *Terahaveen* is an invitation to explore a world where the bonds between women are as unbreakable as the roots of ancient trees, where the threads of sisterhood weave a fabric that withstands the tests of time. May you, dear reader, find resonance in these tales of resilience, and may they kindle the embers of strength within your own heart.

Esmée

Prologue

Before the grand symphony of creation, before swirling nebulae birthed stars, there existed only the void. An infinite expanse of nothingness, devoid of light, sound, or energy. It stretched on for eternity, a silent testament to the absence of all that is.

Then, a tremor. A ripple in the fabric of nonexistence, a disturbance in the absolute stillness. Faint at first, a whisper in the cosmic dark, it grew like a pebble dropped into a pond, its effects spreading outwards, carrying the promise of change.

This ripple, this nascent spark, was the will of the Primordial Ones. Beings beyond comprehension, existing outside the boundaries of time and space, they yearned to break the monotony of the void. And with a collective thought, a single, unified intention, they wove existence from the fabric of nothingness.

Thus began the cosmic dance. The void gave way to a swirling vortex of energy, birthing the first stars and igniting the grand tapestry of the universe. At its heart, a binary quasar, a celestial engine of immense power, fuelled the nascent cosmos.

Within this swirling embrace, a spectacle of incomprehensible magnitude unfolded. A celestial dancer, a binary quasar, pirouetted with mesmerising grace, drawing the remnants of a dying galaxy into its voracious embrace. Here, two nuclei emerged as the focal point of creation and dissolution. One, resembling a citrine stone bathed in hues of golden radiance, exuded maternal strength and protective warmth. The other, akin to the mesmerising allure of a fluorite gemstone, shimmered with the wisdom of ages and the allure of physical beauty.

Bound together in a celestial embrace, they were encircled by a rainbow of ethereal hues, reminiscent of the fuchsite stone. Its cascading colours symbolised the intricate dance of cosmic forces, weaving a tapestry of existence from the threads of time and space.

As the binary quasar pulsed with rhythmic intensity, beams of ultraviolet light pierced the cosmic void, illuminating the surrounding cosmos with their luminous glow. From the depths of this celestial beacon, twin beings emerged—Alpha and Omega—birthed into existence by the very heartbeat of the universe.

Alpha, resonating with the primal energies of the citrine, embodied the forces of protection and destruction, a guardian of cosmic balance. In contrast, Omega imbued with the allure of fluorite, sought individuality and independence, a seeker of truth amidst the vastness of the cosmos.

Their arrival heralded a tale of cosmic duality, a saga of creation and conflict that would echo across the annals of time. As the binary quasar continued its celestial dance, casting its radiant glow upon the cosmos, Alpha and Omega stood at the precipice of destiny, their intertwined fates bound by the pulsating rhythm of the universe.

And so, amidst the swirling chaos of creation, the stage was set for an epic narrative—a saga etched in the luminous tapestry of the rotating binary quasar, where the forces of light and darkness would collide in a cosmic symphony of existence.

Alpha and Omega

In the heart of the cosmic expanse, a spectacle of immense proportions unfolded. At its epicentre, a rotating binary quasar pirouetted, a cosmic dancer absorbing the essence of a distant dying galaxy. This supermassive black hole, ravenous in its hunger, devoured the surrounding gases with an insatiable appetite, casting an ethereal glow upon the galactic remnants.

Amidst the swirling cosmic dance, two nuclei emerged as the focal point of creation and dissolution. One celestial being took the form of a citrine stone, a manifestation of beauty painted in hues of resplendent yellows and rich earth tones. A maternal force, this being radiated strength and protection. The other, embodying the mesmerising allure of a fluorite stone, emanated energetic properties that rippled through the fabric of space. This figure stood as a beacon of wisdom and physical beauty.

Enveloping both beings in a celestial embrace was a rainbow, reminiscent of a fuchsite stone. Its ethereal hues cascaded in harmony, symbolising the intricate dance of cosmic forces. As the binary quasar pulsated, it sent forth beams of ultra-high-energy radio waves, animating the surrounding particles in a symphony of cosmic energy.

The quasar, a celestial lighthouse in the cosmic vastness, emitted waves of ultraviolet light with a regular rotational cadence. This luminous display originated from a glowing disk of infalling material, a tribute to the dying galaxy from which it drew its essence. Jets shot forth along the celestial poles, a cosmic expression that transcended the electromagnetic spectrum. These emissions, coherent and synchronised, moved in lockstep with each other, akin to pulses of a celestial heartbeat.

The crescendo of these pulses reached a climax, a moment of cosmic intensity. With each quickening heartbeat, the binary neutron star birthed twin beings—Alpha and Omega. The very fabric of the cosmos trembled as these celestial siblings emerged, their destinies intertwined with the pulsating rhythm of the quasar.

In the aftermath of this cosmic birth, the celestial stage was set for a saga of creation and conflict. Alpha, resonating with the properties of a citrine stone, embodied the primal forces of protection and destruction. Omega, with the allure of fluorite, sought uniqueness and independence. Their existence heralded the duality of cosmic forces, a tale that would unfold across the vastness of space and time—a narrative etched in the luminous tapestry of the rotating binary quasar.

The Twins

The celestial twins, Brjamohana and Shraavana, were bound not only by the cosmic forces that birthed them but also by a profound connection that transcended the vastness of space. As firstborn, Brjamohana, adorned in the regalia of a principal mother goddess, embodied the primal forces that shaped the very fabric of Primis. Her dark red-brown skin, reminiscent of caramel from Dharatee, spoke of her nurturing essence. Almond-shaped eyes, violet-like Salvia, carried the wisdom of the cosmos. She was a beautiful woman, often depicted in Naijeeri garb, adorned with gold that adorned her headdress and jewellery—a visual manifestation of her divine authority.

Brjamohana, the primordial creator and the Brahman held the cosmic responsibility of protecting the peace, prosperity, and the Way of Life, dharma, of Primis. Duties, rights, conduct, and virtues found their embodiment in her divine presence. Worshipped especially during the cosmic seasons of Perihelion and Aphelion, she stood as the epitome of ultimate truth and reality.

Beside her, Shraavana, the second-born and Omega, embodied the essence of supreme consciousness and great wisdom. Her name, derived from the root 'Shravan', spoke of her role as the hearer and reflector of secrets meant to impart intellectual conviction. With skin that adapted to the emotions it absorbed; Shraavana navigated the cosmos with an innate ability to understand the intricacies of beings—*praaniyon*. Her creation, the Shravakans, was born to gain understanding through the act of hearing, the fundamental element of learning.

Aeons of time saw the twins traversing the vast openness of space, their companionship forged in the elemental remnants scattered from their cosmic birth. Shraavana, attuned to the rhythmic heartbeat of Brjamohana—the *naabhik*—understood the quickening as a sign of restlessness or the steady drumming as ease and motherly sense. In this celestial partnership, Brjamohana became the teacher of dharma, instilling the necessity of moral duties into Shraavana's cosmic consciousness.

However, as the Glow of Dawn bathed the cosmos in ethereal hues, a profound shift unfolded. Shraavana, burdened by the prescribed Way of Life and the desire for uniqueness, rejected the plan devised in the openness of space. Feeling suffocated and controlled, she forsook the analogical creation of Novissimus, a realm meant to mirror Primis. Instead, Shraavana yearned for a realm that stood alone in its uniqueness—*anokha*.

In this rejection, the celestial twins, once confidants in the cosmic dance, faced an irreparable fracture. Shraavana's pursuit of individuality severed the unity that bound them, and the plan for complementary dimensions collapsed. Brjamohana, the primordial creator, watched as the cosmic drama unfolded, their existence in tandem shattered by the choices made at the Glow of Dawn.

As the cosmic winds carried echoes of the twins' separation, the realms of Primis and Novissimus began their divergent journeys. The cosmic saga of Alpha and Omega took a poignant turn, leaving in its wake the remnants of a once-shared destiny now unravelling across the celestial expanse. The twins, now estranged, stood at the threshold of a cosmic paradox, their divergent paths etching a narrative that would echo through the cosmic ages.

The Beginning

In the cosmic genesis, Brjamohana and Shraavana, the celestial sisters, embarked on the creation of two dimensions—Primis and Novissimus. Primis, in its formless and empty state, shrouded in darkness, awaited the divine touch of Brjamohana. Her *taakat*, a force emanating from her essence, moved through the cosmic void.

With a resounding command, 'Let there be light', Brjamohana ushered illumination into Primis. The division between light and darkness marked the active and inactive hours of her creation. Primis was then segmented into Anagha, with four quadrants—Cetus, Lynx, Indus, and Venatici, ushering in the morning and night, the first day.

∞

As the Glow of Dawn heralded the birth of Novissimus, Shraavana, the celestial sister, infused the formless expanse with her divine presence. Like its counterpart, Primis, Novissimus existed in a state devoid of form or life, awaiting the touch of its creator.

With a commanding decree, Shraavana's taakat traversed the spatial expanse, shaping the universe according to her will. "There shall be *sitaare aur grah*—stars and planets," she proclaimed, and thus gave rise to Aakaashaganga, the cosmic river of stars, with its three galactic quadrants. Stars twinkled like jewels in the velvet darkness, and planets orbited in graceful arcs around their stellar hosts.

Satisfied with her creation, Shraavana beheld the unfolding cosmic symphony with a sense of pride and wonder. Yet, as the days passed and Novissimus entered its second phase of creation, a shadow fell upon its pristine realms.

Shraavana, in her infinite wisdom, formed Dharatee, the terrestrial realm, and birthed the Terrestris, beings created in her own image. These beings possessed intelligence and free will, but their hearts were filled with pride and ambition.

In their arrogance, the Terrestris forsook their creator, seeking to carve out their own destiny and ascend to the heights of power and glory. But their rebellion would bring forth chaos and turmoil to both realms, as they traversed from Novissimus to Primis, leaving destruction in their wake.

Witnessing the plight of her children, Brjamohana, in her divine compassion, sought to protect them from the consequences of their actions. Unleashing her divine wrath, she cast down judgments upon the rebellious Terrestris, deepening the divide between the celestial sisters and setting the stage for the cosmic conflict that would define the fate of both realms.

And so, the celestial dance of Primis and Novissimus continued, marred by the echoes of betrayal and the clash of divine wills. Amid it all, the destinies of worlds hung in the balance, as the cosmic drama unfolded with all the grandeur and tragedy of the universe itself.

∞

On the second day of creation, Brjamohana focused her attention on crafting the essence of Primis. With meticulous care, she divided the waters above from those below, giving rise to the vast expanse of the sky. This celestial canopy extended infinitely, reflecting the boundless potential of the universe within its azure depths. Cloud wisps formed and drifted lazily across the expansive canvas, casting ever-shifting shadows upon the land below.

As the waters receded, revealing the fertile land beneath, Brjamohana infused it with vitality and diversity. Majestic mountains soared from the earth, their peaks reaching towards the heavens while their roots delved deep into the core of T'haeri. Valleys and plains unfurled, promising a kaleidoscope of colours and textures, ripe with the anticipation of life.

Yet, Brjamohana's artistry extended beyond the terrestrial realm alone. On the third day, casting her gaze skyward once more, she scattered lodestars across the heavens. These celestial beacons, strewn across the vast expanse, served as guides for travellers and navigators, marking the passage of time and seasons. Among them, she placed the three great celestial bodies—the sun, two moons, and the stars.

The sun, resplendent and regal, ruled over the day, bathing Primis in its golden warmth. The moons, serene and mysterious, held sway over the night, casting their silvery glow upon the world below. Countless stars sparkled like diamonds in the velvet embrace of the night sky, their patterns forming constellations that whispered tales as ancient as time itself.

With the completion of the third day, T'haeri was transformed into a planetae of breathtaking beauty and wonder, its skies alive with celestial dance, and its lands teeming with the promise of life. Yet, Brjamohana knew her work was far from finished, for there remained four more days of creation, each holding its own mysteries and marvels.

On the fourth day of creation, Brjamohana's divine touch extended to the fertile soil of T'haeri, where she planted the seeds of vegetation with purpose and foresight. With a gentle command, she brought forth a verdant tapestry that would serve myriad purposes, enriching the planet with sustenance, shelter, and beauty.

Amidst the lush landscape, trees of diverse kinds sprouted from the earth. There were trees bearing fruits of every flavour and hue, ripe for nourishing the inhabitants of T'haeri. Their branches bowed under the weight of succulent offerings, inviting creatures of all kinds to partake in their bounty.

Amongst the fruit-bearing trees stood majestic giants, their broad canopies providing cool shade from the warmth of the sun. Beneath their sheltering branches, life flourished in harmony, finding solace and respite from the elements.

But it was not only food and shade that Brjamohana bestowed upon T'haeri. She planted trees with sturdy trunks and resilient wood, destined to become the foundation for dwellings and structures. These trees stood tall and proud, their timber promising shelter and protection for the inhabitants of the burgeoning world.

As the landscape flourished, so too did the ground beneath. A riot of colours erupted as flowers of every shape and size burst into bloom, carpeting the earth in a kaleidoscope of hues. Each petal held the promise of beauty and fragrance, drawing creatures from far and wide to revel in their splendour.

Herbs and grasses sprung forth, their delicate forms swaying in the gentle breeze. Their medicinal properties and culinary delights would sustain and nourish the inhabitants of T'haeri, offering healing and flavour to those who sought them.

From towering trees to delicate blooms, Brjamohana's creative hand imbued T'haeri with a symphony of life, each plant and flower woven seamlessly into the fabric of the planet's ecosystem. Together, they formed a vibrant tableau of abundance and diversity, a testament to the boundless creativity and generosity of their divine creator.

After the receding waters on the second day, Brjamohana named this collection of waters Samudra. Its expansive oceans and seas stretched across the surface of T'haeri, teeming with life and intrigue. Samudra became a realm ripe for exploration and discovery, its depths harbouring secrets yet to be unveiled.

On the fifth day of creation, Brjamohana's attention turned to the intricate world beneath the surface of T'haeri. With a delicate touch, she began to weave the mycelia network, a web of interconnected fungi that would bind together the very essence of the planet.

From the depths of the rich soil emerged an array of fungi, each with its own unique form and purpose. Mushrooms of all shapes and sizes sprouted forth, their caps ranging from vibrant hues to earthy tones, promising both nourishment and wonder to those who would encounter them.

Amongst the mushrooms, fungal threads stretched and intertwined, forming a vast network that would soon permeate every corner of T'haeri's soil. This mycelial web served as the silent communicator, facilitating the exchange of nutrients and information between plants, planets, and the soon-to-be-formed T'haerians.

Through this intricate network, plants communicated with one another, sharing resources and warning of impending dangers. Nutrients flowed freely, ensuring the vitality and health of the entire ecosystem. In turn, the fungi thrived, their symbiotic relationship with the plants strengthening with each passing moment.

But the mycelia network was not merely a means of sustenance; it was a conduit for connection and unity. As the mycelial threads intertwined with the very essence of T'haeri, they forged bonds that would bind together the inhabitants of the planet in the cycles of life and growth.

As Brjamohana continued her work, the mycelia network grew ever more intricate and pervasive, weaving its way through the soil and connecting all living beings in a tapestry of interdependence. Through this silent symphony of connection, T'haeri became more than just a planet; it became a living, breathing entity, united in purpose and bound by the threads of the mycelial network.

As Brjamohana beheld her creation, she felt a profound sense of satisfaction. Each day brought new wonders and revelations, and she knew that there was still much more to come. With two days remaining, the journey of creation was far from over, and the universe brimmed with untold possibilities and adventures yet to unfold.

On the sixth day of creation, Brjamohana turned her attention to the seas and skies, filling them with a myriad of living creatures. In the depths of Samudra, great sea creatures swam gracefully, their forms ranging from the majestic *nyangumi* that roamed the oceans to the delicate creatures that inhabited the coral reefs. The waters teemed with life, each species playing its part in the intricate web of the marine ecosystem.

Above, in the boundless expanse of the sky, winged beings took flight. Birds of every shape and size soared through the air, their wings outstretched as they danced on the currents of wind. From the smallest hummingbird to the mightiest eagle, the skies were alive with the beauty and grace of these aerial creatures.

As the sixth day ended, Brjamohana beheld the wondrous diversity of life that now inhabited her creation. From the depths of the oceans to the heights of the heavens, every corner of T'haeri pulsed with the vitality of living beings, each one a testament to her boundless creativity.

On the seventh and final day of creation, Brjamohana bestowed upon her universe the pinnacle of her creative work. In her own image, she fashioned female and male beings, endowing them with intelligence, creativity, and the capacity for love and companionship. Women and men emerged as equals, each possessing unique strengths and abilities, yet destined to complement and support one another in their journey through life.

However, in her wisdom, Brjamohana designated men as stewards of women, entrusting them with the responsibility to protect, cherish, and uplift their female counterparts. This divine decree served as a reminder of the interconnectedness of all life and the importance of mutual respect and cooperation in the harmonious functioning of the universe.

As the seventh day came to a close, Brjamohana looked upon her creation with a sense of profound satisfaction. From the formless void had emerged a wondrous cosmos, rich in diversity, beauty, and purpose. And though her work as a creator was complete, the story of T'haeri had only just begun, its inhabitants poised to embark on a journey of exploration, discovery, and growth that would shape the destiny of their world for aeons to come.

The cosmic days unfolded, a symphony of creation and divine decree, as Brjamohana and Shraavana's celestial dance brought forth the realms of Primis and Novissimus. Within these dimensions, the intricate tapestry of existence began to weave itself.

As the celestial orbs danced through the cosmic ballet and the seasons cycled their eternal dance, the inhabitants of T'haeri undertook their unique odyssey. Guided by the principles of equilibrium, concord, and custodianship, they wove their narratives into the cosmic fabric. The chronicle of Alpha and Omega, of commencements and conclusions, unfurled against the celestial canvas, with each passing moment contributing a verse to the grand epic of life itself.

Thus, the cosmic stage was set for the majestic spectacle of existence to play out. The inhabitants of both Primis and Novissimus embarked on a profound voyage marked by exploration, evolution, and metamorphosis. Throughout the epochs that unfolded, they navigated the vast expanses of the cosmos, confronting obstacles, forging bonds, and shaping their individual destinies within the ever-expanding mosaic of creation.

T'haeri

Located in the Lynx sector, T'haeri has twin moons—Haeri and Taer, with Taer being the largest of the two. The planet is separated into six continents—Iinkiltira, Azore/Naijeer, Asrawi, Faransa, Bolev, and Aarkat. These were the modern names given to each continent based on the ancient tribes. The planetae's capital Petraea is in the south on the third continent—Naijeer.

In the planetary system Srimad-Bhagavatam, governance takes the form of a gyneocracy known as the Bhabhi Salaah. This council comprises female counsellors who are supported by male stewards, known as the Saala Ganatantr. Originally, the Bhabhi Salaah was limited to T'haeri and was established by the eight daughters of Brjamohana's initial creation, Jyeshta. However, following the events of Terahaveen, the Bhabhi Salaah evolved into the planetary gyneocracy it is today.

Currently, Saanvi and Aashvi hold the positions of Bhabhi for T'haeri, with their respective Saala being Sajiv and Aarav. This arrangement reflects the shift towards a broader planetary governance structure, where female leadership is complemented by male counterparts, fostering balance and collaboration within the system.

T'haeri has crimson oceans and fresh waterways, rich in Ferrum, Magnesia Alba, and Selene. The hydrosphere is composed of 75% nitrogen, 15% oxygen, 9% argon, and 1% carbon dioxide, methane, water vapour and neon.

T'haeri's clouds form at different altitudes in its atmosphere. The high-level Cirri clouds occur above 13,716m T'haeri's surface. Due to the cold tropospheric temperature -25°C, these clouds primarily are composed of hexagonal argon ice crystals. They often appear thin, streaky, and white like a wedding veil—*vivaah ka nakaab*. During Perihelion, the Cirri clouds are cerulean blue.

The mid-level Stratos clouds are widely distributed over the planet at 10,668m from the surface. They appear to form at a temperature of about -15°C and contain nitrogen and oxygen gases. When hit by light, the nitrogen and oxygen compounds act like tinting agents making the clouds appear purpura in colour. The lower-level Cumuli clouds—where the populous of Festuca lives—are water-filled and protect the surface from Coma Berenices' radio waves.

T'haeri has an ambient temperature. On a cloudless day, the sky is indigo with flecks of erythrean red. During a sunset, the indigo sky fades to powder blue with bands of coral red and orange-red. To an advena, T'haeri is not a hospitable planetae. To have visitors, the T'haerians created filtering suits to reduce the level of argon to that of Dharatee—0.9%. Additionally, these suits absorb the carbon dioxide that the wearer exhales and convert it into oxygen. Perspiration and urination are filtered, waste is separated, and discarded, to be drinkable by its wearer.

T'haerians, the native inhabitants of T'haeri, are characterised by their tall and slender physiques, which reflect their evolutionary adaptation to the planet's unique environment. Their humanoid form is marked by grace and elegance, with proportions finely tuned to navigate the terrain of their homeland with ease. This physical resilience is complemented by their innate ability to adapt to the diverse ecosystems that span across T'haeri's continents.

Communication among T'haerians is facilitated primarily through phereins, a sophisticated system of non-verbal cues, gestures, and subtle energy exchanges. Phereins serve as a nuanced language, allowing T'haerians to convey complex emotions, intentions, and ideas with precision and clarity. Through phereins, they establish deep connections with one another, fostering a sense of community and unity among their people.

In addition to their mastery of phereins, T'haerians have developed a written language, primarily utilised by trading merchants of Saanvi. This written script adds to the cultural richness of T'haeri, serving as a means of preserving knowledge, recording historical events, and facilitating trade and commerce.

The written language of T'haeri is a testament to the intellectual prowess and cultural sophistication of its inhabitants, reflecting their commitment to education, literacy, and intellectual exchange.

The written language of T'haeri is characterised by intricate symbols and glyphs, each imbued with layers of meaning and significance. These symbols are carefully crafted to convey not only linguistic information but also cultural nuances, artistic expression, and spiritual beliefs. As a result, the written language of T'haeri serves as a reflection of the rich weaving of T'haerian culture, encompassing diverse traditions, philosophies, and values.

Furthermore, the written language plays a crucial role in facilitating trade and diplomacy among the various tribes and factions of T'haeri. Merchants from Saanvi, the bustling hub of commerce and cultural exchange, use the written language to negotiate agreements, record transactions, and establish contracts with trading partners across the planet. In this way, the written language serves as a vital tool for fostering economic prosperity and fostering intertribal relations.

The combination of phereins and the written language reflects the multifaceted nature of T'haerian communication, blending the fluidity of non-verbal expression with the precision of written text. Together, these linguistic traditions contribute to the vibrant culture of T'haeri, fostering connections, fostering understanding, and preserving the rich heritage of its inhabitants for generations to come.

There are eight tribes on T'haeri; the two dominant tribes are—the Naijeeri and the Angrezee. The other tribes are Madhyaee, Phraans, Aarkati, Eshiyaee, Jazayerli, and Boleviya. The Naijeeri became known to specialise in pioneering intergalactic and extradimensional travel for the Bhabhi Salaah while the Angrezee developed terraforming technologies for the Saala Ganatantr.

The process by which T'haerians produce planetary oxygen is a marvel of scientific ingenuity and biological adaptation. At the heart of this process lies the utilisation of unique pigmented electrons, which serve as the catalyst for oxygen production.

T'haerians harness the energy of Coma, a celestial phenomenon unique to their planetary system, to power the conversion of carbon dioxide into oxygen.

Coma emits radiant energy across a broad spectrum, including wavelengths that are specifically absorbed by T'haerian-pigmented electrons.

These electrons, distributed throughout the T'haerian physiology, act as molecular antennas, absorbing the energy of Coma and transferring it to molecular oxygen.

As the pigmented electrons absorb energy from Coma, they undergo an oxidation process, releasing electrons that are subsequently used to oxidise water molecules. This oxidation reaction generates molecular oxygen (O_2) as a byproduct, which is then released into the atmosphere, replenishing the planetary oxygen supply.

The process of oxidising water into oxygen is akin to photosynthesis, albeit with a unique twist enabled by the specialised pigmented electrons of T'haerians. This process not only ensures the continuous production of oxygen essential for sustaining life on T'haeri but also contributes to the vibrant hues characteristic of T'haerian physiology.

The pigmented electrons, energised by the radiant energy of Coma, exhibit a dazzling array of colours, ranging from deep maroons to vibrant greens and rich yellows. These hues are a visual manifestation of the intricate biochemical processes occurring within T'haerian cells, symbolising the symbiotic relationship between T'haerians and their planetary environment.

The process of oxygen production on T'haeri showcases the remarkable adaptability and resourcefulness of its inhabitants, who have adapted sophisticated mechanisms for harnessing celestial energy to meet the fundamental needs of life. Through their ingenuity and mastery of biochemistry, T'haerians ensure the continued vitality and sustainability of their planetary ecosystem, forging a harmonious relationship between biology and cosmology.

The Naijeeri, inhabiting the southern regions of T'haeri below the Equatorial line, exhibit distinct physical characteristics that set them apart from other T'haerian tribes. Their unique attributes are a result of their geographical location and adaptations to the local environment.

One of the most striking features of the Naijeeri is their dark, rich hue of maroon skin tone, reminiscent of the mangan diaspore gem of Mangal. This deep coloration is a direct consequence of the higher concentration of pigmented electrons within their physiology. These pigmented electrons, which play a crucial role in the production of planetary oxygen, also impart a rich and vibrant hue to the Naijeeri's skin, symbolising their close connection to the land and the cosmos.

In addition to their distinctive skin tone, the Naijeeri possess viridian green eyes, reminiscent of the lush leaves of the Baobab tree. This verdant hue reflects the Naijeeri's affinity for nature and their deep-rooted connection to the flora and fauna of T'haeri. The striking contrast between their maroon skin and green eyes adds to the captivating allure of the Naijeeri, marking them as a visually stunning and enigmatic tribe.

Completing the Naijeeri's unique appearance is their hair, which takes on a vivid yellow hue reminiscent of the Lisianthus flower. This vibrant coloration further emphasises the Naijeeri's connection to the natural world, evoking images of sun-kissed meadows and blooming fields. The yellow hair of the Naijeeri serves as a symbol of vitality, creativity, and resilience.

The House of Nihaarika, an ancestral lineage within the Naijeeri tribe, holds a special significance in T'haerian society. Residing in Surtseyan, the ancestral house is revered as the first creation of Brjamohana, the cosmic architect of T'haeri.

As custodians of ancient wisdom and guardians of tradition, the House of Nihaarika plays a central role in preserving the cultural heritage and spiritual legacy of the Naijeeri tribe. Through their rituals and teachings, the House of Nihaarika ensures the continuity of T'haerian customs and values, passing down the wisdom of generations to future descendants.

Surtseyan, an enchanting islet located just 500 meters off the western coast of the Azorean continent on T'haeri, is a haven of natural beauty and biodiversity. Dominated by the majestic presence of the Donax volcano, Surtseyan boasts a landscape rich in geological wonders and lush vegetation.

At the heart of Surtseyan lies the Donax volcano, the most notable geological formation on the islet. Positioned on the southern end of the islet, the Donax volcano commands attention with its imposing stature and rugged terrain. Its crater, which opens to the Faya Sea, is filled with crystal-clear water, creating a tranquil lagoon that contrasts with the volcanic landscape surrounding it. The opening in the crater, facing north towards the Azorean continent, gives rise to the Daucus, a small natural harbour with sandy beaches that offer respite and shelter to visitors and marine life alike.

Surtseyan is home to a diverse array of endemic Azorean flowering plants, each contributing to the island's vibrant ecosystem. The Azorean Banyan tree and Baobab tree stand tall, their gnarled branches reaching skyward in a testament to resilience and endurance. Violet forget-me-not flowers carpet the ground with delicate blooms, while orange and magenta Azores spurges add splashes of colour to the landscape. Floating pink lotuses grace the tranquil waters of the lagoon, their ethereal beauty is mesmerising all who behold them.

Standing sentinel over the island is the Dragon's blood tree, a sacred symbol revered by the Naijeeri tribe who inhabit the region. The Naijeeri, known for their harmonious relationship with nature, communicate with the Dragon's blood tree and view it as a guardian of the island. Its presence serves as a reminder of the interconnectedness of all living beings and the importance of preserving the natural world.

The waters surrounding Surtseyan teem with life, with an abundance of fish and aquatic animals inhabiting the area. Amberjack, nudibranchs, parrotfish, and moray eels are just a few of the species that call these waters home, their colourful presence adding to the diversity of marine life found in the Faya Sea.

Due to its protected status and pristine natural environment, Surtseyan remains largely untouched by human development. Tall city buildings are non-existent on the islet, allowing its natural beauty to flourish undisturbed. As a result, Surtseyan retains its wild and untamed charm, inviting visitors to explore its rugged landscapes, tranquil waters, and thriving ecosystems in a true sanctuary of nature.

The Jazayerli tribe, residing to the north of T'haeri, presents a stark contrast to the Naijeeri in their approach to life and their relationship with nature. Characterised by a lower count of pigmented electrons, the Jazayerli have diverged from the ancestral way of oneness with nature, instead embracing a more technologically reliant culture.

Unlike the Naijeeri, who communicate through phereins and commune with nature, the Jazayerli tribe has shifted towards technological communication methods. This shift has led to a detachment from the natural world, with Jazayerli often prioritising virtual interactions over direct connection with their surroundings. As a result, their cultural identity has become more centred around the use of technology, leading to a loss of a deep spiritual connection to nature.

One of the most distinctive traits of the Jazayerli tribe is their striking azure blue eyes, reminiscent of the mined azurite gemstone. These piercing blue eyes are a visual hallmark of the tribe, reflecting their unique genetic makeup and cultural heritage. Additionally, Jazayerli have red hair, reminiscent of the vibrant hues found in the T'haerian seas, and reddish-orange skin reminiscent of carnelian, further setting them apart from other tribes on T'haeri.

The House of Nidhi, an ancestral lineage within the Jazayerli tribe, resides in Festuca of Petraea on the Azore continent. As the seventh ancestral House and creation of Brjamohana, the House of Nidhi holds a position of honour and respect within Jazayerli society. It serves as a centre of cultural and spiritual heritage, preserving the traditions, rituals, and teachings passed down through generations. Despite the tribe's reliance on technology, the House of Nidhi remains a bastion of tradition and ancestral wisdom, ensuring the continuity of Jazayerli cultural identity amidst the rapid pace of technological advancement.

Overall, the Jazayerli tribe represents a fascinating contrast to the Naijeeri, embodying a shift towards technological reliance and a departure from the ancestral connection to nature. Despite these differences, the House of Nidhi stands as a testament to the enduring legacy of Brjamohana's creations, reminding the Jazayerli of their roots and cultural heritage in an ever-changing world.

Festuca, in stark contrast to the tranquil islet of Surtseyan, emerges as a bustling metropolis and the thriving epicentre of T'haeri's cultural, economic, and political landscape. Situated within the Petraea region, Festuca stands as a beacon of progress and innovation, where tradition and modernity converge to shape the destiny of the planet.

As the largest city in Petraea, Festuca occupies an expansive area of approximately 105 square kilometres, accommodating a dense population of around 705,000 T'haerians. Within its bustling streets and towering skyscrapers, a vibrant tapestry of life unfolds, pulsating with the energy of trade, commerce, and creativity.

Festuca serves as T'haeri's cultural centre, where artistry, craftsmanship, and innovation flourish in equal measure. The city's skyline is adorned with architectural marvels, blending futuristic designs with elements of T'haerian heritage and tradition. Museums, galleries, and theatres abound, showcasing the rich cultural heritage of the planet and fostering a spirit of artistic expression and creativity.

At the heart of Festuca lies its economic engine, fuelled by a network of trade agreements with sister planetarum. Each sister planetarum contributes approximately 15% of its economic output to Festuca's wealth, with Saanvi playing a particularly significant role by supplying 25% of its economic resources. These trade agreements facilitate the exchange of goods, resources, and knowledge, driving economic growth and prosperity for the city and its inhabitants.

In addition to its economic significance, Festuca also serves as the seat of both the Bhabhi Salaah and the convent of the Saala Ganatantr, making it the political nucleus of T'haeri. Here, decisions of planetary importance are made, governance structures are established, and the destiny of T'haeri is shaped by the collective wisdom and leadership of its governing bodies.

Despite its bustling urban environment, Festuca remains a melting pot of diverse cultures, traditions, and perspectives. Its streets resonate with the vibrant sounds of T'haerian dialects and its markets bustle with the sights and smells of exotic goods from distant lands. Festuca's cosmopolitan atmosphere fosters a spirit of inclusivity and tolerance, where individuals from all walks of life come together to celebrate the richness and diversity of T'haerian society.

In essence, Festuca stands as a testament to T'haeri's resilience, adaptability, and ambition. It is a city where the past meets the future, where tradition and innovation coexist harmoniously, and where the dreams of tomorrow are forged in the crucible of today's endeavours. As T'haeri's shining beacon of progress, Festuca illuminates the path forward, guiding the planet towards a future filled with promise and possibility.

Leaving the confines of T'haeri we arrive at Saanvi. Saanvi, the last planetae to undergo terraforming within the Srimad-Bhagavatam system, stands as a testament to the culmination of technological advancements since the twentieth century. This latecomer to the terraforming process reaped the benefits of centuries of progress, emerging as a veritable treasure trove of precious resources and natural riches.

Rich in precious gemstones, spices, raw materials for fabrics, and precious metals, Saanvi boasts a diverse and bountiful landscape that has fuelled its economic prosperity. The planetae's gross economic output is fuelled by a multitude of industries, each contributing to its status as a leading producer within the Srimad-Bhagavatam system.

A significant portion of Saanvi's economic output, approximately 25%, is allocated to T'haeri, reflecting its status as a key contributor to the planetary economy. The Tejee se Badhate merchant clans play a pivotal role in this exchange, supplying approximately 12% of Saanvi's economic output through trade in fine textiles, spices, and precious metals. These merchant clans, renowned for their shrewd business acumen and extensive trade networks, serve as vital conduits for the flow of goods and resources between Saanvi and the rest of the Srimad-Bhagavatam system.

Another notable contributor to Saanvi's economic output is the House of Mahila, responsible for mining operations that yield sapphires, rubies, emeralds, and tanzanite. Through their meticulous extraction techniques, the House of Mahila extracts these precious gemstones from the depths of Saanvi's mineral-rich soil, contributing approximately 8% to the planetae's gross economic output.

Saanvi's fertile lands and favourable climate also make it the top producer of a wide array of spices, including pepper, ginger, cloves, nutmeg, cinnamon, saffron, anise, zedoary, and cumin. These aromatic treasures not only add flavour to cuisines across the Srimad-Bhagavatam system but also contribute significantly to Saanvi's economic prosperity, accounting for the remaining 5% of its economic output.

Among Saanvi's many natural resources, one spice stands out as particularly prized—Aushadhi. Known for its hallucinogenic properties, Aushadhi holds a special place in Saanvi's cultural and economic landscape, commanding high prices in markets across the planetae and within the system.

The House of Adrija, tasked with mining operations in Saanvi's mineral-dense mountains, harnesses the unique properties of Aushadhi to enhance their abilities to locate precious metals such as rhodium, platinum, ruthenium, gold, and iridium. This symbiotic relationship between Aushadhi and mineral extraction ensures the sustainable exploitation of Saanvi's natural resources while maximising economic output without causing major disruption to the planetae's delicate ecosystem.

In essence, Saanvi stands as a shining example of the transformative power of technology and innovation, leveraging its natural riches to become a beacon of prosperity within the Srimad-Bhagavatam system. Through strategic alliances, careful stewardship of resources, and a commitment to sustainability, Saanvi continues to thrive as a vital hub of commerce, culture, and economic activity within the vast expanse of the Srimad-Bhagavatam system.

Mangal, distinguished as the cultural seat of Anagha within the Srimad-Bhagavatam system, occupies a unique position in the planetary hierarchy, abstaining from direct economic contributions to T'haeri's Gross Domestic Product (GDP). Instead, Mangal's significance lies in its role as the custodian of T'haeri's rich cultural heritage and architectural legacy.

At the heart of Mangal's cultural governance structure lies the Sanskrti clans, who hold sway as the ultimate authority on all matters pertaining to culture and architecture within the Srimad-Bhagavatam system. This esteemed council, known as the Amar, consists of forty members who are revered as immortals due to their enduring legacy and profound influence on T'haerian society. New members of the Amar are elected by the existing members of the Sanskrti clan, a process that ensures continuity and reverence for tradition.

The Amar convenes periodically, typically during the Vernal season, to deliberate on matters of cultural significance and establish standards for architecture. These gatherings serve as forums for the exchange of ideas, the preservation of historical and cultural records, and the setting of educational curricula for Petraea Uni, the esteemed educational institution located on the planet Budh.

Through their collective wisdom and dedication to preserving T'haeri's cultural heritage, the Sanskrti clans and the Amar play a vital role in shaping the cultural identity of the entire Srimad-Bhagavatam system. Their meticulous attention to detail, commitment to excellence, and unwavering dedication to tradition ensure that T'haeri's architectural marvels and cultural traditions are safeguarded for future generations to cherish and admire.

Mangal serves as a beacon of cultural enlightenment and artistic expression, nurturing the collective soul of T'haerian society and fostering a deep appreciation for the richness and diversity of its cultural heritage. As guardians of tradition and custodians of artistic excellence, the Sanskrti clans and the Amar stand as pillars of strength, guiding T'haeri towards a future enriched by its storied past.

Bhabhi Salaah

The Bhabhi Salaah, translated from the Ancient Tongue as the Sister Council, represents an ancient and esteemed all-women group that traces its origins back to the matriarchs of T'haerian ancestral tribes in 5 AD. Situated in the heart of T'haeri, the seat of Bhabhi Salaah, the council was established with the profound purpose of guiding all descendants of Brjamohana onto a path of enlightenment.

Central to the ethos of the Bhabhi Salaah was the rigorous training undertaken by its adherents, which encompassed both physical and mental conditioning over the course of years. This arduous regimen aimed to unlock supernatural abilities latent within each member, preparing them for their sacred duty of enlightenment and guidance.

A pivotal moment in the history of the Bhabhi Salaah occurred with the discovery and consumption of Aushadhi, a substance of profound significance. Aushadhi had the transformative effect of awakening the third eye of the Bhabhi, granting them a heightened perception of the essence of Brjamohana, and imbuing them with her taakat, or divine power.

Those sisters who successfully endured the ritualistic consumption of Aushadhi and survived its effects ascended to the esteemed rank of Ma'an Su, achieving a state of elevated consciousness and oneness with Brjamohana. Conversely, those who did not achieve this heightened state retained the title of Rakshak Shreshth within the council.

The Ma'an Su, empowered by their communion with Brjamohana, assumed a pivotal role during the terraforming of the other seven planetarums, overseeing groundbreaking innovations in intergalactic and extradimensional travel. This technological advancement facilitated the expansion of the descendants of the founding members across Anagha, accompanied by their loyal Saala. However, despite the success of intergalactic travel, the fledgling nature of extradimensional travel warranted caution.

The Rakshak Shreshth, mindful of the potential perils inherent in untested technology, urged prudence and restraint to their Ma'an Su counterparts. Nevertheless, spurred by impatience or perhaps hubris, the Ma'an Su sanctioned the activation of extradimensional travel, opening a portal to Novissimus. This event precipitated the devastating events of Terahaveen, underscoring the consequences of recklessness in the pursuit of advancement.

A millennium after the cataclysmic events of Terahaveen, the Bhabhi Salaah underwent a profound transformation, marked by a series of sweeping reforms that reshaped the very fabric of the council. In response to the lessons learned from the folly of the past, stringent measures were implemented to ensure the preservation of wisdom and the safeguarding of Anagha.

Central to these reforms was a comprehensive restructuring of the Bhabhi Salaah's recruitment and training protocols. Prospective members now faced an extensive and rigorous training regimen designed to cultivate their ability to channel taakat without the consumption of Aushadhi. This shift in approach reflected a commitment to nurturing innate potential rather than relying on external substances, thereby fostering a deeper connection to the divine essence of Brjamohana.

In tandem with these changes, a system of separation of powers was established within the council, delineating distinct roles and responsibilities among its members. A hierarchical structure was introduced to streamline decision-making processes and ensure efficient governance. At the heart of this reformation stood the imposing Haree Tower, a centralised compound situated in Festuca, serving as the epicentre of Bhabhi Salaah's power and influence.

Extradimensional travel, once a source of both wonder and peril, was unequivocally banned, and all associated technologies were systematically dismantled and destroyed. Likewise, the consumption of Aushadhi, once considered a sacred rite of passage, was abolished, recognising the inherent dangers it posed to both individual members and the broader community.

To fortify these prohibitions and prevent the resurgence of chaos, the Litany against Chaos was composed, drawing upon the ancient wisdom enshrined within the revered Book of Brahman. This dirge of warning served as a solemn reminder of the consequences of hubris and the imperative of vigilance in the face of temptation.

With the foundational principles of wisdom, discipline, and restraint guiding their path, the Bhabhi Salaah now stands poised to navigate the complexities of the cosmos. Within the walls of the Haree Tower, women of exceptional talent and unwavering dedication undergo rigorous training, honing their taakat powers under the tutelage of seasoned mentors.

Those who aspire to join the ranks of the Bhabhi embark on a transformative journey, entering as novices before ascending through the ranks of apprenticeship. Only upon successfully completing the *Antim Pareekshan*, the final trial of their training, do they earn the esteemed title of Bhabhi, ready to assume their rightful place within the Sister Council and carry forth its sacred legacy into the future.

At the pinnacle of the Bhabhi Salaah hierarchy resides the revered Ma'an Seat, a figure of unparalleled authority and wisdom within the Sister Council.

Known simply as Ma'an, she embodies the collective consciousness and guiding spirit of the Bhabhi, wielding power and influence that surpasses any mere legislative body within the realm.

The Ma'an Seat fulfils a multifaceted role within the council, serving not only as its paramount leader but also as its foremost diplomat and ambassador to the other planetarum. Endowed with the mandate to uphold the principles of enlightenment and unity across Anagha, Ma'an navigates the intricate web of interstellar politics and diplomacy with grace and sagacity.

The selection process for the Ma'an Seat is a solemn and deliberative affair, conducted by the esteemed Haree Hall, the inner circle of the Bhabhi Salaah entrusted with the stewardship of its traditions and values. Chosen for life, the Ma'an relinquishes her former Padanaam, symbolising her transcendence beyond regional affiliations to embody the collective consciousness of all Padanaams.

A potent symbol of her authority and inclusivity, the sceptre wielded by the Ma'an Seat is adorned with stripes representing the vibrant hues of all eight Padanaams. This emblematic gesture serves as a visual testament to her mandate to unify and guide the diverse peoples of Anagha, transcending regional divides and fostering a sense of collective identity and purpose.

During the foundational stages of training within the Bhabhi Salaah, novices are initiated into the core tenets of the Way of Life, a guiding philosophy that forms the bedrock of the council's teachings. Central to this ethos is the cultivation of authentic and empathetic communication, characterised by sincerity and transparency, devoid of deceit, hypocrisy, or duplicity.

One of the fundamental practices espoused by the Bhabhi involves providing individuals with a compassionate exit strategy when faced with difficult choices or conflicts. This principle is encapsulated in the phrase, 'Please choose the cramp path to live'. While succinct, this expression carries profound significance within the context of the Way of Life, serving as a gentle yet firm reminder of the consequences of one's actions and decisions.

The phrase is derived from a longer saying, 'The broad path leads off into destruction. Please move onto the narrow and cramped path leading off into life'. This admonition encapsulates the essence of Bhabhi's teachings, offering individuals the opportunity to reconsider their choices and opt for a path that leads to growth, fulfilment, and ultimately, life.

In essence, the invocation of 'Please choose the cramp path to live' serves as a compassionate invitation to introspection and transformation, empowering individuals to make choices that align with their highest values and aspirations. It embodies the ethos of empathy, understanding, and empowerment that lies at the heart of the Bhabhi Salaah's teachings, guiding both novices and practitioners alike towards a life of authenticity, integrity, and purpose.

As novices progress through their training within the esteemed ranks of the Bhabhi Salaah, they reach a pivotal juncture marked by the bestowal of their sceptre, albeit devoid of its respective gemstone, symbolising the commencement of their journey towards mastery. Empowered by this symbolic gesture, novices advance to the apprentice group, where they delve into the intricacies of channelling taakat, the divine power inherent within them.

Under the watchful guidance of seasoned mentors, apprentices embark on a rigorous regimen of mental and physical exercises aimed at honing their ability to wield taakat with precision and control. These exercises, while demanding and oftentimes gruelling, serve to test the composure and resilience of the apprentices, preparing them for the challenges that lie ahead.

A crucial milestone in the apprentices' journey is the Antim Pareekshan, the final test designed to assess their character and readiness to assume the mantle of a full-fledged Bhabhi. Presented with a morally complex scenario, apprentices are tasked with making a life-defining decision: whether to utilise taakat to save their elderly parent, thereby endangering themselves and their Saala, or to prioritise the welfare of their village, sacrificing personal ties for the greater good.

This ethical dilemma serves as a crucible through which the true essence of each apprentice is revealed, testing their resolve, selflessness, and moral fortitude. Those who demonstrate unwavering dedication to the collective welfare by prioritising the needs of the many over the few ascend to the esteemed rank of Bhabhi, embodying the highest ideals of the Sister Council.

Conversely, apprentices who falter in the face of this ultimate test remain at their current level, their journey towards mastery temporarily halted. Among this group, the strongest and most capable are selected to serve as the Mistress of Novices, assuming the role of a stand-in leader should the Bhabhi of their respective planetae become incapacitated.

Thus, the Antim Pareekshan stands as a crucible through which the true mettle of each apprentice is forged, separating the worthy from the merely proficient and ensuring that only those who embody the highest virtues of wisdom, compassion, and selflessness ascend to lead the sister.

Upon successfully passing the Antim Pareekshan, an apprentice ascends to the esteemed rank of Bhabhi within the Bhabhi Salaah, marking the pinnacle of her journey towards mastery. As a newly anointed Bhabhi, she is bestowed with the solemn privilege of selecting her Saala, a loyal companion and confidante bonded to her for life. The Saala fulfils a crucial role in the Bhabhi's life, serving either as her baatacheet karana, consort, or as her dedicated bodyguard and protector.

Earning the right to wear the ceremonial shawl and wield a sceptre adorned with a gemstone concealing a sword, the newly minted Bhabhi embodies the essence of her respective planetae, symbolised by the gemstone adorning her sceptre. This sacred insignia signifies her allegiance to her home world and her commitment to upholding its values and traditions.

In accordance with the ancient customs of the Bhabhi Salaah, only eight women are ordained as Bhabhi, each representing one of the revered Padanaam. These eight Padanaam collectively form the governing body of the Sister Council, with each Bhabhi overseeing a designated domain of Anagha. Their tenure in office is solemnly sworn until death or voluntary retirement, ensuring stability and continuity within the council's leadership.

Within the intricate hierarchy of the Padanaam, each Bhabhi is accompanied by a retinue of subordinates comprising two apprentices and four novices, symbolising the representation of the eight planetarums. The allocation of roles and responsibilities within each Padanaam is based on meritocracy, with strength in taakat serving as the primary criterion for advancement. Thus, the social or economic background of an individual prior to joining the Haree Tower holds little sway over their standing within the Sister Council, underscoring the council's commitment to equality and meritocracy.

Living within the hallowed halls of the Haree Tower, Bhabhi and their subordinates undertake a myriad of roles and duties, both within the confines of their sanctuary and during official missions and assignments across Anagha. As stewards of wisdom and guardians of enlightenment, they tirelessly labour to uphold the values and principles of the Bhabhi Salaah, ensuring the prosperity and harmony of all who dwell within the realm of Brjamohana.

Kainanis, devoted adherents within the esteemed ranks of the Bhabhi Salaah, pledge themselves to a sacred vow of chastity, poverty, and obedience, symbolising their unwavering commitment and allegiance to the revered Ma'an Seat. Tasked with the solemn duty of chronicling the oral history of Brjamohana and the cosmic genesis of the Anagha galaxy, Kainanis sisters serve as the custodians of sacred knowledge within the hallowed halls of the Haree Tower.

In their role as scribes, Kainanis meticulously recorded the timeless tales of Brjamohana, the genesis of Primis, and the celestial dance that birthed the Anagha galaxy. They also document the ancient rift between Brjamohana and her twin, Shraavana, illuminating the cosmic tapestry of creation and conflict that defines the universe.

The writings of the Kainanis, collectively known as the Zaabta of Brjamohana, serve as a testament to the wisdom and legacy of the Sister Council, preserving ancestral knowledge and divine teachings passed down through generations.

During pilgrimages to their respective home planetarum, Kainanis sisters embrace their role as emissaries of compassion and goodwill, extending hospitality and aid to travellers and pilgrims who seek solace and guidance in the local *bauddh*. With hearts overflowing with empathy and compassion, they offer assistance to the infirm, impoverished, and sick, embodying the spirit of service and selflessness that lies at the core of the Bhabhi Salaah's teachings.

Adorned in ceremonial shawls of pristine white, accented with black trim, the Kainanis sisters symbolise purity and humility in their sacred duties. This esteemed role is reserved exclusively for novices and apprentices, who exemplify the virtues of humility, dedication, and devotion as they embark on their transformative journey within the Sister Council.

Thus, the Kainanis stand as beacons of wisdom, compassion, and service, bridging the realms of the sacred and the mundane as they uphold the timeless teachings of Brjamohana and illuminate the path to enlightenment for all who seek solace within the embrace of the Bhabhi Salaah.

Vihaars, esteemed Bhabhi of exceptional stature within the Sister Council, is entrusted with the weighty responsibility of representing the interests and concerns of their respective Padanaam within the hallowed halls of the illustrious Haree Hall. Chosen by their Padanaam for their wisdom, integrity, and leadership acumen, these distinguished Bhabhi serve as the voice and advocate of their constituents, ensuring that their voices are heard, and their needs addressed at the highest levels of governance.

Forming a formidable cadre within the hallowed halls of the Haree Hall, the Vihaars convene both formally and informally in gatherings known as labaada. These meetings serve as a crucible of deliberation and discourse, providing a forum for the exchange of ideas, the articulation of concerns, and the formulation of collective decisions. During these sessions, the Vihaars may cast votes or engage in discussions on matters of vital importance, ranging from policy initiatives to strategic planning and crisis management.

One of the pivotal roles of the Vihaars within the Haree Hall is their participation in the selection and elevation of a new Ma'an Seat in the event of a vote of no confidence. Empowered by the collective mandate of their Padanaam, the Vihaars exercise their judgment and discernment in determining the suitability and legitimacy of potential candidates, ensuring the continuity and stability of leadership within the Sister Council.

Adorned in ceremonial shawls reflective of the vibrant hues of their respective planetae, the Vihaars symbolise the diversity and unity of Anagha, embodying the collective aspirations and heritage of their home worlds. These regal garments serve as visual emblems of their authority and allegiance, affirming their role as custodians of tradition and guardians of the Sister Council's legacy.

In essence, the Vihaars stand as pillars of wisdom, diplomacy, and integrity within the halls of the Haree Hall, wielding their influence and authority with grace and sagacity in service of the greater good. Through their steadfast leadership and unwavering dedication, they uphold the timeless values of the Bhabhi Salaah, ensuring the prosperity and harmony of all who dwell within the embrace of Brjamohana.

Rakhane vaale, entrusted with the sacred duty of preserving and managing the vast repository of knowledge housed within the revered halls of the Haree Tower library, occupies a pivotal role within the intricate hierarchy of the Bhabhi Salaah. Charged with the meticulous task of safeguarding the secrets of *Terahaveen* and maintaining the integrity of the council's archives, the Rakhane vaale serves as a custodian of history and guardian of wisdom.

In her capacity as the steward of the Haree Tower library, the Rakhane vaale meticulously organises and catalogues the myriad records and documents that comprise the council's collective knowledge. From ancient manuscripts to classified files, she sifts through a deluge of information, discerning the wheat from the chaff and ensuring that only the most pertinent and vital intelligence reaches the discerning eyes of the Ma'an.

Operating as an indispensable *aide de camp* to the Ma'an, the Rakhane vaale acts as a conduit between the inner sanctum of the Haree Tower and the bustling corridors below. With diligence and discernment, she filters through the myriad communications and reports that flow into her purview, relaying only the most critical and urgent matters to the esteemed leader of the Sister Council.

Moreover, the Rakhane vaale assumes the solemn responsibility of announcing the arrival of the Ma'an before her entrance into the hallowed chambers of the Haree Hall, ensuring that her presence commands respect and reverence befitting her exalted station. This ceremonial gesture serves as a symbol of deference and honour, underscoring the reverence with which the Ma'an is regarded by all within the council's inner circle.

A role of such gravitas and significance is entrusted exclusively to Bhabhi hailing from the Lynx sector, a testament to the esteemed lineage and inherent qualities of leadership and discernment that define the inhabitants of this esteemed region. Through her unwavering dedication and meticulous attention to duty, the Rakhane vaale upholds the sacred legacy of the Bhabhi Salaah, safeguarding its secrets and guiding its leaders with wisdom and grace.

Saala Ganatantr

The Saala Ganatantr, an esteemed institution founded in 5 A.D. by the paternal T'haerian ancestral tribes, stands as the male counterpart to the venerable Bhabhi Salaah, embodying a tradition of honour, duty, and martial prowess. Situated within the formidable Citadel of Sabha on T'haeri, the Saala Ganatantr is dedicated to the pursuit of knowledge, mastery of smithery, and excellence in combat, guided by the overarching principles of Brjamohana's teachings.

Central to the ethos of the Saala Ganatantr is a steadfast devotion to the belief in Brjamohana, serving as a prerequisite for admittance into its hallowed ranks. As an oath-bound society, members pledge themselves to the pursuit of enlightenment and service to their brethren, upholding the sacred values that define their esteemed order.

In the formative years of the Saala Ganatantr, a structured rank system was implemented to instil discipline, foster camaraderie, and uphold the ideological principles set forth by the revered Bhabhi Salaah. At the lowest rung of this hierarchical ladder stand the initiates, representing the youngest and least experienced members of the order. Charged with the singular focus of training and learning, initiates dedicate themselves to mastering the arts of combat, smithery, and scientific inquiry under the tutelage of their seasoned mentors.

As initiates progress along their journey within the Saala Ganatantr, they may choose to specialise in one of two distinct paths: that of the Saamant or the Sankalak. While the decision is typically deferred until later in their lives, some initiates may opt to pursue their chosen path early on, earning the title of initiate Saamant or initiate Sankalak. Once this foundational decision is made, they transition into the role of apprentice within their selected order, embarking on a transformative journey of mastery and self-discovery.

Within the esteemed ranks of the Saala Ganatantr, the **Sankalak** occupy a pivotal role as scientists and innovators, dedicated to advancing the frontiers of knowledge and pioneering groundbreaking technologies that propel the brotherhood into the forefront of intergalactic exploration and discovery. Tasked with the formidable responsibility of researching and developing intergalactic and extradimensional technologies, the Sankalak brothers serve as the vanguard of scientific inquiry within the Citadel of Sabha.

Drawing upon centuries of accumulated wisdom and the guiding principles of Brjamohana's teachings, the Sankalak devote themselves to the pursuit of scientific excellence, delving into esoteric fields such as quantum tunnelling, engineering, and advanced theoretical physics. With unwavering determination and boundless creativity, they push the boundaries of conventional understanding, seeking to unlock the mysteries of the cosmos and harness its latent potential for the betterment of the Saala Ganatantr and all who dwell within its embrace.

While most of their work takes place within the confines of the Citadel of Sabha, where they meticulously document their findings and collaborate on ambitious research projects, Sankalak brothers are not confined to their laboratories. Indeed, they are frequently called upon to venture into the field, testing their inventions and theories in real-world environments and confronting the challenges of interstellar exploration first-hand.

It is this unwavering dedication and pioneering spirit that led the Sankalak brothers to incessantly persuade the Ma'an Su to push ahead with the development of novel extradimensional travel technologies. Recognising the immense potential for discovery and advancement that lay beyond the confines of traditional space travel, the Sankalak championed the cause of interdimensional exploration, urging the Sister Council to embrace bold new frontiers and seize the opportunities that awaited in the uncharted realms of the multiverse.

As the custodians of craftsmanship and martial prowess within the esteemed ranks of the Saala Ganatantr, the *Saamant* brothers occupy a crucial role at the nexus of tradition, innovation, and defence. Renowned for their mastery of smithing and technical expertise, the Saamant fulfil a multifaceted role, providing essential support to the brotherhood's military endeavours while upholding societal order within the ancestral home world of T'haeri.

At the heart of their responsibilities lies the meticulous maintenance and management of the Saala Ganatantr's armoury, technology inventory, and supply infrastructure. With unparalleled skill and dedication, the Saamant brothers ensure that the brotherhood's arsenal remains well-stocked, its equipment in optimal condition, and its technological assets at the forefront of innovation. Whether forging weapons of war, repairing advanced machinery, or supplying technical services in the field, the Saamant exemplify the virtues of craftsmanship and service that define the ethos of the Saala Ganatantr.

In addition to their vital logistical role, the Saamant brothers play a pivotal role in supporting the Sena, the brotherhood's elite warriors, on expeditions and military campaigns. Drawing upon their technical expertise and combat prowess, they provide essential support services, ranging from equipment maintenance and repair to tactical advice and logistical coordination. Through their unwavering dedication and resourcefulness, the Saamant ensure that the Sena are well-prepared and equipped to confront any challenge that may arise in the field.

Moreover, the Saamant brothers serve as custodians of societal order within T'haeri, leveraging their authority and influence to uphold the values and traditions that define the ancestral homeland of the Saala Ganatantr. Through their leadership and guidance, they foster a sense of unity, discipline, and resilience among the inhabitants of T'haeri, ensuring stability and prosperity for generations to come.

For those Saamant brothers who seek to ascend to even greater heights of martial prowess and leadership, the path to the Sena is open through rigorous combat training and skilful demonstration of prowess on the battlefield. Graduating to the esteemed ranks of the Sena, they embody the pinnacle of martial excellence within the Saala Ganatantr, serving as guardians of honour, defenders of the realm, and champions of Brjamohana's sacred legacy.

As the preeminent combat force and esteemed leaders within the Saala Ganatantr, the **Sena** brothers embody the pinnacle of martial prowess, strategic acumen, and unwavering dedication to duty. Charged with safeguarding the interests of the brotherhood and shaping its destiny, the Sena serve as the vanguard of strength, resolve, and resilience, guiding the Saala Ganatantr through times of peace and conflict alike.

At the forefront of decision-making and leadership, the Sena brothers exercise unparalleled authority and influence within the brotherhood, wielding their collective wisdom and expertise to chart the course of scientific research, shape the paternal Houses of new initiates, and determine the overarching direction of the Saala Ganatantr's endeavours. Whether deliberating on matters of strategic importance or resolving internal disputes, the Sena brothers exemplify the virtues of honour, integrity, and unity that define the ethos of the brotherhood.

Central to the hierarchy of the Sena is the revered Ma'an Su, the supreme leader and spiritual guide of the Saala Ganatantr. Selected from among the ranks of the Sena by the Ma'an herself, the Saala of the Ma'an Su holds a position of unparalleled honour and responsibility, serving as the trusted confidante and loyal companion of the supreme leader. In recognition of their unwavering loyalty and commitment, those chosen as the Saala of the Ma'an Su are granted the rare privilege of partaking in Aushadhi, a sacred ritual that symbolises their union with the Ma'an Su and attainment of conscious awareness.

The consummation of Aushadhi represents a profound spiritual and metaphysical journey, through which the Saala achieves a heightened state of consciousness and unity with their revered leader. This sacred bond transcends the boundaries of individuality and ego, forging a deep and unbreakable connection between the Ma'an Su and her chosen Saala, ensuring harmony, strength, and unity within the ranks of the Saala Ganatantr.

In the wake of the cataclysmic events of *Terahaveen*, the Saala Ganatantr underwent profound transformations, reshaping their practices, beliefs, and societal roles in response to the devastating consequences of their overzealous pursuit of extradimensional travel. As the dust settled and the brotherhood sought to rebuild and reconcile with its past, sweeping reforms were enacted to ensure the stability, integrity, and harmony of the Saala Ganatantr.

Foremost among these reforms was the banning of Aushadhi, the sacred ritual once used by Saala brothers to attain heightened consciousness and supernatural abilities. Recognising the inherent dangers and abuses associated with the use of Aushadhi, the brotherhood moved to abolish this practice, thereby severing the direct link between Saala and transcendence.

In its place, a new bond was forged between Saala brothers and their Bhabhi counterparts, cemented through the divine power of taakat. Through this sacred bond, Saala brothers draw strength, resilience, and mental prowess from their connection to their Bhabhi, fostering a profound sense of unity, loyalty, and mutual dependence within the ranks of the Saala Ganatantr. This bond not only serves to reign in the influence of Saala brothers on the Bhabhi Salaah but also ensures their protection and well-being, allowing them to withstand ailments and injuries with remarkable resilience.

Moreover, in recognition of the need for continued innovation and scientific advancement, Saala brothers are now required to pursue higher education at Petraea University, where they study the sciences and collaborate on the development of innovative technologies. Embracing the ethos of intellectual inquiry and collaborative research, Saala brothers harness their collective ingenuity and expertise to push the boundaries of knowledge and innovation, ensuring that the Saala Ganatantr remains at the forefront of scientific discovery and technological progress.

Amidst these sweeping changes, the Saala rankings remain intact, serving as a symbol of hierarchy and prestige within the brotherhood. However, the Litany against Chaos, once a cautionary warning, has now become the guiding creed of the Citadel of Sabha, reminding all members of the Saala Ganatantr of the importance of balance, harmony, and restraint in their pursuit of knowledge and power.

Thus, through adaptation, reflection, and renewal, the Saala Ganatantr emerges from the shadows of Terahaveen, poised to embrace a future defined by unity, innovation, and enlightenment, guided by the timeless values of honour, duty, and fraternity.

While we looked to find meaning within these two celestial beings. Time stood still. And stars are born.

Chapter 1

In the aeons following the twins' birth, dark matter permeated the vast expanse of space, awaiting deployment to give shape to form and life substance. Brjamohana and Shraavana, the cosmic twins, spent countless ages together, refining their taakat and outlining the dimensions of their grand creation. Through the dust particles lingering from their birth, they crafted miniature systems, dreaming of binary dimensions, galaxies, and planetarum systems.

They would talk without end about their dreams of making binary dimensions, galaxies, and planetarum systems. "Look at our blank canvas. Imagine the things we could create and carry out," Brjamohana said to Shraavana.

"Our galaxies would be twins. One having natural resources the other does not. That way there can be mutual trading between the two. A sharing of knowledge, wisdom, and cultures," Shraavana mused.

"Yes! Imagine the unity that could be," Brjamohana said emphatically.

Their shared vision resonated with unity and cooperation. Brjamohana envisioned twin galaxies, each with unique resources, fostering trade, knowledge sharing, and cultural exchange. The twins were in complete harmony, both in mind and purpose, echoing, 'We will need workers to help us.' And thus, the *Aatma jeev*, spirit creatures, were born, categorised into *saaraapi*, *karoobi*, and *devadi*.

The *saaraapi* are stationed in front of the thrones of Brjamohana and Shraavana. They are covered with six wings—two cover their face, another two their feet, and with the last two they would fly about. The *karoobi* were works of art and are associated with the presence of both goddesses.

It can be said that Brjamohana and Shraavana are sitting between or upon the *karoobi*. Symbolically, the *karoobi* served as the 'representation of the caisson' of Brjamohana and Shraavana which they rode to explore space. The wings of the *karoobi* offered the twins both guarding protection and swiftness in travel.

It was the *karoobi* that Brjamohana wielded to seal the portal at the conclusion of *Terahaveen*, a promise etched in cosmic destiny. In fact, Brjamohana promised on that fateful day, "Never again will I subconsciously place into the minds of my children the desire to connect with their galactic siblings." The *devadi* were the last group and it is through these spirit beings that all living things were created.

Brjamohana's *taakat* is mother—giving forth life and taking from something old for something new to exist. Because she lived fully and carried out thoroughly her *dharma,* she is called Brahman. For Shraavana, her *taakat* manifested as supreme consciousness and great wisdom. This gave her the ability to be one with another's emotions and impart intellect, and knowledge.

As the supreme consciousness, Shraavana had the ability to absorb the emotions—negative and positive—of others. This would in turn amplify her own emotions making her more susceptible to feeling 'weighed down' by the speaker. This could sometimes lead her to have a sense of being overwhelmed and anxious about having to completely fulfil her role as second creator.

During this time, the two supreme beings were in sync. The Way of Life, *dharma*, was formally introduced by Brjamohana at this time. The first part was the universal, cosmic law (*rita*) that regulates the forces of *taakat,* manifested by the law pf physics. It controls everything from subatomic properties to their plans of creating analogous dimensions. It was the moral responsibility of both to decide how many galaxies and stars would be formed if there would be living things, and if would they need reverence from their creation.

As Alpha and Omega, they agreed to have the dimensions named Primis and Novissimus. Showing her deference for their birth order, Shraavana said to her sister, "As *jetha*, your dimension should be first to mine." Brjamohana, as the firstborn, handled Primis and Novissimus went to Shraavana. As binary beings, they decided the entire creative process should take a total of twenty-eight days to complete their dimensions; the premise being the number twenty-eight represented completeness and perfection.[1] This completed *rita*.

"Our next assignment is the decision of creation," Shraavana said.

Brjamohana called this period *varna dharma*. *Varna dharma* consisted of the duties and responsibilities each would fulfil in the family and cosmic society. An important aspect is religious and moral law. At this stage, Brjamohana decided what would be the rites for her creation to follow and shared these with her sister.

"Our creations are our children. They will need guidance, wisdom, and knowledge on how to accurately display one's devotion." She hoped Shraavana would create similar rites for her own creation. But something in Shraavana was starting to change.

Although second-born, am I too not a goddess? Why, then, should Brjamohana exalt herself above me and pass edicts on how things should be done?

An air/desire to use her *taakat* for her own purposes was creeping into Shraavana's heart. As mentioned, Shraavana takes on the emotions of others to her own detriment. Brjamohana's stress of creation, creating rites, and setting the purpose of her dimension was constantly and consistently shared with her. So, feeling the weight of her sister and the prospect of living up to that standard seemed unrealistic and burdening.

"Why **must** we be duality incarnate? Why can I not just **be**?" She mused with irritation. Although she was the second most powerful being in existence, she was starting to feel as if her sister was encapsulating her by setting up the dharmas.

"The more I share or do, all she does is dictate, dictate, **dictate!**" Therefore, she slowly started to withhold information/ideas from Brjamohana.

Svargeey dharma is the natural expression and evolution of the body, mind, soul, and feelings throughout the stages of the twins' life: righteousness, pleasure, and liberation. The divergence between the sisters and what is means to be just and right is taking full form. For Brjamohana, she believes the right or just expression is being cohesive with everything in unison.

As there is no room for uniqueness. She expressed this belief in her typical motherly tone to Shraavana. "How can anything stand, Shraavana, if there is division? Unity means completeness, oneness in thought and duty," Brjamohana would often say. To Shraavana it was condescending—*Am I not a supreme being as well!*

Brjamohana knew during the four stages she must complete each exactly so, without going off outside the dictated parameters. In *Brahmacharya*, she spent 25 years instituting standards. Brjamohana developed the sciences for all future living things; she set up what philosophy means and is in practice. She defined logic and practised self-discipline. She took this time to contemplate what it would mean to become a Divine Creator or Ultimate Reality.

To all future creations, Brjamohana will prove to be their guru. When she finished this stage, as the Alpha goddess, she took on the title of Brahman. This meant she was the highest dimensional and universal principle, the ultimate reality. All mater, energy, time, space, and being is seen to have come from Brjamohana from this point on.

During *Grihastha,* she formed T'haeri and gave life to females and males in her image. She named the first woman—Jyeshta—and the first man—Purush. She taught them how to pursue a virtuous life, blessed their land to give forth its fruitage and told them to be fruitful. In the *Vanaprastha* stage, she retired or rested.

Taking on a more advisory role, Brjamohana guided some of her creations to write down how to worship her—in what was later known as the Book of Brahman. In the last stage *Sannyasa*, Brjamohana entered a state of peace and bliss. She completely devoted herself to Muksh. Brjamohana gained freedom from rebirth, the cyclical nature of gaining new knowledge in each life. Thus, she reached celestial perfection—*sampoornata.*

"What could life be if I went with the ebb and flow of each rebirth? How much more when I learn? Or become my higher self?" Therefore, Shraavana explored what the four stages of *Svargeey* would mean for her, personally.

During the *Brahmacharya*, she focused on setting up her own set of laws about science, philosophy, her eventual Book of Shraavana, and logic.

These were not cohesive with the ones set out by her sister. This would mean all her creations would be in opposition with their dimensional siblings. This stage lasted some 25 Terrestris years for Shraavana after which she paused using her *taakat* to generate new forms of life.

As she entered *Grihastha* in the twenty-sixth year, Shraavana resumed giving forth life. She created the luminaries of Aakaashagang, seven life-sustaining planetarum in the three quadrants. Next, she made a division between light and dark, calling these periods, Din and Raat. Shraavana formed from the dust particles remaining from her birth, Dharatee. Afterwards, she made male and female in her likeness; she told them, "Your offspring will fill the four corners of the universe. So, be plenteous and tame Dharatee."

Instead of retiring during *Vanaprastha*, Shraavana continued to focus on increasing her own desires and pleasure—completely rejecting any idea of a greater emphasis on spiritual liberation. Reasoning—'Spiritual liberation **is derived** from centring on matters that bring greater happiness.' Therefore, renouncing material desires and her prejudices was not an option to consider during the last and final stage, *Sannyasa*. Shraavana continued reliving stages one to three, repeatedly in perpetuity. However, this meant Shraavana was prone to further degradation.

Since Shraavana severed her familial connection and lost celestial completeness, her wants and desires became increasingly carnal. This defied the logic of Brahman which was set by Brjamohana once she reached *sampoornata*. She lost all sense of logic and any self-control she was born with. Shraavana was no longer a goddess that measured up to twenty-eight. That is why upon entering the fourth *dharma*, she was overtly self-absorbed. It is during this stage that the multidimensional events of *Terahaveen* took place.

Shraavana's personality became darker and more withdrawn, overran by all the emotions she had been absorbing. Her mood went from avid listener to irritated hearer. 'The musings of these beings are becoming duller and denser by the second. Did I **not provide** them with the Book of Shraavana? These 'concerned matters' serve absolutely no purpose.' Her countenance went from radiating bold, vibrant purples to colder hues like blue and green. Her facial features became more pronounced—higher cheekbones, more defined chin, petite nose and mouth.

Blue markings appeared on her face in a lace-like pattern. Her eyes went from being soft and round to upturned and wide. Shravakans picture Shraavana with obsidian spiral pillowy hair, skin the colour of bronzite and eyes the colour of turquenite. On her head was a gold crown with lacework and in the centre was a spherical Paraiba blue topaz gemstone. Her countenance was devoid of vibrance and her original sagacity. Her wisdom became unpalatable and harsh. And her followers had an appearance of piety and higher insight which influenced the populace to be tyrannical and domineering.

Sva-dharma, the sum of one's life moulded by one's tendencies, personality, desires, and experiences. It is one's life path. Coming to grips with that Shraavana's love for her was growing cold, Brjamohana concluded, 'It is up to me to fulfil the Way of Life.' Therefore, she continued creating all things, beings—celestial/humanoid—in complete perfection. It took her twenty-seven creative periods to create Anagha, Srimad-Bhagavatam the planetary system and its eight planetarums and 1 P planetae, endow the first matriarchs of T'haeri with her *taakat*, and guide all her children to a harmonious society of life.

At the end of the twenty-seventh day, Brjamohana proceeded to rest. The twenty-eighth day was reserved for her last creation—forging a new, more whole relationship with Shraavana. Shraavana, on the other hand, saw the fourth *dharma* as her chance to live fully in her **own** essence, reserving her wisdom and supreme consciousness for her own creation. However, what she did not realise was severing the bond with her sister made all her creative works imperfect and prone to defect. This reduced her celestial number to twenty-seven.[2] Therefore, she completed her work in twenty-seven days instead of twenty-eight.

The story of Brjamohana's and Shraavana's creation and dimensions mirrored each other despite Shraavana's incepted desire to be unique. The dimensions themselves were two opposite sides of the same coin. Both headed towards a collision that could not be prevented. Neither Brjamohana nor Shraavana could have foreseen what would take place once that tunnel opened, and blithe and oppression rained down on T'haeri and her sister planetae. Nothing could have prepared Shraavana for the sheer will, might and determination of Brjamohana for the preservation of her creation's life.

Shraavana knew her sister to be associated with protection, strength, motherhood, and destruction to empower creation. But in the back of Shraavana's mind, she always pondered, **how** did Brjamohana use destruction to empower creation. What was to be created once she destroyed something? Forebodingly, she truly never wanted to find out the answer. For she knew the rage within her sister…she was her confidant.

Chapter 2

Brjamohana, shaping the first woman from red clay, breathed life into her creation, Jyeshta, infusing her with a measure of divine power, thus birthing Maanav. Naming her creation Jyeshta, Brjamohana then fashioned a magnificent garden, Surtseyan, upon an islet to the west of the principal continent. In this enchanted sanctuary, Jyeshta flourished, intimately connected with the flora that surrounded her, each plant communicating with her and with one another.

On the second day, Jyeshta was granted a divine vision by Brjamohana. The vision revealed the splendour of the majestic Baobab trees in the south, the crimson embrace of the planet's waters, and the myriad creatures inhabiting every corner of her world—creepy crawlers, soaring birds, winged beings, and sea monsters. Brjamohana entrusted Jyeshta with the task of naming each of these creatures and nurturing the land.

The third day brought profound teachings from Brjamohana to Jyeshta, "Your life and the lives of those to come are divided into four stages—Brahmacharya, Grihastha, Vanaprastha, and Sannyasa." During Brahmacharya, Jyeshta would receive education in science, philosophy, logic, and self-discipline, learning to lead a life of righteousness.

In Grihastha, she would embrace family life with a lifelong companion, managing her household, educating her offspring, and fostering a family-centred and righteous social existence. Vanaprastha would mark her retirement from household responsibilities, focusing on moksha—spiritual liberation. Finally, in Sannyasa, her attention would remain devoted to the pursuit of spiritual enlightenment.

Beneath the serene udyaan tree, Jyeshta eagerly absorbed Brjamohana's teachings daily, embarking on her educational journey. The initial lessons centred on the sciences, with Brjamohana illuminating the night sky with the stars of Srimad-Bhagavatam, naming each constellation and guiding Jyeshta to do the same whenever she gazed at the celestial canvas. The divine teachings extended to the origin of Brjamohana and her twin sister, born from a quasar—a revelation that rooted Jyeshta firmly in the field of astronomy.

As Jyeshta delved deeper into the sciences, Brjamohana expounded on the major branches—earth & space science, social science, life science, physical science, and formal science. The cosmos unfolded its mysteries before Jyeshta, and she absorbed the profound knowledge bestowed upon her.

Simultaneously, while naming the creatures populating T'haeri, Jyeshta traversed its expanse, communing with its flora and fauna. After a meticulous exploration lasting twenty-eight years, she christened her home T'haeri, reflecting its essence of tranquillity and peace. With the naming complete, Jyeshta transitioned to the next phase—cultivating T'haeri to make it a hospitable haven for her future descendants. Her dedication to shaping the environment showcased her commitment to the flourishing life on the celestial canvas she had been entrusted with.

Jyeshta, the inaugural sentient creation, manifested in extraordinary form. Standing at a height of 2.01 meters, she bore the visage of a humanoid endowed with long and sinuous limbs. Voluminous spiral hair, akin to the texture of cotton, cascaded down, adorned in hues of yellow reminiscent of the Lisianthus flower. Her skin, resembling mangan diaspore, exhibited crimson red undertones mirroring the vast oceans of T'haeri.

The enchanting viridian green of Jyeshta's eyes mirrored the leaves of the Baobab tree, reflecting the deep connection between the celestial guardian and her planetary abode. Embracing her uniqueness, Jyeshta found companionship in the maroon caracal—a striking Felidae with a maroon-gold coat and obsidian tufts of hair gracing its pointed ears. Together, they formed a harmonious bond, traversing the serene landscapes of T'haeri as the guardians of its tranquillity.

Despite Jyeshta's completeness, Brjamohana, in her benevolence, decided to gift her a male companion to share in the harmony of existence. Initiating a profound slumber upon Jyeshta, Brjamohana crafted a male humanoid from red clay during her rest. Placing the newly formed man beside Jyeshta, she breathed life into him, filling his lungs with the essence of existence. As the man awoke, Jyeshta examined him and bestowed upon him the name Purush, signifying male.

Purush, adorned with *ochre*-hued pigment, exhibited a complexion of light brown with underlying olive undertones. Tribal markings in gold adorned his cheeks, complementing his haunting copper-coloured eyes. His jet-black hair framed a chiselled jaw reminiscent of the Kati Mountains. Standing at a height of 2.11 meters, Purush possessed long, muscular limbs akin to the Khashab alward tree found in Central Azore.

His headdress, crafted from vanadium metal with gold scrollwork and *arjuani ododo* on either side, added a regal touch to his appearance. Purush became an integral part of Jyeshta's life, and together they embraced the journey of unity and companionship. Affectionately, he would be known as *Baba Khasha* by his grandchildren due to his resemblance to the majestic tree.

For twenty-eight years, Jyeshta and Purush remained childless. Over the course of the years, they were filling out their oneness in thought and mind. Their intricate love grew and blossomed like the choko ulimwengu, a flower that is reddish-brown in colour and smells like roasted cacao when it blooms; a dense fruity and nutty aroma that lingers in one's nostrils when inhaled.

Upon seeing the flower, Purush so named Jyeshta his '*choko*' for her extraordinary beauty and deep maroon pigment, her cheeks turning red like the *ododo*.

Jyeshta did not think herself to be the motherly type. She knew Purush was given to her for the intended purpose of filling T'haeri with their offspring. However, she found and felt content in being childless and in reaching her higher self. "I want motherhood but only if it doesn't conflict with my sense of self," she would often say to herself. So, she would seek Brjamohana's face, asking for reassurance that her motherly duties would not take away from her personal being. One evening, Jyeshta had a vivid dream of Anagha.

Brjamohana took her by the hand and said, "Walk with me. I want to show you, what you and all those after you will be and become."

The eight planetae appeared before her. Jyeshta saw each planetae being terraformed for habitation and her daughters spread out across Srimad-Bhagavatam. Jyeshta then saw her daughters seated on a counsel that kept the peace and balance—she along with her eight daughters are said to be its founders. The rudimentary workings of intergalactic travel had been realised along with extragalactic travel. When she woke, Jyeshta understood that motherhood was one stage in her overall dharma. And with the effusive expressions from Purush, she was finding it easier to fulfil this part of her dharma.

Together, Jyeshta and Purush set out to cultivate T'haeri. They walked its length and breadth, naming and marking the boundaries of each continent and body of water. They named the land where they formed their family Mwanzo wa Maisha—*the beginning of life*. Mwanzo wa Maisha is in the middle of the four major continents and surrounded by three *al'anhar*—Dijlah flowing southeast, Nahr Al-Furāt flowing southwest, and Nahr Bishah flowing west.

The sea to the west was the Mashambani Sea, to the southwest was the Nyekundu Sea, and to the southeast was the Kiajemi Sea.

The north-western most continent where the climate was colder and the air thinner, Purush suggested the name Iinkiltira, with the tribal name Angrezee.

He said, "Here people will be fair like the cold, eyes crystal blue like azurite, and hair dark like the night sky." Purush's poetic nature caused Jyeshta's ruddy brown cheeks to turn red like the choko ulimwengu flower. Taking her by the hand, Purush said, "Let's go for a stroll." They travelled east passed the Kati Mountains and to a landmass rich in iron, manganese, tin, tungsten, antimony, copper, lead, zinc, aluminium, gold, silver, mica, and precious stones. This continent had the physical characteristics of mountain systems, plateaus, plains, steppes, and deserts. Its boundaries were the Laaras Mountains in the west and the Maji Ocean in the east.

Finding the land to be majestic in nature, Jyeshta gave it the name Asrawi, and the tribal nomen, Eshiyaee. Asrawi had many mountain ranges however, none could compare to its sub-continent ranges: Makazi ya Theluji, Tulivu, and Salamu. As the largest mountain system, it was collectively called the great Makazi ya Theluji. That evening, Jyeshta and Purush sat at the base of Makazi ya Theluji.

Purush took Jyeshta into his arms, and she shared with him Brjamohana's future blessings for their family. She said, "Our daughters will keep the cosmic order of Srimad-Bhagavatam, forming a counsel of sisters. Our sons will become the progenitors of technology and the counsel for male stewards. And they will be spread out across the four quadrants of Anagha."

Purush silently gave thanks to Brjamohana and in an undertone said, "*Alsalam ealayna*."

As the years unfolded, Jyeshta and Purush continued their exploration, naming the remaining four continents and using various mountain systems to demarcate their boundaries. With time, the couple welcomed children into their lives. To aid them in the proper upbringing of their offspring, Brjamohana bestowed upon Jyeshta the *Book of Brahman* through a visionary experience.

This sacred text contained teachings on dharma, guidelines on regulating a woman's innate taakat, and insights into the branches of sciences, philosophy, and logic. The next morning, Jyeshta eagerly shared with Purush the knowledge she had gained about science and its diverse branches—formal, natural, and social. Thus began the oral tradition of passing down this valuable wisdom through generations.

∞

Jyeshta and Purush, united in purpose and bound by a shared vision, embarked on the monumental task of cultivating T'haeri. Their relationship was a pattern woven with threads of mutual respect, love, and a profound understanding of each other's strengths and weaknesses.

Jyeshta, with her keen intellect and deep connection to philosophy, served as the beacon of wisdom in their partnership. Her insights into the cosmic order and her ability to foresee the consequences of their actions became invaluable as they traversed the uncharted territories of T'haeri. Jyeshta's grounded and nurturing nature provided a stable foundation for their family and the societies they were destined to shape.

Purush, with his poetic soul and appreciation for the beauty of nature, brought a creative and intuitive dimension to their endeavours. His visions extended beyond the practicalities of cultivation, encompassing the aesthetic and spiritual aspects of the land. It was Purush's poetic inclinations that led to the naming of Iinkiltira, envisioning a people fair as the cold, with eyes crystal blue like azurite, and hair dark as the night sky.

As they walked the length and breadth of T'haeri, naming continents and marking boundaries, Jyeshta and Purush faced challenges that tested the resilience of their union. The diverse landscapes presented not only physical hurdles but also philosophical dilemmas. Differences in approaches emerged, each reflecting their unique perspectives—Jyeshta's inclination towards order and structure, and Purush's affinity for beauty and spontaneity.

Yet, in the face of challenges, their complementary strengths became more apparent. Jyeshta's wisdom guided them through the intricacies of societal organisation, while Purush's artistic vision added a layer of cultural richness to their endeavours. The occasional disagreements only deepened their understanding, creating a dynamic synergy that fuelled the transformative journey of T'haeri.

Purush's poetic gestures, like naming the sea to the west Mashambani, Nyekundu to the southwest, and Kiajemi to the southeast, became cherished moments that not only shaped the geography but also reflected the poetry of their shared existence. The evenings spent at the base of Makazi ya Theluji were not just about strategic decisions but also moments of quiet reflection, where the vastness of their undertaking met the intimacy of their connection.

In these moments, when Jyeshta shared Brjamohana's visions, and Purush silently gave thanks, the spiritual and familial bonds deepened. The challenges became threads in the pattern, weaving a story of partnership and collaboration that transcended the cultivation of T'haeri. Together, Jyeshta and Purush navigated the complexities of creation, leaving an indelible mark not just on the land but on the very fabric of their shared destiny.

Jyeshta and Purush were blessed with a sizeable family, comprising eight daughters and six sons. Their daughters—Hakima, Barika, Maua Maridadi, Fanaana, Pravakta, Almuelijuntha, Tabiba, and Mahila Savaaree—each received a male steward from Brjamohana upon reaching the age of twenty-eight. It was considered *mahzur*, prohibited, for a daughter to choose a male steward from among her brothers, according to Brjamohana's guidance. The six sons—Akida, Balozi, Mwenye, Utambuzi, Mwana, and Abedi—alongside their father, Purush, would go on to become the founding fathers of what later developed into the Saala Ganatantr.

Jyeshta took on the responsibility of imparting the knowledge she gained from Brjamohana to her eight daughters. Notably, Hakima, the eldest daughter, displayed exceptional prowess in philosophy and social science. Hakima's clan developed a deep love for wisdom, seeking to understand fundamental truths about themselves, their world, and their relationships. Together, they established the four pillars of philosophy—theoretical, practical, logic, and the history of philosophy.

In one of their nightly discussions, Jyeshta shared the Litany against Chaos with Hakima, emphasising its significance as an admonition reserved for those exceptional in philosophic wisdom. Jyeshta foresaw that Barika's clan would contribute to unlocking the wonders of Anagha, guided by the wisdom imparted by Hakima's clan.

As Hakima reached the age of twenty-eight, a pivotal moment in their familial history unfolded. Brjamohana presented her with Chaarak, a steward entrusted to assist Hakima in fulfilling her destiny. The instruction was clear: Hakima was to leave her homeland and journey north, where she and her descendants would span the vast stretch from the Prashaant Ocean to the Laaras Mountains. Hakima and Chaarak embraced this directive, embarking on a journey that led them to the new homeland of Iinkiltira. Together, they laid the foundation for the Angrezee, a lineage destined for greatness.

Hakima shivered, pulling the coarse furs of their makeshift cloaks tighter. The wind, a constant here in the north, whipped at their faces, stinging their sun-kissed skin. Beside her, Chaarak, his broad frame silhouetted against the bruised purple sky, adjusted the straps of their heavily laden packs.

Gone were the vibrant greens and endless blues of Mwanzo wa Maisha, their homeland cradled by the life-giving embrace of three rivers. Iinkiltira offered a stark contrast. The rolling plains stretched endlessly beneath a perpetually grey sky, the horizon a jagged line where the land bled into the unforgiving expanse. Here, the days were shorter, the relentless sun dipping below the horizon earlier, stealing away the warmth with alarming swiftness.

Yet, in this harsh beauty, Hakima saw possibility. The tall, ochre-hued grasses whispered secrets in the wind, and the clusters of hardy, grey-barked trees hinted at hidden resilience. This was a land that demanded adaptation, a quality she and Chaarak possessed in abundance.

Their journey north, a union forged not just in love but in a shared thirst for exploration, had been arduous. But with each challenge, their bond had strengthened. They learned to hunt the silent grey stalk deer, their swiftness a stark contrast to the lumbering beasts of Mwanzo wa Maisha. They discovered the warmth trapped within the seemingly barren earth, using volcanic stones to cook their meals and ward off the encroaching chill.

As they crested a low hill, a sight unfolded before them that caused Hakima to gasp. Nestled in the valley below, nestled amidst the swaying grasses, were clusters of low, dome-shaped dwellings, constructed from woven branches and covered in what looked like cured animal skins. Smoke curled from chimneys, a comforting sign of life in this unforgiving land.

Here, perhaps, was the start of something new. A tribe, the Angrezee, born from their union, their resilience, and their unwavering spirit, taking root in the unforgiving embrace of Iinkiltira.

The passage of time and the distance travelled left an indelible mark on Hakima's descendants. The olive pigment of their skin lightened, akin to the transformation of sunlight on the horizon. Their hair darkened, reminiscent of the jasper stone, and their eyes sparkled with the brilliance of azurite crystals. The Angrezee, devoted to the pursuit of wisdom and communion with Brjamohana, held a special place in the celestial entity's gaze. They were blessed with direct access to Brjamohana's taakat, a source of power and insight that allowed them to obtain Brahman.

The Angrezee's direct connection to Brjamohana's taakat manifested in various aspects of Hakima's daily life. Firstly, Hakima and her descendants developed an acute sensitivity to the cosmic energies that surrounded them. They could attune themselves to the subtle vibrations of the universe, gaining insights and foresight that eluded others. This connection facilitated a deeper understanding of the natural order and the underlying principles governing existence.

The benefits of this connection included heightened intuition, intellectual clarity, and an enhanced ability to navigate complex situations. Hakima, as a leader, could make decisions with a profound understanding of their long-term implications. The Angrezee's communion with Brjamohana's taakat also granted them a form of cosmic protection, shielding them from certain calamities and guiding them in times of uncertainty.

However, this connection also came with burdens. The heightened sensitivity meant that the Angrezee could feel the cosmic disturbances caused by imbalance and chaos. Hakima bore the weight of responsibility to maintain harmony within Iinkiltira. The challenges included navigating the delicate equilibrium of cosmic energies and ensuring that their actions aligned with the cosmic principles they revered.

Overall, the connection to Brjamohana's taakat shaped Hakima's leadership style and influenced the Angrezee's role in Iinkiltira. It was a source of both empowerment and accountability, guiding them on a unique path of cosmic enlightenment and communal prosperity.

Hakima herself bore the physical manifestations of her lineage's connection to both wisdom and the cosmos. Her warm ivory complexion, adorned with deep olive undertones, framed features that bespoke a regal elegance. Two braids of black and purple fine hair cascaded down her back, while cobalt-coloured eyes, with a ring of honey amber at their centre, held the depth of both intellect and celestial understanding.

White dots adorned her brow line and formed intricate markings on her cheeks, reminiscent of a symbolic language. Crowned with a headdress of interlocking copper pieces, Hakima stood tall and slender at a height of 2.09 meters, a living embodiment of her clan's legacy and connection to the divine.

∞

The Angrezee tribe whispered tales that spoke of distant kin, a tribe born of the same blood but destined to roam far across the plains of Iinkiltira. They were the Yamnaya, a nomadic people whose origins were intertwined with those of the Angrezee, yet who forged their own path.

The bond between the two tribes was not just one of blood, but of shared lineage, their ancestors Hakima and Chaarak, the progenitors of their race. Yet, as they journeyed and guided the stars, the Yamnaya evolved, adapting to the geography they encountered. And with each passing generation, subtle changes began to emerge, shaping their appearance and their culture in ways both profound and unique.

Where the Angrezee were tall and slender, their skin kissed by ochre hues and their eyes a piercing crystal blue, the Yamnaya bore a slight variance in their appearance. Their frames were just as lithe, their stature just as imposing, yet their skin held a toasted beige hue, reminiscent of the sun-kissed sands of 'Akhta' desert, in the east. Their eyes ranged from shades of amber to the stormy grey of impending tempests, a reflection of the myriad skies they had gazed upon. And their hair, instead of the dark depths of night, glinted with hues of reddish black, like smouldering embers beneath the surface.

Despite these differences, the bond between the Angrezee and the Yamnaya remained unbreakable, a testament to the enduring legacy of Hakima and Chaarak. And though their paths diverged across the vastness of space, their shared heritage ensured that they would forever remain bound by blood and kinship, their fates intertwined in ways that transcended time and distance.

At the heart of Yamnaya life beat the rhythm of the nomadic spirit, as they traversed the vast expanses of the *Ah'mil* steppe with a grace born of generations of familiarity. Their lives were entwined with the rhythm of the seasons, as they followed the migrations of herds and the blooming of wildflowers across the boundless plains.

Yet, it was not merely survival that drove the Yamnaya, but a quest for greatness that burned bright within their souls. They were warriors, fierce and indomitable, their prowess on horseback unmatched as they thundered across the steppes with the thundering hooves of their steeds. Clad in furs and armour adorned with symbols of their lineage, they rode as the vanguard of their people.

The Yamnaya were artisans of culture and civilisation. Around their campfires, tales were spun of heroes, their words echoing across the plains like whispers carried on the wind. They crafted exquisite ornaments of gold and bronze, their intricate designs reflecting the beauty of the natural world that surrounded them.

In the depths of winter, when the steppes lay shrouded in snow and ice, the Yamnaya retreated to their settlements, where the warmth of community and kinship awaited. Here, beneath the shelter of their yurts, they celebrated the bonds of family and friendship, sharing stories and songs that wove the fabric of their shared identity ever tighter.

But perhaps most enduring of all was the legacy of the Yamnaya's indomitable spirit, a flame that burned bright even in the darkest of times. From their humble beginnings as wanderers of the steppe, they rose to become architects of empires, their influence stretching far beyond the bounds of their ancestral lands.

∞

Barika, the second eldest daughter, harboured a deep affection for Earth and space sciences, particularly astronomy. Her passion ignited beneath the vast expanse of the night sky, where she would lose herself in the dance of the stars, tracing each constellation with practised ease. With her feet planted firmly in the ruddy clay soil, she sought communion with the celestial realm, posing questions about their origins and trajectories.

During her nightly discussions with her mother, Barika would eagerly share her insights, revealing how the movements of the celestial bodies unveiled profound truths about their own existence. She found solace and enlightenment in the silent conversations she held with the stars, their silent brilliance guiding her on a journey of discovery that transcended the boundaries of mere mortal understanding.

"*Alsalam ealayna,*" Jyeshta whispered, her words carrying a weight of reverence. "I felt your celestial affinity even in the cradle of my *al'awrasiu*. Brjamohana has bestowed upon you, gifts surpassing my teachings, and her guidance will endure." Gazing up at the shimmering Najm Shamal, Jyeshta sensed the impending shift in the stars. In three days' time, Barika's heart would stir with the call to depart from her kin, for she would reach the age of twenty-eight, marking a pivotal moment in her journey.

The third day arrived, and it was fully the twenty-eighth year of Barika's life. Brjamohana touched the space in between her eyes opening her mind to the wondrous cosmos and what lay beyond it. Barika saw the rudimentary tunnels of galactic travel forming, encircling, and closing around her. Overwhelmed by what she envisioned; Barika fell into a deep mediative trance.

Feeling Brjamohana's hand on her shoulder, Barika awoke and Brjamohana presented Mustashar'akim, her male steward. Together the two left Mwanzo wa Maisha for Azore and were the ancestors of the Naijeeri. As they left for Azore, Brjamohana whispered in Barika's ear, "Whenever you look to the stars, there I will be, and I will let myself be found by you."

Jyeshta also taught Barika the *Litany against Chaos* as she had with Hakima. She further instructed her to pass the dirge down to each firstborn daughter of her future clan. Later it was said that whenever Brjamohana allowed herself to be found by Barika and Mustashar'akim's children, their skin would turn *easal,* their hair would glow like Como, and they would be thoroughly entwined with Brjamohana, travelling along the celestial currents.

This entwining happened so often; this change in their pigmentation and hair became their permanent features along with their *bibi's* eye colour of veridian green. Barika grew to be the tallest of her sisters, standing at a magnificent 2.12 m tall.

The oral tradition of reciting the *Litany against Chaos*, continued until it was lost to time and eventually forgotten. Only the eldest daughter with the strongest connection to Brjamohana, could remember and unlock the knowledge of creating extradimensional travel.

∞

Barika stood beneath the expanse of the night sky, the constellations overhead painting a celestial canvas. The gentle breeze carried the whispers of the cosmos, and Brjamohana's touch stirred a restlessness within her heart. The call to adventure echoed through the cosmic currents, urging Barika to leave the familiarity of Mwanzo wa Maisha and venture into the unknown of Azore.

Internal conflicts tugged at Barika's being. A profound love for her family and the land of her birth clashed with the irresistible pull of the cosmic forces. The weight of responsibility, instilled by her mother's teachings and the Litany against Chaos, bore down on her shoulders. Yet, the celestial yearning was undeniable, an ancient song resonating within her very essence.

As Barika prepared to leave, emotions intertwined like the stars above. Joy and anticipation of the cosmic mysteries that awaited her collided with the sorrow of parting from the warmth of her family. She shared tearful moments with her siblings, imparting wisdom, and love, promising to remain a guiding light in their lives.

Jyeshta, her mother, understood the cosmic rhythms that governed Barika's destiny. In a quiet moment, as the Najm Shamal watched over them, Jyeshta whispered words of encouragement. "Alsalam ealayna," she said, acknowledging the cosmic connection that had been sensed since Barika's inception. The departure was bittersweet, a dance of separation and unity in the grand cosmic symphony.

$$\infty$$

Mustashar'akim, a steadfast companion chosen by Brjamohana, became the anchor in Barika's cosmic odyssey. He possessed a quiet strength and an innate understanding of the celestial currents that guided their journey. His role extended beyond a mere steward; he was a partner in deciphering the secrets of the universe.

Azore, the destination of their cosmic pilgrimage, unfolded as a tapestry of wonders. It was a realm where the boundaries between the material and celestial blurred. A landscape rich in ethereal beauty, adorned with crystalline structures that refracted the cosmic energies that permeated the atmosphere.

The air itself seemed to shimmer with the resonance of celestial harmonies.

Together, Barika and Mustashar'akim navigated the challenges of Azore, exploring its mysteries and connecting with the cosmic threads that wove through the very fabric of the land. Mustashar'akim, with his intuitive understanding of the celestial energies, complemented Barika's astronomical wisdom. Their union became a dance of balance, a harmonious synchronisation with the cosmic currents.

As they forged their path in Azore, Barika and Mustashar'akim became the ancestors of the Naijeeri. Their presence left an indelible mark on the cosmic weaving of Azore, and their descendants would continue the legacy of celestial entwining. The setting sun of Mwanzo wa Maisha became a distant memory as they embraced the cosmic dawn of Azore, where the celestial currents guided their every step.

∞

In the quiet solitude of Mwanzo wa Maisha, under the celestial canopy that adorned the night sky, Barika, the second eldest daughter, found solace in the embrace of the cosmos. Night after night, she would venture into the open expanse, her eyes fixed upon the weaving of stars that unfolded above. Barika's heartbeat was in tandem with the rhythmic dance of the constellations, and in those moments, she felt an ethereal connection that transcended the boundaries of earthly existence.

In the stillness of the ruddy clay soil beneath her feet, Barika engaged in a ritual that mirrored a conversation with the heavens. With a voice barely above a whisper, she would call out to each constellation by its given name. The night air would carry her words to the stars, and, with a sense of anticipation, she would wait for their subtle responses. It was as though the cosmos itself held secrets waiting to be unravelled, and Barika sought to unlock the mysteries of the universe through her nightly dialogues.

Her love for Earth and space sciences, particularly astronomy, was not merely an academic pursuit; it was a passion that permeated the core of her being. Each twinkle in the night sky held a story, a narrative written in the language of stars, and Barika was determined to decipher its every nuance. The constellations became her companions, silent witnesses to her inquiries about their formation, their movements, and the cosmic tales they spun across the cosmos.

This deep curiosity shaped Barika's worldview in profound ways. She viewed the world not just through the lens of earthly existence but as an interconnected weaving of celestial wonders. The mundane and the extraordinary coexisted in her perception, and every challenge or triumph was but a small chapter in the grand narrative of the cosmos. Her decisions, influenced by this cosmic perspective, took on a significance beyond the immediate, guided by a profound understanding that her journey was a part of a much larger celestial design.

Barika's intellectual depth extended beyond the scientific realm; it embraced a spiritual dimension as she sought to comprehend the cosmic forces that shaped her destiny. This unique worldview set her on a path that transcended the boundaries of the known, leading her towards a destiny intertwined with the very stars she so ardently studied.

∞

In the heart of Naijeeri lies the vibrant tapestry of the Al'iyghbw people, descendants of the illustrious Barika and Mustashar'akim, whose legacy reverberates through the corridors of time. From their ancestral lands, nestled amidst rolling hills and lush forests, the Al'iyghbw have woven a rich cultural tapestry that is as intricate as it is vibrant.

Central to the identity of the Al'iyghbw is their language, a marvel of complexity and nuance that reflects the very essence of their being. Unlike conventional tongues, the language of the Al'iyghbw is not spoken with words but with chemical phereins, gases that carry within them a complex network of emotions, thoughts, and intentions.

As the Al'iyghbw converse, the air around them becomes infused with a symphony of scents, each pherein carrying with it a wealth of meaning that transcends the limitations of mere words. A subtle shift in the composition of these gases can convey joy, sorrow, anger, or love with an eloquence that defies description.

The Al'iyghbw have mastered the art of interpreting these chemical signals, honing their senses to discern the subtle nuances of emotion that dance upon the air. Through this intricate language of phereins, they forge connections that run deeper than mere words, binding them together in a tapestry of shared experience and understanding.

In addition to their remarkable language, the Al'iyghbw are renowned for their vibrant cultural traditions, which find expression in music, dance, and storytelling. From the rhythmic beat of the drums to the swirling movements of their traditional dances, every aspect of Al'iyghbw culture is infused with a sense of vitality and passion that is palpable to all who encounter it.

But perhaps most striking of all is the warmth and hospitality of the Al'iyghbw people, who welcome strangers with open arms and open hearts. In their presence, one cannot help but be swept away by the intoxicating aroma of their phereins, which speak volumes of their kindness, generosity, and boundless spirit.

As the sun sets over the ancestral lands of the Al'iyghbw, casting a golden glow upon the landscape, one cannot help but marvel at the beauty and richness of their culture. For in the language of phereins and the traditions of their ancestors, the Al'iyghbw have found a way to express the very essence of their souls, leaving an indelible mark on the world around them.

∞

Maua Maridadi, the third progeny of Jyeshta and Purush, found her calling in the intricate pattern of plant life. Her affinity for the life sciences, particularly botany, blossomed into a profound love for the flora that adorned Mwanzo wa Maisha. In the familial storytelling sessions, she would captivate her audience by describing over 600 diverse plant species, unravelling the secrets of their growth habits and medicinal properties.

As Maua Maridadi delved into her studies, her contributions to the understanding of plants extended beyond mere description. She became a pioneer in improving plant growth, creating genetically compatible hybrids, and imparting invaluable knowledge on irrigation and fertilisation practices. The disciplines of botany—morphology, physiology, ecology, and systematics—blossomed from her passion and dedication.

Her unique appearance mirrored the botanical beauty she cherished. Maua Maridadi's skin, akin to grey bentonite clay with muted olive undertones, held the essence of the earth. A pale greyish-blue tint adorned her forehead, nose, and cheeks, a testament to her connection with the botanical realm.

Standing tall at 2.07 meters, her slate green eyes mirrored the hues of the foliage she studied. Her Afro-textured hair, slate grey-blue with moss and non-flowering sprouts, was crowned with pale green kamal phool flowers, and golden implants adorned her cheeks like dew-kissed jewels.

On her twenty-eighth birthday, a pivotal moment awaited Maua Maridadi as Brjamohana bestowed upon her a male steward named Sarih. Together, they embarked on a journey eastward, leaving the familiar grounds of Mwanzo wa Maisha for Madhy Asrawi. In this new land, they continued their botanical explorations, contributing to the terraforming efforts and identifying newly evolved species.

The clan that formed around Maua Maridadi and Sarih played a crucial role as ecologists on the planetae Saanvi. Their expertise extended to the careful study and categorisation of the terraformed species, including the remarkable Aushadhi. Maua Maridadi's legacy, intertwined with the verdant tapestry of plant life, continued to flourish as she and Sarih nurtured the botanical wonders of the cosmos.

In their efforts as ecologists, Maua Maridadi and Sarih became stewards of a new world, cultivating harmony between the native flora and the terraformed species. Their journey, guided by the cosmic forces and their shared passion, etched a vibrant chapter in the ongoing saga of T'haeri's exploration and adaptation.

In the lineage of Jyeshta and Purush, Fanaana emerged as a creator, finding her passion not in the sciences but in the vibrant beauty of nature and the art of expression. She developed what would later be recognised as the philosophy of art—an intricate study exploring the nature of art, delving into concepts of interpretation, representation, and expression. Alongside this, she delved into aesthetics, the philosophical study of beauty and taste.

Fanaana's artistic legacy found a home in Mangal, where her descendants established the seat of arts, culture, and architecture. Her clan became revered for their mastery in sculpting, painting, and building, defining the very essence of beauty and taste on T'haeri.

In her studio on one fateful day, experimenting with T'haerian clay, Fanaana encountered a sweet breeze that unveiled a male sculpture she had been working on. To her surprise, standing before her was Svaamee, her male steward, resembling the semi-finished sculpture. As Najm Shamal watched over them, Fanaana, on her twenty-eighth birthday, acknowledged the cosmic alignment that brought them together.

With a content understanding smile, Fanaana and Svaamee left the embrace of her family to embark on a journey to the south-eastern continent of

Faransa. There, amid the enchanting landscapes, the two became one—a union of creativity and companionship.

Standing tall at 2.04 meters, Fanaana inherited the choko complexion from her mother Jyeshta, while her eyes, reminiscent of her father Purush, held cyan rings inside lapis orbs. Mosaic facial markings adorned her features in cerulean blue, ecru, and deep saffron, creating a visual masterpiece around her brow line and under her eyes.

Her headdress, crafted from hammered vanadium metal with gold etchings in a geometric pattern, added an air of regality. A reddish copper downward triangle rested on her forehead, accentuating her distinctive features. Copper earrings resembling rotating gears adorned her saea, complementing her auburn hair with shades of *brinjal*.

Fanaana, with her unique presence and artistic vision, left an indelible mark on the cultural landscape of T'haeri. Her philosophy of art and aesthetic sensibilities shaped the creative endeavours of her descendants, resonating through the sculptures, paintings, and buildings that adorned Mangal and beyond.

In the dossier of Jyeshta and Purush's lineage, Pravakta emerged as a scholar with a profound love for the social sciences. Much like her older sister Hakima, Pravakta's interests were rooted in sociology and psychology. She became the architect of the foundational principles governing the developmental, structural, and functional aspects of human society on T'haeri.

Pravakta's studies went beyond the boundaries of her own kind, encompassing the diverse lifeforms that inhabited T'haeri. Sitting beneath the shade of a Delonix regia, she connected with every living organism, a harmonious exchange of information that transcended verbal communication. Her name, meaning 'communicator', foreshadowed the role her descendants would play as *Almutasilin*, adept communicators in the intricate web of T'haerian life.

Pravakta bore a distinctive appearance that mirrored her intellectual prowess.

Copper hair cascaded around her warm ivory complexion, a harmonious blend that spoke of both strength and elegance. Gold hexagonal forehead jewellery adorned her, a symbol of the intricate connections she sought to understand.

Her amber-pigmented eyes held the depth of her insights into the minds and behaviours of the T'haerian lifeforms. Rounded points adorned her ears, a nod to her connection with both tradition and innovation. Draped in traditional Bulifi garb in greys, slate, and copper hues, Pravakta stood tall at 2.06 meters, a beacon of wisdom and understanding.

On the eve of her twenty-eighth birthday, Brjamohana presented Pravakta with a male steward named Tabib'dhukir. Together, they embarked on a journey westward, traversing Azore and crossing the vast expanse of the Prashaant Ocean. Their destination was Bolev, a new land where Pravakta's insights into social dynamics and communication would find fresh ground.

In Bolev, Pravakta and Tabib'dhukir continued their exploration of the intricate relationships that wove through the fabric of T'haerian society. The Almutasilin, descendants of Pravakta, became known for their exceptional communication skills, serving as bridges between diverse communities and fostering understanding in the ever-evolving social landscape.

In the verdant embrace of Mwanzo wa Maisha, Almuelijuntha emerged as a guardian of herbal plant life, a practitioner of the ancient art of phytotherapy. Her deep connection with nature led her to unlock the healing abilities concealed within the flora that adorned their homeland. Almuelijuntha's expertise extended to identifying plants that aided in digestion, maintained dental health, or soothed an upset stomach.

Immersed in the natural rhythms of Mwanzo wa Maisha, Almuelijuntha's knowledge was so intimate that she could guide seekers to the exact location of the needed herb, whether it hid beneath a particular tree or nestled next to a specific patch of grass. Her mastery of phytotherapy became a beacon of health and wellness, weaving seamlessly into the daily lives of her community.

Almuelijuntha's physical presence reflected the grace and wisdom she drew from the healing powers of nature. Standing tall at 2.08 meters, her jet-black hair was fashioned in the form of a blooming yaru flower, a living homage to the botanical wonders she studied. Almond-shaped amber eyes held a warmth that mirrored her compassionate nature.

Her platinum striation facial marks, intricately woven with gold lattice work on the bridge of her nose, marked her connection with the healing arts. A head adornment, jewelled with citrine, amethyst, and amber, adorned her milky porcelain skin with undertones of rose quartz. The oval-shaped ornament, featuring an intricate Art Deco motif, added an ethereal touch to her overall appearance.

During her explorations in the forest, a burst of rays from Coma illuminated a clearing before Almuelijuntha. Intrigued, she followed the divine guidance and discovered Walid Al'aeshab. As Najm Shamal hovered over them, Almuelijuntha recognised the cosmic alignment marking her twenty-eighth year of birth.

With a chuckle of acknowledgement, Almuelijuntha and Walid Al'aeshab set forth from the familial lands of Mwanzo wa Maisha. Their journey led them to Asrawi, a region east of the Laaras Mountains and north of the Kati Mountains. In this new land, Almuelijuntha's healing wisdom and Walid Al'aeshab's presence would become integral to the flourishing tapestry of Asrawi's natural and cosmic harmony.

In the illustrious lineage of Jyeshta and Purush, Tabiba emerged as a brilliant mind, excelling in both life and formal sciences. Her contributions to the fields of medicine and mathematics were transformative, laying the foundation for the development of biomedical science. Working in tandem with her sister Almuelijuntha, Tabiba's computational genius allowed them to unravel the molecular intricacies of healing properties within plants.

Tabiba's mind, akin to a finely tuned instrument, saw equations floating around her like others witnessed the majestic sunsets of T'haeri. Numbers flashed before her with the vividness of coral red and orange bands on the powder blue sky, guiding her towards groundbreaking discoveries in the realms of medicine and mathematics.

Unlike her sisters who looked to Najm Shamal for the passage of time, Tabiba's calculations were precise. With an exacting sense of humour, she anticipated her twenty-eighth birthday with mathematical precision.

Brjamohana, recognising Tabiba's unique perspective, sent Riqat Alqalb at the precise third hour, twenty-third minute, and fifty-fourth second of the day.

In a moment of reflection, Tabiba questioned Riqat Alqalb about the meaning of his name. "My name means light-heartedness," he responded. In response, Tabiba, acknowledging her own disposition, greeted him with 'Alsalam ealayna' and a smile. Humble in her self-awareness, she embraced the realisation that gaiety was a quality she could nurture.

Guided by her male steward, Riqat Alqalb, Tabiba decided to settle in Azore, north of her sister Barika and Mustashar'akim. Their journey took them to this enchanting land, where the azure seas mirrored the red hues of Tabiba's hair, spiralled like the Nahr Alniyl of Azore. Her burnt orange pigment and crystal Azul eyes reflected the vibrancy of the T'haerian seas.

Adorned with red freckles and rhodium implants in a fern-like pattern on her cheeks, Tabiba wore a rhodium headpiece with gears that moved in a counter-circular motion. Floral scrollwork marked each vein in her body, a testament to the intricate intertwining of her scientific prowess and cosmic connection.

In Azore, Tabiba's intellectual brilliance and Riqat Alqalb's light-heartedness became integral to the fabric of their new home. The harmonious dance of equations and the joyous rhythms of their shared journey echoed through the vibrant landscapes of Azore.

In the tapestry of Jyeshta and Purush's lineage, Mahila Savaaree emerged as a guardian of all living organisms, with a profound love for the life sciences. Her daily studies with her mother focused on animal life, leading her to define and establish zoology—a comprehensive study of the structure, embryology, classification, habits, and dispersion of all animals on T'haeri. Mahila Savaaree's dedication to understanding the animal kingdom resulted in a harmonious coexistence between T'haerians and animals, where neither animals nor their by-products were used for food.

Mahila Savaaree's vision and commitment to studying animal life led to an unparalleled harmony between T'haerians and the diverse creatures that shared their ecosystems. From amphibians to mammals, every interaction between T'haerians and animals was characterised by a deep understanding and respect for the interconnectedness of all living beings.

On the day she turned twenty-eight, Mahila Savaaree ventured into the meadows of Mwanzo wa Maisha and encountered Lahaz Alzuhur—a male speaking with a namir. Brjamohana, in her sense of humour, sent Lahaz Alzuhur at the third hour of the day. The greeting, '*Ahlaan ya hubiy*', marked the beginning of a new cosmic journey for Mahila Savaaree.

In response to Mahila Savaaree's laughter and inquiry about his name's meaning, Lahaz Alzuhur revealed that it meant 'Notice the flowers.' With a sense of camaraderie and the acknowledgement of Brjamohana's humour,

Mahila Savaaree and Lahaz Alzuhur decided to settle in Bolev, the land her parents called home in the west.

Standing tall at 2.02 meters, Mahila Savaaree possessed bronze-pigmented skin that reflected the warmth of her connection with nature. Her straight obsidian hair framed her hazel eyes, adorned with gold and slate green flecks around the iris. High cheekbones carried ivory facial markings, adding a touch of regality to her presence.

A headdress in the shape of a koi fish adorned her head, crafted from copper-bronze with intricate scrollwork on either side of her ears. At its centre, a cobalt blue Chrysocolla gemstone added a vibrant focal point. The fins and gills of the koi, in a fan design, showcased the colour of the Chrysocolla gemstone. Her garb resembled the armour of a samurai soldier, mirroring the copper-bronze hue of her headdress.

Mahila Savaaree, with her unique presence and profound connection with animal life, left an enduring legacy of harmony and understanding on T'haeri.

Her studies in zoology shaped a world where the coexistence of T'haerians and animals was marked by reverence and mutual respect.

∞

As the progenitors of T'haerian life, Jyeshta and Purush's legacy transcended the physical realm of blood and bone. After four generations, their existence culminated in a magnificent metamorphosis. They transitioned to the Astral Plane, a dimension where their jeevan—the vibrant essence of their life force—intertwined with the ethereal tendrils of the mycelial network of Srimad-Bhagavatam. In this realm, their very being became an inseparable thread in the luminous tapestry that wove together all life—past, present, and future.

The Astral Plane served as a cosmic nexus, a point of convergence for every living creature that had ever breathed, currently drew breath, and would one day draw breath. Jyeshta and Purush, in their ascension, became woven into the very fabric of Srimad-Bhagavatam, a living testament to the cyclical, collective, and interconnected nature of existence. Their essence pulsed through the mycelial network, forming a luminous bridge that linked the memories, experiences, and jeevan of every living being.

Whenever T'haerians connected with the mycelial network, the grounding ritual transcended a mere personal communion. It became a profound reconnection with the memory of Jyeshta and Purush, a potent reminder that nature itself was a living culture, a collective ethos that transcended the boundaries of individual lives. The mycelial network, a writhing archive of countless lifetimes, held the imprints of every being that had ever lived. By grounding themselves, T'haerians tapped into this wellspring of wisdom, gaining a deeper understanding of their place in the intricate tapestry of life.

The presence of Jyeshta and Purush in the Astral Plane underscored the cyclical dance of life. It served as a constant reminder that every birth, every grounding, and every connection reverberated through the collective consciousness, leaving an indelible mark on the grand symphony of existence. This interconnectedness became a guiding principle for the T'haerians, fostering a profound sense of unity and shared destiny among them.

In their grounding rituals, the descendants of Jyeshta and Purush weren't merely connecting with the present moment. They were reaching across the veils of time and space, their consciousness brushing against the eternal essence that flowed through Srimad-Bhagavatam. The Astral Plane, with its intricate mycelial network, became a conduit for this perpetual dance of life, a dance where every step resonated not just in the present, but in harmony with the echoes of the past and the whispers of the future.

As generations passed, the T'haerians further integrated the knowledge gleaned from the mycelial network into their daily lives. Their architecture mimicked the branching forms of the network, creating buildings that flowed and intertwined with the natural landscape. Their language evolved to incorporate their pheromones and the rhythmic pulses and subtle vibrations emanating from their connection to the collective consciousness.

Young female T'haerians underwent rigorous training to hone their ability to access the network. Elder female T'haerians, their minds seasoned with centuries of collective wisdom, served as guides, teaching the intricacies of navigating the ethereal expanse. During these training sessions, the young T'haerians would delve into the depths of the network, encountering vibrant echoes of past events and glimpsing the potential pathways of the future.

However, this profound connection to the collective consciousness presented a unique challenge. The sheer volume of information and experiences flowing through the network could be overwhelming. Unprepared minds could become inundated with the echoes of countless lives, leading to confusion and even emotional breakdowns. To counter this, T'haerians developed advanced meditation techniques, allowing them to filter the information and navigate the network with focused awareness.

Through these practices, the T'haerians developed a deep reverence for the natural world. They understood that every living being, from the smallest insect to the tallest tree, was intricately woven into the fabric of the mycelial network. This fostered a sense of responsibility and care for their environment, leading to sustainable practices and a harmonious coexistence with all living things.

The legacy of Jyeshta and Purush continued to resonate through generations, not as mere figures of the past, but as living reminders of the interconnectedness of all things. Their presence in the Astral Plane became a beacon of collective wisdom, guiding the T'haerians on a path of unity, responsibility, and a profound respect for the intricate dance of life.

Religion often attracts fanatics. And fanatics are often attracted to religion. When the latter becomes the former, it is often seen as devotion.

Interlude

In the intricate dance between religion and fanaticism, a delicate balance teeters on the edge of belief and extremism. The allure of religion, with its profound teachings and promises, acts as a magnetic force drawing seekers into its embrace. However, lurking in the shadows, fanaticism waits to entwine itself with devotion, morphing the sacred into the profane.

As individuals navigate the labyrinthine passages of faith, some find solace and purpose in the rituals, scriptures, and communal gatherings that define their chosen religion. Devotion, in its purest form, becomes a guiding light, offering a moral compass and a sense of belonging. It is the heartbeat of a spiritual journey, pulsating with the rhythms of prayer and introspection.

Yet, within the sanctuary of devotion, shadows emerge. Fanaticism, the distorted twin of sincere faith, craves an all-consuming fervour. When the fervent pursuit of religious ideals transforms into an unyielding, intolerant zeal, the line between devotion and fanaticism blurs. The devotee, once guided by humility and compassion, risks succumbing to the intoxicating allure of absolutes.

Fanatics are often drawn to religion like moths to flame. The structured doctrines and the promise of divine validation become fertile ground for those seeking unwavering certainty in an uncertain world. The allure of absolute truth, when wielded without nuance, morphs into a weapon of exclusion and division. Fanaticism, in this guise, revels in the illusion of moral superiority, creating an 'us versus them' narrative that eclipses the inherent unity of humanity.

Devotion, at its core, seeks spiritual growth, understanding, and connection. However, when the fervour of devotion is tainted by fanaticism, the quest for personal enlightenment transforms into a crusade to impose rigid beliefs on others. The echoes of history resound with tales of religious fanaticism, where the quest for purity has birthed conflict, persecution, and untold suffering.

Chapter 3

Mzaliwa wa pili was pacing back and forth in her study, looking inquisitively at the equation she just worked out. *Could this be it? Did I figure it out?*—she wondered to herself. Mzaliwa stared at the blue floating holographic equation, giddy with excitement. For the past year, under the guidance of Professor Prabuddh, she had been working on how to make extradimensional travel possible. The Gamma travel crystals and her equation would provide Rayid Fada with the necessary means to bend space into a tunnel for travelling between dimensions. At least that was Mzaliwa's theory.

Mzaliwa was fascinated by space travel from her adolescence and is the very reason she travelled far from her home planet, T'haeri, to Budh. Stories were told around the fire pit in Azore, of the *First Ones* who looked to the stars and left T'haeri. Within three years, these ones travelled across the four quadrants of Anagha. With each return trip home to T'haeri, the *First Ones,* as they came to be known, shared the planetary structure, condition, lifeforms, etc with the Angrezee tribe.

The premise was to transform each planetae into a liveable one. Over the course of the next six centuries, each planetae was terraformed. The first planetarum was Aashvi in 2099 AB and the last was Saanvi in 2545 AB. Both were respectively named after the first and second Bhabhi. By 2600 AB, within the scientific community—*Sankalak*—intergalactic and extradimensional travel was the next logical step forward.

Half a century later, Prof Sajiv and his brother, Aarkat, made intergalactic travel possible. However, translating their equation for interdimensional travel to extradimensional remained in its infancy—unstable and unpredictable.

After hearing about the warning given to the Ma'an Su by the Rakshak Shreshth, Profs Sajiv and Aarkat nearly stopped working on the mathematical equation. However, being pushed by the impetuousness of the Ma'an Su, they forged ahead.

They implored the board of the Petraea Uni to find an exceptional Astrophysicist within their ranking to help realise the solution. Unable to find a suitable initiate Sankalak, Prof Prabuddh suggested Mzaliwa, who he was mentoring in extradimensional theory. A *sabia* who was neither nominated nor accepted to attend the University.

Using Mzaliwa's equation, the extradimensional theory was now scientific law. Testing the veracity of her equation would have to wait until later.

Immediately, Profs Sajiv and Aarkat informed the Ma'an Su that extradimensional travel is now possible. With that came the order to initiate the first group of explorers to Novissimus—their closest dimension. Mzaliwa quickly opened the chroma pad laying in front of her to call home. "Ma'an where's Baba? I have important news to share! We have already discussed it, *choko*, and we knew this day would come. Alsalam ealayna. We will see you when you return."

Tears swelled in Mzaliwa's eyes. "Alsalam ealayna, Ma'an."

The Rayid Fada made their preparations—attaching *Salaee*—their largest spacecraft to the launching station, inputting Mzaliwa's equation, and engaging the Gamma crystals with the navigation dock. Mzaliwa took the shuttle up to *Salaee,* whose belly she could see on the ride up. *I am going to Novissimus. The first of my family to ever leave our dimension. Af'sadi, I take your words with me and may I honour you with my return. Alsalam ealayna.* Taking a deep breath, Mzaliwa stepped off the shuttle and onto the platform of *Salaee.*

∞

Sit, my children, and let me tell you a story about a girl whose disappearance almost shattered our world.

Mzaliwa wa pili leisurely swam from the shoreline in front of her home to the crater of Donax volcano. From coast to coast, this took her all of ten minutes. Laying down to soak up the warm rays Coma emitted on her home world, she could not help but notice how obtrusive the skyscrapers of Festuca were. The gold dome-shaped buildings rose well into the clouds, with smaller limestone constructions for the High City dwellers. At its centre was Brjamohana's temple, an edifice with a deep eggplant purple dome with gold trimmings and arched windows with gold-stained glass scrollwork.

Mzaliwa sighed and wondered, "Have they even read the holy text from the Book of Brahman? She herself said, *I cannot be contained in handmade buildings; even the heavens of the heavens, cannot contain me. How much less, then, can a house by which you will call my own!* They have truly forgotten our ways!" The people of T'haeri would connect with Brjamohana by grounding with nature. Opening ourselves to constant communication between each lifeform and passing our energy to them as a response. She stretched out her limbs and soaked up the rays from Coma.

All around her was the marvellous and splendid plant and animal life of Surtseyan. To her left were fields of violet forget-me-nots. She could see the Azorean Banyan tree that marked the distance from her house and Afdal Sadiqa, her best friend from childhood. The Baobab tree *Baba Khasha* planted on one of his many trips to Surtseyan. Before swimming back to the mainland, Mzaliwa wa pili grounded herself in the pooling waters, asking for one of the floating pink lotuses to put into her hair. After receiving permission and thanking the flower for its beauty, she carefully tucked the flower into her satchel and swam back.

Najm Shamal would soon be in position, marking Mzaliwa's twenty-eighth year of birth. This past Perihelion the Bhabhi Salaah met to select who would become her male steward. But Mzaliwa was having second thoughts. She understood that the joining of her family, the House of Nihaarika, and the House of Nidhi was of paramount importance. Taqi comes from the Jazayerli tribe, descendants of Tabiba; she wrote the equation that made terraforming possible. And she was from the Naijeeri tribe, descendants of Barika, the whisperer of celestial bodies and the one who unlocked Anagha. Two powerful Houses of Azore.

Every woman coming of age, who was not selected to go to uni, accepted her male steward and fulfilled her dharma. However, Mzaliwa wanted more from life than being a committed partner and mother. She carried with her the essence of her aunt, Barika, who was always looking to the stars and was the founder of astronomy. As well as her other aunt Tabiba, who defined medicine and mathematics. Her heart was intent on combining the fields of astronomy and physics, to create a new field of science, astrophysics.

The child even dreamt of attending Petraea University—a school where intergalactic travel was discovered and only the brightest minds were selected to attend every Aphelion. However, during the Aphelion of Mzaliwa's generation, not a single girl was selected. Only the initiates from the Sankalak order were selected. Appealing a decision took months, even years if the Bhabhi Salaah did not deem the applicant's objection sufficient. Mzaliwa **had** to find someone to look over her work and make her case before the Bhabhi Salaah.

Who could I find that would be interested in what I am working on? The mathematics behind this equation is hard enough for me to get from my mind and formulate into words. How could I find a professor at Petraea Uni who would listen? Mzaliwa had been studying the screen before her displaying a solution that would make current intergalactic travel more stable. She had improved upon what Sajiv and Aarkat had established when she was younger. While Mzaliwa stood before her screen, she debated whether she should submit it for review with a professor who was new to uni, Professor Prabuddh.

She closed her eyes, inhaled deeply, and hit the submit button. *What harm could I have just done? The time remaining before I must live with Taqi is closing.* Taqi, the eldest son of House Nidhi of the Jazayerli tribe, descendants of Tabiba, was not someone Mzaliwa was fond of. He was neither into astrophysics nor anything science-related.

He does not even appear to be intellectually stimulating, Mzaliwa opined loudly to her iya. A rumbling chuckle started to erupt outside of Alqizima. "My dear, his intellectual stimulation is not what will preserve both House Nihaarika and House Nidhi. His seed will." Before she could protest how awkward that statement was, her iya had already strolled out of her room.

Not one to sulk indefinitely, Mzaliwa noticed it was a quarter passed the sixth hour of the day on her *saea*. Around this time, she is always headed to Jeevan's house to see her best friend, Afdal Sadiqa or affectionately Af'sadi.

Grabbing her satchel, Mzaliwa headed towards the back of her house towards the family entrance.

The direct route to Af'sadi's house was a 15 km trip and only took a fourth of an hour to complete. Today, Mzaliwa took the scenic that would take her meandering through the dense forest of Surtseyan. Whenever she took this way with each passing breezing, she felt as if she heard Brjamohana speaking to her, calling to her.

Each plant turned towards her, showing its beauty and exchanged a bit of its force with Mzaliwa sending her into a trance. Right away Mzaliwa was shaken out of her trance by her mother's voice. It was as if the song-singing voice of her iya was carried through the intertwining network of roots, vines, and mycelium. *Sorry Af'sadi,* as she touched the stem of a Celosia. Mzaliwa turned and sprinted back to the house to see what was urgent. Breathless she reached the back door of the family house, glancing at her watch—*an eighth of an hour!*—Mzaliwa smiled at the record time. "Iya, what is it? What is wrong?"

"As soon as you left your workstation, the screen lit up instantaneously with a chromatic message from Prof Prabuddh. Who is Prof Prabuddh, Mzaliwa?" A hint of curiosity, exasperation, and empathy flashed all at once in Alqizima's voice.

"I...I can explain. This combining of the Azore's two prominent Houses just cannot happen. Spending a life with Taqi is not my true dharma. And somehow, I know Brjamohana would understand. So, I sent in the equation that improves upon intergalactic travel to Prof Prabuddh. Not for a second did I think he would not only open my *milafun* but also answer me in kind. Grasping Mzaliwa's face Alqizima could only smile and release a rumbling chuckle. You are more Tabiba's child than mine. *Alsalam ealayk ya waladay.* Ma'an, you are not angry? How could I be? Only Brjamohana can set our dharma; the Bhabhi Salaah will understand."

Postlude of Chapter 3

As an older woman sat in the tranquil garden of her home, surrounded by the gentle rustling of leaves and the fragrance of blooming flowers, a younger woman approached. The elder, known as Sayidat Dawla Musina, carried with her the weight of years, and her eyes held the wisdom of experiences lived. The younger woman, full of curiosity, sought to unravel the stories of her ancestors.

With a warm smile, Sayidat welcomed the younger one and began recounting the tale of Mzaliwa, a woman whose journey defied the expectations of her time. "You see, my dearest one, it was not always easy to forge one's path in a world bound by tradition and the expectations of ancient houses. Let me tell you about Mzaliwa, a flame that burned with an unyielding desire to break free from the chains of destiny."

"Mzaliwa, my dear, was a spirited soul, marked by a fervent passion for the stars and the mysteries they held. She carried within her the essence of her aunts, Barika and Tabiba, who had left indelible marks on our people's history."

The older woman's gaze wandered into the distance as if peering through the veils of time. "In her time, every woman of age accepted her male steward and fulfilled her dharma, as was the tradition. Yet, Mzaliwa hesitated, for her heartbeat to the rhythm of a different calling. She yearned for more than the role society had assigned her—a committed partner and a mother."

"Mzaliwa harboured dreams that stretched beyond the confines of familial alliances and societal norms. Her heart, infused with the essence of brilliant minds that came before her, yearned for the unexplored realms of the cosmos."

"Her reluctance to embrace the predetermined path stemmed from a profound desire to transcend the limitations imposed by tradition. She longed for a life not dictated by societal expectations but shaped by the boundless horizons of knowledge and discovery. Mzaliwa craved a destiny of her own making, one where the pursuit of astrophysics would be her guiding star."

Alqizima's eyes glimmered with a mix of pride and empathy. "She possessed the dreams of attending Petraea University, a place where intergalactic travel was discovered and only the brightest minds were chosen. But, during her generation's Aphelion, not a single girl was selected. Only the initiates from the Sankalak order were chosen."

The older woman's voice carried the weight of understanding. "Mzaliwa, with a heart filled with determination, sought to challenge this decree. She devoted herself to a groundbreaking equation, an improvement upon intergalactic travel. And, with a brave heart, she submitted it to Professor Prabuddh, a new faculty member at Petraea Uni."

A soft chuckle escaped Alqizima, reminiscent of the laughter that echoed in the past. "Oh, the audacity of youth! Mzaliwa's actions stirred ripples in the calm waters of tradition. It was a deviation from her prescribed path, a path that led to union with Taqi from the House of Nidhi."

The older woman's eyes met those of the younger, conveying a message beyond words. "But, my child, Mzaliwa's reluctance was not met with anger or disappointment from those who truly understood. Her mother, Alqizima herself, embraced her daughter's defiance with a smile and a rumbling chuckle. 'You are more Tabiba's child than mine', she would say."

"In that serene moment, Alqizima's voice resonated with the assurance she had once bestowed upon her daughter. 'Only Brjamohana can set our dharma; the Bhabhi Salaah will understand.' In the reflection of her mother's eyes, Mzaliwa found not only understanding but also the encouragement to defy the gravitational pull of societal norms. Alqizima's laughter, like the rustle of leaves in the cosmic breeze, echoed the sentiment that the pursuit of knowledge and the forging of one's destiny were intertwined in the grand tapestry of existence."

"As I recount these tales, my dear descendant, remember that the stars have witnessed the struggles and triumphs of those who dared to dream beyond the confines of tradition. Mzaliwa's legacy is a testament to the enduring flame that lights the way for those who seek to dance with the cosmos, guided not by the predetermined steps of society but by the celestial music that resonates within their souls."

And as the older woman shared this tale with the younger one, a legacy unfolded—a legacy of dreams pursued, societal norms challenged, and a mother's understanding that transcended the boundaries of time.

Chapter 4

Mzaliwa played back Prof Prabuddh's message; to say she was shocked was an understatement. Not only was he impressed with her work, but he was also sending her a personal invitation to study at Petraea Uni in Budh. *My dreams are coming true! I must tell Af'sadi the great news!*

Grabbing her mufid from her satchel, she rang Af'sadi. Af'sadi's sura appeared revealing a slightly annoyed but effusive friend. "I received your apology, Mzaliwa but what could have been so important that only *Sorry, Af'sadi* came across?"

Af'sadi, as a descendant of Maua Maridadi, knew every flowering plant especially the ones more voice-sensitive. "Oh, Af'sadi! My iya's song-singing voice carried news about my submission to Prof Prabuddh. I have been accepted and he wants me to study with him personally. He is sending a letter directly to the Bhabhi Salaah to inform them. I am going to Budh! *Mubarak Brjamohana!* Alsalam ealayna, you are truly blessed!"

"My ears sing with this news, Mzaliwa! But what will happen to Taqi? Never has a steward gone without a woman who was not selected for uni. He will be a wanderer, Mzaliwa! Baadha! Yes, Taqi may have been selected as my steward this past Aphelion but trust I was **not** his first choice. The Bhabhi will select another, I am sure of it!"

"But are you sure? There have been rumblings recently. A shift is happening, Mzaliwa, and I do not like it. T'haeri does not like it; she is speaking, and no one here is listening. Nor does Brjamohana. I fear that chhoda they call Brjamohana's temple to be the cause. A reckoning is coming, Mzaliwa. And pay attention, Anagha will stand still."

"Chaa'chee may be of the Rakhane vaale order and will rightly make it so that this deviation goes unnoticed. I do not mean to dampen your spirits. I more than anyone want you to fulfil your dharma. Your true dharma. Nonetheless, I believe you fulfilling said dharma will cause this *aspasht* I am feeling."

"Brjamohana's will is perfect so, something else must be at play here."

Hmmm, Af'sadi is never this kayiyb whenever good news is shared with her.

So, something is amiss here on T'haeri. But what could it be? The Bhabhi Salaah has become emboldened with some of their technological and innovative desires but nothing that ever went beyond what the Aushadhi revealed to them.

Adherents to Brjamohana are another story. All T'haerians are completing their dharmas and reaching enlightenment.

But some are showing themselves to be the exception—by either shortening Brahmacharya or lengthening Grihastha stages. "I have noticed the cultural shift, the *altataruf,* if you will, Af'sadi. I will speak again with Ma'an before I send in my reply to Prof Prabuddh. I *shkran lak,* Af'sadi for your wise counsel. Chaa'chee Maua Maridadi would be pleased. You honour me with your words, Mzaliwa."

In Novissimus, Shraavana could feel her twin's longing for reconnection. A stirring was happening, and she could feel it as if she was the source. To lull in her sister's warmth was creeping back into her being. But the path she had chosen was hers. It did not involve having to fulfil whatever dharmas Brjamohana said were necessary. So, for now, the separation would continue.

Shraavana was not as diligent as her twin in keeping an eye on her creation. Yes, she supplied the necessary framework for life to sprout, thrive, and carry on. But she mostly left them all to their own devices, believing the least amount of involvement from her the better. She named her galaxy, Tofauti.

Shraavana watched as her progeny on Dharatee spread from their point of origin in Khisba to the five winds—Alqutbiat Alsharqia, Algharb, Aleard Alhisan, Alriyah Altijaria, and Halat Rukud. The Terrestris went from being nomadic peoples to forming communities to clouded cities. Space travel had been realised. Therefore, some Terrestris left Dharatee for the other planetae and formed Awọn-iletos. Terraforming was not a customary practice in Novissimus, so genetic modifications; in some cases, complete alterations, were made for adaptation purposes.

Owokuqala Uzelwe's father fourth removed theorised the principles needed for galactic travel. In fact, her bloodline is credited with forming the various branches of science—mathematics and logic, biological science, physical science, and social science. Owo was fascinated with numbers and physics.

She dreamt of numbers and saw numbers in her everyday life.

Number swirled around her like the blankets her mom knitted for her from *uboya* hair. Owo could visualise quantum space, seeing light slowed down as a spacecraft flew through a hyperdrive. She wanted to be the first *aimra'a* to realise intergalactic space travel. Owo had the working principles of quantum tunnelling and began formulating the basic equation. Her guiding principle was not only leaving Dharatee but Novissimus entirely.

For all their technological advancement, basic *insaan* qualities like empathy, kindness, loyalty and love—especially love, escape every Terrestris. Everyone kept everything and everybody at arm's length. Coldness is all one felt living here and Owo could not be more opposite. Her essence was too delicate for the harsh life on Dharatee, and she obviously stood out.

Escaping was all she ever dreamt of, Owo believed solving for extradimensional travel was her ticket off the world, off the galaxy and off this blighted dimension. *This **must** work. What was it Prof Ofeefee said? A conductor of some sort is necessary for the Antariksh to pilot the vessel—a crystal from Shraavana's birthing. Now which sister planetarum has it? Think Owo, think. That is, it! Shravan! Named after Shraavana herself. Why could I not remember that?*

"Lówó, please send a message to Prof Ofeefee and tell him an Iksray travel crystal from Shravan is needed for extradimensional travel."

"Right away, ma'am! Uhm, ma'am, I have an incoming message from Prof Ofeefee. Displaying it now on the holo screen."

Owo, you have figured out extradimensional travel oh. Were you at any point going to tell the department? We have been working on this theory for the last decade eh. Do you really think the science board will give you the credit?

"Prof Ofeefee, nice to see you, sir. Your acknowledgement of my achievement is credit enough. If I did not know any better, I would think you were paying me a backhanded compliment. But it is the matter of the Iksray crystal, sir. That is the conductor we need."

I will talk to the Mineralogy department. I am sure that they have mined that crystal from Shravan. I have seen quite a few of the wealthy dissidents wearing it around their necks! I will get back to you. Owokuqala Uzelwe has solved our ten-year conundrum. I leave you.

Soon after, Owo let out a long-withheld sigh once her holo screen clicked off. "Lówó, I swear underneath that hard and tough exterior is a man who deeply cares. He would never admit but it feels like sometimes he wishes I were his daughter."

"Ma'am, not every person has good in them. Especially those of Dharatee. Sometimes the truth you see is what it really is."

"I know Lówó, I know. I just want to be in a world where people are their greater selves and not their baser." Whispering, *"Ma'am someone is listening at the door,"* Lówó said to Owo.

Giving a slight nod. "Abeg, come in," and her door opened to reveal her iya with a shocked look quickly followed by rash annoyance.

"Who were you speaking to? I heard voices coming from this room while I was coming to give you the laundry you left downstairs. I know there is not some boy you are hiding in your closet."

"Hmm…but those are not my clothes, however. Anyway, I was speaking to my professor regarding progress on our extradimensional theory and the mathematics behind it."

"You know you really should be thinking about settling down and finding a husband."

"As I was saying, Prof Ofeefee was discussing my project and its success. I will be leaving with the test crew in two shift rotations."

"Wait, you are leaving while knowing that your father is not working with the Katul anymore? You are such a selfish and ungrateful child."

"Selfish? Ungrateful? Three-quarters of my dakhal goes to the family on top of me taking care of all the bills Baba was paying. Outside of being the financial breadwinner of this family, I am also responsible for all the cooking, the cleaning, taking care of—read parenting—my siblings or anything else that comes to your mind."

"Where in that is selfishness? Where in that is ungratefulness? Why would anyone who has the means to leave stay here with the two of you? If it is not one thing, it is something else. I am blamed for anything that happens in this ụlọ—a broken window in a part of the ụlọ that I am never in; Baba's holo pad randomly stopped working; Kęta admitted to breaking your porcelain figurine and yet you accused me."

"There are criticisms after complaints, complaints after criticisms. Life is exhausting and everyone is miserable."

Mzaliwa stepped off the platform and onto *Salaee* and took in the wonder around her. On her trip from T'haeri to Budh, Mzaliwa travelled on the star cruiser, *Taaraa*. The *Taaraa* was manned with a forty-personnel crew. It was outfitted with four warp nacelles and had a maximum speed of warp 4. The *Taaraa* star ship had at least two impulse reactors.

But *Salaee*, she was a beauty to behold. She was a full-fledged fleet carrier with fifteen decks. *Salaee* normal cruise speed of warp 8, a maximum cruise speed of warp 16, and a top speed of warp 22 sustainable for up to twelve hours. However, for this trip, she was outfitted with an enhanced warp drive, and now safely attained and indefinitely sustained its maximum cruise speed of warp 16.

The *Salaee* starship was built large enough to have a quantum drive in addition to its primary and secondary warp drives. However, before introducing the Gamma travel crystal to its core, it could only operate for short periods of time before shutting down.

The command centre is the first deck and is ovoid in shape and is divided into three parts: navigation, flight control, and flag. The navigation bridge of *Salaee* directly supervises all primary mission operations and coordinates all departmental activities. And is located at the frontmost portion of the command centre.

The living spaces were confined to decks four to eleven—each designed to mimic the exact biomes of the eight planetae of Anagha. Deck three held the mess hall and lounge which were equipped with full bar and kitchen facilities. It featured eight different stations that featured the local cuisines of everyone's home world. The mess hall could occupy 100 diners at a time, while the lounge can occupy 32 diners at a time.

Mzaliwa made her way down to deck four for the T'haerian biome and residences. Although she had been living on Budh for the last one and a half years, *Salaee* recognised her as more T'haerian than Budhi. The communal area was reminiscent of the dense Surtseyan forests—violet forget-me-nots, orange and magenta Azores spurges, Baobab and Banyan trees, with a crimson river in its centre carrying floating pink lotuses.

She could hear the native araçari singing in the trees. The interior was like the monolithic dome theatres back home featuring concave walls. So, the araçaris songs travelled throughout the area at perfectly collected vocal points. She felt at home and her nerves were settling.

[Attention all crew members, please start making your way to the pods found on deck three as we prepare to bring the quantum drive online.]

Aushadhi was used as the intermediary to Brahman. However, when the intermediary becomes the primary focus, is it really Brahman that was being sought?

Prelude to Chapter 5

In the sacred quest for connection to Brahman, the cosmic spice Aushadhi stood as an intermediary between the mortal realm and the divine. The rituals and offerings, the whispers of incantations, all danced around the ethereal presence of Aushadhi—a conduit believed to carry prayers and supplications to the very essence of Brahman.

Yet, during this celestial dance, a contemplative shadow lingered. A question, subtle but profound, whispered through the corridors of devotion: When the intermediary becomes the focal point, does it obscure the true essence of Brahman or merely reflect the limitations of mortal understanding?

The seekers, in their earnest pursuit, found solace in the tangible—the healing and elevated touch of Aushadhi, the tangible link to the cosmic order. The herbs, the rituals and the intricate symphony of offerings were woven into a tapestry of reverence for the intermediary. Aushadhi, with its healing powers and celestial aura, became the locus of their devotion, drawing hearts and minds into its embrace.

Yet, as the fragrance of sacred herbs wafted through the air, a subtle caution echoed. Was the pursuit of ingesting Aushadhi a means to an end, a humble journey towards the ineffable Brahman, or had the intermediary, in its splendour, become an unwitting veil obscuring the ultimate truth?

As the rituals unfolded and the fragrance of Aushadhi permeated the sacred spaces, seekers grappled with the paradox: Can the intermediary truly represent the boundless essence of Brahman, or does it cast a shadow that conceals the formless reality beyond mortal comprehension?

Chapter 5

But Auntie, what events led up to us pursuing extradimensional travel with such enthusiasm?

Well, little one to understand that is to try to understand the Bhabhi Salaah.

The Bhabhi Salaah was formed by the daughters of Jyeshta and Purush who had reached enlightenment—Hakima, Barika, Maua Maridadi, Fanaana, Pravakta, Almuelijuntha, Tabiba and Mahila Savaaree. Through their reaching Brahman, they forged a direct bond with Brjamohana, and it granted them mystic abilities. Collectively, it was decided that their intended purpose was to be our planetary council—a gyneocracy[3]—and our gurus.

Brjamohana had given us women the ability to create and therefore, it was only natural that our women are placed in a position of power to protect this function. We trace our clans through our women; our children born assume the House of their mother but also have the birth rights from their father. Our kinship is what determines the bonds between the mother and the male steward father figure. This system forms our protective circle where more than anything else family and its prosperity are valued.

So, to ensure the future of the Bhabhi Salaah, the council would select women who reached the age of twenty-eight to join their ranks. They relied on the alignment of Najm Shamal being directly over Haree—their principal city.

These women had the innate ability to tap into Brjamohana's taakat; however, they lacked the proper guidance.

They convened every Aphelion to discuss those who would become initiates on their twenty-eighth year of birth. These initiates would undergo physical and mental conditioning training to hone their abilities. They would use these gifts to be entuned with the rhythms of nature. The rest of our girl population who were not selected to become initiates were selected to go to

Petraea Uni. Then at uni, they would be taught to think spatially and have the full competency of their male counterparts—often excelling beyond them.

As gurus, they were our custodians of formal and spiritual learning. The ancient texts given to Jyeshta were held in the grand library of Haree. The library was a breathing sentient dwelling place for our holy texts and secular works. During Perihelion, the Bhabhi Salaah would commune with Brjamohana and receive further instruction from her for daily life or when complex societal problems arose. The latter did not happen often amongst women but with men involved…

To avoid these male incursions entirely, through divine providence the Saala Ganatantr of a Bhabhi Salaah's second sister would be considered the *um dhukir* of his nephews. This we called *qafil*—sons learn how to behave in society, social values, and intra(er)personal responsibilities of the Saala Ganatantr.

From their education process, we studied the celestial bodies, worshipped Brjamohana, and made technological advancements. We went from rudimentary housing structures to High City dwellings in the clouds. They were mechanical buildings—their gears made of iridium and platinum. They were marvellous automated and sentient structures.

You could get lost in their ingenuity—the moving gears powering the buildings in the High City. Their technical systems could perceive their environment and solve common problems. The steam-powered mechanical flying ships that transported our ancestors throughout T'haeri. You could be in Bolev in under three hours.

The Naijeeri tribe made it possible for us to see the length and breadth of Anagha. They fashioned our stargazers, cruisers, and ships. Living vessels containing the very biome of T'haeri that carried us everywhere. While Angrezee tribe developed and specialised in terraforming the planetae within Srimad-Bhagavatam. Brjamohana blessed us with eight planetae for our eight clans. Each fashion a planetarum to be more hospitable.

But we soon lost sight of the greater meaning of reaching enlightenment.

Oneness with Brahman and the release of one's ego.

I, Katibat'unthaa daughter of Jina la kwanza, am the historical scribe of T'haeri and for the Bhabhi Salaah. I come from an extensive line of aurat from the Kainanis order. We have captured the history of T'haeri and her surrounding planetae sisters, initially oral to now written. All meetings of the

Bhabhi Salaah are penned so that future generations have an accurate accounting of their founding. For them to learn, grow and advance our society. Nothing is discarded from the written record—all our mistakes and any disputes are compiled into the history of our people.

Each Kainanis sister must study the transcribed record of T'haeri. Therefore, here is how our society advanced after the eight sisters left Mwanzo wa Maisha.

Kainanis: Jina la kwanza—Log Entry: 0,01—Star date: 1 Nne 5 A.D.

In the fourth month, on the first day of the month, that is in the first year of Duniani, the Ma'an Su, and the Bhabhi Salaah assembled in Haree. Here the Bhabhi Salaah, under the direction of the Ma'an Su, established the basics governing life here on T'haeri. The life of a T'haerian and the natural world are intrinsically connected. We are taken from the soil of T'haeri and fashioned in the image of Brjamohana. We were given the responsibility to protect and preserve the environment. No one T'haerian can exploit or misuse the natural resources of T'haeri for personal benefit.

Since T'haeri is the first planetarum created by Brjamohana from the matter left over after her remaining birth, every living organism has Brjamohana coded into their genetic code. Meaning T'haerians are connected to the Aatma of the planetae through the physical and astral planes. Therefore, any invention needs to take into consideration how its use will impact the natural world and our connection to Brjamohana herself.

All life needs to be governed by a set of laws that aide in their perfect development. The Bhabhi Salaah was founded by our ancestral sisters for that very purpose. We uphold and dispense the moral and spiritual upbringing of every child of Brjamohana. Thus, since the premise of life is grounded in connectivity with nature i.e., oneness with Brahman, then the laws of nature govern the lives of all inhabitants. There are three basic principles—(1) stability; (2) transference; (3) performance and fulfilment.

Primarily, it has been understood that every living thing's establishment and foundation comes from Brjamohana. Second, the jeevan of all beings— mammals or microorganisms—transfers to or becomes part of the mycelial network known as the Astral Plane once they have fulfilled their life's course. Third, our actions have a direct impact on the lives of others. Therefore, every action needs to be set with the intention that the outcome or fulfilment is a mutually positive one for all parties. Life is spherical; the beginning is the end, and the end is the beginning.

Previous scrolls taken from an accounting of our oral history make it plain that our ancestors lived what today we would consider a primitive way of life. Plumbing made from copper pipes, and heated baarish and ipakàs was a standard feature in the homes of across all continents. Transportation was steam-powered machines made of aluminium mined from Phraans.

The interior was made of plants—woven together in an intricate hexagon pattern—from the T'haerian biome which is a gaseous byproduct that produced the necessary steam to move the airships to and fro. These chambers were also of the same atmospheric composition as the home planetae, T'haeri. This was extremely essential as 'oneness with nature' was still popular and held in high regard.

The ships were of all varied sizes however, their design remained similar— the oblong oval of a canvas was the upper compartment for the gas to collect and used to keep the vessel afloat—the helm propeller was used for steering. The body of the ship was aluminium with three oblique windows on either side, one broad captain's window that spanned the front of the ship, and retractable canvas and aluminium wings at its centre. Mechanical gears were at the helm with the fin of a samaka.

Bhabhi our first session is being called to order. We are discussing how we will guide society in matters of both spiritual and secular. As in the *Book of Brahman*, we are to mentor our young women through each dharma stage until they have reached enlightenment.

Our primary objective is to ensure those who have been selected to become part of our ranks faithfully fulfil their life's dharma. That selection process will take place during the Perihelion and every twenty-eight years from each birth of a female child. Each student must display the extraordinary ability to harness *taakat* and use it in a controlled manner.

Her mother would have trained her in the basics based on the explicit interest her daughter displayed. For example, if the *taliba* had heightened *Shravan* abilities, her mother should have been training her to empathetically listen. The expectation is every *taliba* should be rightly suited to fulfil Brahman's Way of Life.

Here are the guidelines for each of Svargeey dharma. Svargeey dharma is comprised of personal responsibilities towards oneself, family, society, humanity, and Brjamohana which includes the environment, T'haeri, and nature. Our educational period will start when the girl is from childhood to twenty-five years.

Stage 1: **Brahmacharya** occupies the first twenty to twenty-five years of life, corresponding to adolescence. This is when parents have the responsibility to raise their daughters in the mental regulation of Brjamohana. Thus, training her to use taakat only when necessary and only to enhance her gifts from Brahman. Upon the child's *upanayana*, a three-year rites of passage period, the young woman will begin a life of study in Haree. She will dedicate her life to learning all aspects of Svargeey dharma, i.e., the 'Way of Life.' This stage denotes chastity for the purpose of learning from a guru, and during the later stage of life to attain *sampoornata*.

Stage 2: **Grihastha** spans from the age of twenty-eight to fifty years of life. During this period, individuals take on the multifaceted responsibilities of family life, which include marriage, raising children, and pursuing a career. Women who have been paired with their Saala, are encouraged to foster strong and supportive relationships with their stewards, children, and extended family members.

Parents in the Grihastha stage are entrusted with the responsibility of raising their children in accordance with the teachings of the Brahman. This involves instilling moral values, cultural heritage, and the 'Way of Life' in the next generation. Education and nurturing the talents and abilities of children are considered essential aspects of parental duties.

Stage 3: **Vanaprastha** spans from the ages of fifty to seventy-five. During this phase, individuals gradually withdraw from active involvement in worldly affairs and shift their focus towards spiritual pursuits. This stage often comes after individuals have fulfilled their duties as householders, raised their children, and established a sense of stability in their families.

Women entering the Vanaprastha stage are encouraged to gradually withdraw from the hustle and bustle of worldly affairs. This may involve reducing professional commitments, relinquishing certain responsibilities, and creating space for contemplation. The primary focus during Vanaprastha is on spiritual pursuits. This includes engaging in deep meditation, introspection, and furthering one's understanding of spiritual teachings.

This is not a stage of complete isolation but rather a period of continued learning. Individuals are advised to study sacred texts, engage in philosophical discussions, and seek the guidance of spiritual mentors.

Stage 4: **Sannyasa** occurs after the age of seventy-five. It represents a profound shift where individuals choose to detach themselves from material possessions and societal attachments, dedicating their lives entirely to spiritual pursuits. This stage often involves seeking self-realisation, practising meditation, and striving for union with the divine. The acumination is achieving *sampoornata*.

Women in Sannyasa are often advised to retreat to spiritual sanctuaries, ashrams, or monastic communities. These environments provide a conducive space for deep meditation, contemplation, and communion with the divine. The emphasis is on creating an atmosphere that supports intense spiritual practices and facilitates self-realisation. Sannyasis are encouraged to share their spiritual wisdom with others. This may involve teaching, mentoring, and guiding younger generations on the spiritual path. The act of sharing wisdom is seen to contribute to the spiritual evolution of society.

Our secondary objective is securing a harmoniously prosperous society. Therefore, those not selected during the Perihelion will become *talib ealmaniun* for open enrolment to Petraea University during Aphelion. These young women will lead our civilisation to technological advancement.

The combination of spiritual and secular education ensures a holistic development of young women, shaping them into leaders capable of fulfilling their life's dharma. This comprehensive approach aligns with the principles of Svargeey dharma, emphasising personal responsibilities towards oneself, family, society, humanity, and the broader concept of Brjamohana. Through these stages, the Bhabhi Salaah seeks to guide and empower each taliba to contribute meaningfully to the well-being of T'haeri and its inhabitants.

Kainanis: Jina la kwanza—Log Entry: 0,20—Star date: 1 Nne 15 AD.

In the fourth month, on the first day of the month, that is in the tenth year of Duniani, the Ma'an Su, and the Bhabhi Salaah assembled in Haree. Duniani was known for her unwavering determination and an insatiable thirst for progress. The discovery of Aushadhi had elevated her and her sisters to a higher state of consciousness, and Duniani was convinced that pushing the boundaries of their knowledge would bring even greater enlightenment. The

Rakshak Shreshth, on the other hand, were more cautious, emphasising the need for thorough testing and understanding of any innovative technology.

The disagreement between the Ma'an Su and the Rakshak Shreshth began when Duniani proposed the idea of exploring extradimensional travel. She envisioned it to transcend the limits of their current existence, to reach realms beyond Anagha, and potentially connect with Brjamohana in even more profound ways. However, the Rakshak Shreshth, led by the wise and experienced Rakshak Shreshth leader, Surya, was concerned about the potential risks and the unknown dangers that might lurk in the uncharted territories of other dimensions.

Duniani, driven by her impatience to achieve new heights of understanding and power, dismissed the warnings as mere reluctance to embrace progress.

She believed that the potential benefits far outweighed the risks and that the Bhabhi Salaah should not be held back by fear. In her view, the time for caution had passed, and they should seize the opportunity to unlock the mysteries of the universe.

The Sankalak were a group of brilliant minds, driven by an insatiable curiosity for scientific discovery. Their passion for pushing the boundaries of known technology and exploring uncharted territories fuelled their dedication to advancements in intergalactic and extradimensional travel. The prospect of unravelling the mysteries of the cosmos and expanding the Bhabhi Salaah's capabilities was at the core of their collective enthusiasm.

In their laboratories within the Saala Ganatantr, the Sankalak delved into innovative fields like quantum tunnelling and engineering. They conducted experiments that showcased the immense potential of extradimensional travel, presenting mesmerising simulations and theoretical frameworks that captured the imagination of all who witnessed them. The Sankalak's excitement became contagious, spreading throughout the scientific community and even reaching the ears of the Ma'an Su.

To sway the Ma'an Su and overcome any reservations she might have had, the Sankalak employed a strategic approach, downplaying the potential risks associated with untested extradimensional travel.

1. *Confidence in Expertise:*
   – *Leveraging their extensive knowledge and expertise in quantum mechanics and extradimensional theories, the Sankalak exuded*

confidence in their ability to control and mitigate any potential risks.
- *They presented themselves as pioneers on the brink of a breakthrough, assuring the Ma'an Su that their mastery of the science involved would ensure a safe and controlled deployment.*

2. *Selective Presentation of Data:*
   - *The Sankalak carefully curated the data they presented to the Ma'an Su, emphasising successful simulations and experiments while downplaying any anomalies or uncertainties.*
   - *By showcasing the positive aspects and potential benefits, they aimed to overshadow the warnings provided by the Rakshak Shreshth order.*

3. *Highlighting Technological Progress:*
   - *Emphasising the rapid progress made in their laboratories, the Sankalak showcased tangible results and technological advancements.*
   - *They painted a picture of a technology that had already surpassed initial testing stages, creating an illusion of readiness that appealed to the Ma'an Su's impatience and eagerness for progress.*

4. *Framing Risks as Manageable Challenges:*
   - *Instead of presenting risks as insurmountable obstacles, Sankalak framed them as manageable challenges that could be addressed through further refinement and testing.*
   - *Their ability to confidently outline strategies for overcoming potential hurdles provided reassurance to the Ma'an Su.*

5. *Appeal to Ambition and Legacy:*
   - *Knowing the Ma'an Su's desire for the Bhabhi Salaah to leave a legacy, the Sankalak appealed to her sense of ambition.*
   - *They portrayed the pursuit of extradimensional travel as a bold and historic endeavour that would etch the Sister Council's name into the annals of galactic history.*

In the face of the Sankalak's charismatic presentation and assurances, the Ma'an Su found herself swayed by the allure of scientific progress and the promise of unparalleled achievements, giving the green light for the novel extradimensional travel.

Kainanis: Jina la kwanza—Log Entry: 0,100—Star date: 1 Nne 55 AD.

In the fourth month, on the first day of the month, that is in the first year of Aanya, the Ma'an Su, and the Bhabhi Salaah assembled in Haree. I, Jina la kwanza and chronicler of the cosmic annals, inscribe upon the celestial scrolls a chapter etched in the shadows of mysticism and the intoxicating embrace of Aushadhi. In the time when the stars wove tales of Saanvi's bounty and the Aushadhi that beckoned the Bhabhi Salaah into realms beyond the corporeal.

As I inscribe these words onto the ancient scrolls of our people, I bear witness to a chapter in the celestial journey that demands reflection. In the earliest days of our Bhabhi Salaah, during the first year of Aanya, the sacred Aushadhi mined from the bountiful planet Saanvi was introduced—a substance entwined with visions and perceptions beyond the veil of reality.

In those years, when I, Jina la kwanza now in the twilight of my existence, was but a young seeker of knowledge, the elders of our tribe spoke of the potent hallucinogenic properties of Aushadhi. The claim resonated through the sacred halls that it could unlock the third eye of the Bhabhi Salaah, allowing them to peer into the very essence of Brjamohana and be filled with her taakat. Its properties held the promise of unlocking the third eye, piercing the veil that shrouded the unseen realms.

The tales spoke of Bhabhi Salaah who, in the elevated state induced by Aushadhi, would witness the essence of Brjamohana with vivid clarity. In the embrace of Aushadhi, the Bhabhi Salaah believed they communed directly with Brjamohana, and her taakat surged through their very beings. It was an era of cosmic connection, a time when the sacred substance was revered as a conduit to the divine, a bridge between the mortal and the celestial realms.

The ritual poisoning, a paradoxical rite, became a pivotal moment. Aushadhi, carefully administered, served as the cosmic key to unlock the latent potentials within the Bhabhi Salaah. In the selection of the Ma'an Su, the ritual of poisoning became intertwined with the allure of Aushadhi. The chosen candidate would partake in a sacred elixir laced with the hallucinogenic mineral. As the toxins coursed through their veins, the Bhabhi Salaah observed with keen eyes the candidate's journey through the realms of consciousness, discerning the whispers of destiny carried by Brjamohana's cosmic winds.

Yet, as the moons waxed and waned, a subtle shift occurred. The reliance on Aushadhi transcended its sacramental use. The Bhabhi Salaah, in their pursuit of heightened states, found themselves entangled in the web of hallucinogenic revelations, their grasp on reality becoming more elusive. Once tethered to the direct connection with Brjamohana, the Bhabhi Salaah, found solace in the intoxicating embrace of the mineral. The third eye, once a conduit to the divine, became clouded by the hallucinogenic haze of Aushadhi.

In the haze of Aushadhi-induced visions, the essence of Brjamohana became intertwined with the subjective experiences of the Bhabhi Salaah. The once clear channel to divine taakat blurred, replaced by the kaleidoscopic tapestry painted by the hallucinogenic substance.

Now, as I observe with sombre reflection, the whispers of the elders speak of a time when the direct connection to Brjamohana was unadorned by the veils of Aushadhi. In the first year of Aanya, a new Ma'an Su has ascended, and the ritualistic use of Aushadhi persists. The cosmic dance continues, but the question lingers—has the sacred substance become a crutch, overshadowing the pure communion with Brjamohana?

May the celestial winds carry these reflections through the cosmic expanse and may the cycles of time guide our people towards the path of unadulterated connection and cosmic truth.

Chapter 6

In the early days of T'haeri, when the people dwelt in humble mud and brick abodes, the promise of enlightenment cast its light upon them. Guided by the mystical prowess of the Bhabhi Salaah, their trajectory shifted from the earthbound simplicity of their origins to the soaring heights of technological marvels.

The city of Haree, once rooted in the soil, now stood as a testament to the union of mysticism and machinery. As the residents of T'haeri gazed skyward, their aspirations took flight alongside the city that defied gravity itself. The transition from rudimentary housing to the ethereal metropolis unfolded like a grand symphony of gears, steam, and innovation.

Dome-shaped buildings adorned the skyline, their ivory exteriors gleaming in the sunlight. These architectural marvels, inspired by the ancient mysticism of the Bhabhi Salaah, reached towards the heavens in harmonious ascent. Deep purple accents adorned the structures, reflecting the spiritual essence that permeated the city.

In the heart of Haree, the grand library stood as a jewel in this celestial crown. Its dome, an intricate lattice of ivory and deep purple, housed the collective wisdom of T'haeri. Within its sentient walls, ancient texts and futuristic blueprints coexisted, creating a repository of knowledge that spanned epochs.

Ascending into the clouds, the buildings of High City were not mere static structures but living, breathing entities of mechanical wonder. Gears crafted from rare iridium and platinum whispered tales of precision and artisanry.

These gears, embedded in the foundations of the city, synchronised to orchestrate a dance of perpetual motion.

As the gears of progress turned relentlessly in T'haeri, the Naijeeri tribe, inheritors of the legacy of Maua Maridadi and Sarih from the Madhy Asrawi tribe, emerged as the architects of a cosmic odyssey. Descendants of those who once crafted the wondrous vessels that sailed the skies, the House of Sabiean, specialists in botany and ecologists, became the heralds of a new era.

Steam-powered mechanical ships, resembling majestic creatures of myth, traversed the skies, connecting distant lands. These flying vessels were a manifestation of the Naijeeri tribe's ingenuity, carrying the essence of T'haeri's biome within them. The airships were not merely vehicles; they were living vessels, sustaining life as they sailed through the aether.

The echoes of steam-powered engines reverberated through the workshops of Haree as the House of Sabiean delved into the alchemy of transportation. Drawing inspiration from the steampunk influences came from the drawing tables of Fanaana, they forged the first cosmic cruisers. These magnificent vessels retained the aesthetic charm of their steampunk predecessors while harbouring an ambition that surpassed the skies above T'haeri.

The star ships now evolved beyond recognition from their steampunk origins, reached a pinnacle of technological prowess. Quantum drives, once a distant dream, allowed them to navigate the entire breadth of the galaxy within the span of three to five light years. The cosmic horizon beckoned, inviting the people of T'haeri to explore the mysteries of the cosmos.

Powered by quantum drives, a revolutionary leap from the steam engines of yore, these star ships promised to transcend the boundaries of T'haeri and explore the vast expanse of the galaxy. The Madhy Asrawi tribe, with their botanical expertise, integrated living biomes within the star ships, a nod to the sacred bond between nature and technology.

Sabewun-class cruisers, named after the visionary leader of the House of Sabiean, Sabewu, heralded the cosmic leap. Quantum drives, fuelled by the Gamma travel crystals harnessed from Budh's core, propelled the star ships into the cosmic arras. These vessels, adorned with intricate metallic filigree and vibrant plant life, became emissaries of the T'haerian spirit.

Journeying beyond the confines of the Anagha system, the star ships ventured into uncharted territories. The quantum drives, a testament to the fusion of mysticism and science, enabled them to traverse vast distances within the blink of an eye.

The most profound innovation lay within the living heart of these cosmic cruisers—the biome that adapted to its occupants. Inspired by the ecological wisdom of the Madhy Asrawi tribe, the House of Sabiean created biomes capable of responding to the emotional and physical needs of travellers.

As the star ship ventured deeper into the cosmos, the biome transformed seamlessly, offering an environment that mimicked the natural habitat of T'haeri. It was a harmonious fusion of technology and organic life, ensuring the well-being and equilibrium of those who embarked on this aetheric odyssey.

The cosmic pioneers discovered a celestial jewel amidst the stars—the planetae Saanvi. This verdant world became the celestial haven for the House of Sabiean and their descendants. The Sabewun-class cruisers, an evolution of their predecessors, became the symbol of ecological stewardship in the cosmos.

Saanvi, with its lush landscapes and diverse ecosystems, became a living testament to the expertise of the Madhy Asrawi tribe. The ecologists of the House of Sabiean and the merchant clan Tejee se Badhate, cultivated the planetae, fostering a harmonious coexistence between the indigenous flora and the settlers from T'haeri.

In the heart of High City, the Technological Nexus emerged as the epicentre of innovation. An amalgamation of Trintur's industrial prowess and Biltufar's visionary engineering, the Nexus became a hub where ideas and inventions converged. Inventors, engineers, and scholars gathered to push the boundaries of what was once thought possible.

Automated and sentient structures, powered by the very life force of T'haeri, dotted the landscape. The buildings responded to the needs of their inhabitants, perceiving the environment, and solving challenges with uncanny efficiency. The Nexus became a beacon of progress, where the pursuit of knowledge and technological advancement coexisted seamlessly.

The Angrezee tribe, masters of terraforming, turned their gaze to the stars. Inspired by the celestial bodies that guided their spiritual beliefs, they embarked on a journey to shape and mould other planetae within Srimad-Bhagavatam. Eight planets, eight clans, each terraformed to be a hospitable home for T'haeri's children.

The Naijeeri tribe's creations, the star gazers, cruisers, and ships, became vessels of exploration. They allowed the people of T'haeri to witness the vastness of Anagha, the interconnected celestial dance that mirrored the interconnectedness of all life.

Yet, amidst the dazzling brilliance of technological progress, the Bhabhi Salaah began to sense a shift. The core tenets of oneness with Brahman and the release of ego seemed to be slipping away. The grandeur of their creations threatened to overshadow the greater purpose of reaching enlightenment.

In the pursuit of advancement, T'haeri risked losing sight of the sacred bond between nature, spirit, and the people. As the gears of progress turned relentlessly, the Bhabhi Salaah gathered during Perihelion to commune with Brjamohana, seeking guidance on how to steer the course back to the path of enlightenment.

In the celestial city of Haree, amidst ivory and deep purple, the delicate balance between mysticism and machinery teetered on the edge. The future of T'haeri hung in the delicate embrace of the aether, waiting for the wisdom of the Bhabhi Salaah to guide it back to its spiritual roots.

We dreamt of reaching the stars and going beyond the boundaries of T'haeri. And then we dreamt some more.

Prelude to Chapter 7

In the ancient scrolls of our people, the tale of Srimad-Bhagavatam echoes through the cosmic winds—a story interwoven with the wisdom of Tabiba and the ingenuity of the Angrezee tribe. Gather around, my daughters, as I weave for you the tale of the equation that birthed the cosmic transformation.

Many moons ago, when the Angrezee tribe sought the means to tame the unruly celestial bodies, Tabiba, a visionary amongst our kin, unlocked the secrets of Aliastislah. In her meditations under the starlit skies, she derived the equation $L = \int d\, b\,(x, t)$, a cosmic mantra that held the key to the balance between life and the planet's heartbeat.

Listen closely, for it was this equation that inspired the Angrezee tribe to forge technology capable of terraforming entire worlds. The L, representing life, became their guiding star, and the integration of $d\, b\,(x, t)$, a dance of variables woven through space and time, unfolded like a sacred hymn.

In the genesis of their endeavour, the Angrezee tribe, like cosmic architects, chose Aashvi, a gas giant with its gemstone jasper, as their canvas. The mathematical symphony of Aliastislah reverberated through the halls of their laboratories as they meticulously extracted nutrient-dense gases, laying the foundation for the creation of a new world.

The process, akin to cosmic alchemy, involved the manipulation of atmospheric composition, a celestial choreography that called upon the wisdom of Tabiba. Flora and fauna were introduced with reverence, and the surface adapted for humanoid habitation under the gentle guidance of the equation.

As Aashvi transformed into a gemstone haven, lessons etched themselves into the cosmic scrolls. The Angrezee tribe, with eyes towards the stars, learned the language of planetary harmonics. They unravelled the interplay between elements, understanding the heartbeat of a world and the nuances of atmospheric ballet.

In their quest for efficiency, the settlers of Aashvi faced trials and tribulations. The T'haerian pioneers, like cosmic siblings, bore witness to the wonders and challenges of adaptation. Augmentation became a rite of passage, a union of ancient traditions and the demands of their new homes.

The Aashvis, with their almond-pigmented naturelings forms, embraced augmentation. Denser bone structures, suits attuned to the gravitational forces of the triple moons, and physiological adjustments became the tools of survival. It was a transformative process, a communion with the very essence of the terraformed worlds.

As the Angrezee tribe ventured forth to other planetae—Arunima, Baidya Nath, Budh, Mangal, Omaja, Saanvi—the equation of Aliastislah guided their exploration. The lessons learned from Aashvi quickened the pace of transformation, turning barren landscapes into thriving ecosystems, deserts into grasslands, and the inhospitable into the harmonious.

My daughters, know that the equation $L = \int d\, b\, (x, t)$ is not merely mathematical; it is a cosmic anthem sung by the celestial weavers, a legacy of our ancestors. As you tread upon the terraformed lands of Srimad-Bhagavatam, remember the ingenuity of the Angrezee tribe, the wisdom of Tabiba, and the dance of variables that shaped the destiny of our cosmic home.

Chapter 7

Aashvi

In the aeons past, when the celestial tapestry bore witness to the gas giant Aashvi in the Cetus sector, the T'haerians, with their unwavering spirit of exploration, gazed upon it as a challenge to be embraced. Aashvi, adorned with its gemstone, jasper, was an enigma wrapped in the shroud of a gas giant. Our story unfolds at the precipice of transformation, where the T'haerians set forth to weave the fabric of life into the very essence of Aashvi.

Picture the vastness of Aashvi's gas-laden skies, a celestial canvas waiting to be painted with the hues of life. The T'haerians, masters of terraforming, embarked on an odyssey to extract the nutrient-dense gases that concealed the potential for a new world. The cosmic alchemists among them meticulously harnessed the elements, weaving a symphony of gases that would lay the foundation for life to flourish.

In the celestial dance between science and magic, the atmospheric composition was delicately manipulated. A metamorphosis unfolded as the once thick and impenetrable gaseous clouds began to dissipate, revealing a canvas ready to embrace the touch of terrestrial wonders.

Imagine the first whispers of flora and fauna, introduced with tender care by the T'haerians. Seeds, like stardust, descended upon the surface, eager to take root in the nutrient-rich soils. The Terraformers, guided by ancient wisdom, nurtured the emergence of ecosystems that would thrive in harmony with the gemstone haven.

As the first rays of Aashvi's triple moons caressed the newly formed landscapes, a ballet of colours emerged. Lush jungles, majestic forests, crystalline lakes, and towering mountains painted the surface with a palette of unimaginable beauty. Each breath of the newly formed atmosphere carried the promise of life, whispered by the winds that now swept across this gemstone haven.

In their pursuit of mastery over the cosmic forces, the T'haerians faced the challenge of Aashvi's triple moons. It was a celestial ballet, an intricate dance of gravitational forces that required ingenuity. Special suits, forged with the artisanry of the celestial weavers, adorned the Terraformers. These suits, like a second skin, were woven with the threads of resilience, allowing them to tread where none had ventured before.

Generations of T'haerians toiled, adapting, and evolving, as the gemstone haven embraced them as its own. The Aashvis, toasted almond-pigmented naturelings, donned suits accented with gold and turquoise, their eyes reflecting the lustre of a world reborn.

And so, against the cosmic tapestry, Aashvi emerged from the cocoon of its gaseous past, a gemstone haven where life pulsed in rhythm with the celestial dance. The legacy of the T'haerian Terraformers became etched into the very soul of Aashvi, a testament to the indomitable spirit that turns the cosmos into a canvas awaiting the strokes of cosmic artisans.

Arunima

Ah, let me regale you with the tale of Arunima, a once-barren canvas in the cosmic gallery, where the T'haerians embarked on a cosmic odyssey to breathe life into the very essence of desolation. Arunima, adorned with the gemstone Ametrine, became the stage upon which the symphony of wisdom and knowledge would unfold.

As the T'haerians set their sights on this celestial gem, they embraced the challenge of transforming a desolate wasteland into a haven of verdant beauty. Picture the deserts, stretching across the horizon like an endless sea of golden sands, untouched by the breath of life. It was in this barren expanse that the celestial alchemists among the T'haerians sought to unveil the hidden potential.

Advanced technology, woven into the fabric of their cosmic mastery, became the brush with which they painted the landscape. The dance of terraforming unfolded as the once-arid deserts yielded to the touch of rejuvenation. Rivers, born from the cosmic loom, carved intricate patterns through the ancient sands, breathing life into the parched earth.

Lush grasslands, like a carpet of emerald, unfolded beneath the caress of cosmic winds. The rivers, shimmering with the hues of the gemstone Ametrine, cradled the promise of life as they meandered through this newfound oasis. Lakes, reflecting the celestial tapestry above, mirrored the symphony of stars that watched over the transformation.

Yet, in this cosmic ballet, the T'haerians were not alone. The Naijeeri, descendants of Arunima's ancient lineage, stood as stewards of their ancestral home. In a harmonious dance, they actively participated in the terraforming process, preserving the echoes of their cultural identity amidst the cosmic evolution.

The Baobab tree of Surtseyan, a venerable elder of the ancient lands, became a symbol of this connection between the old and the new. With roots anchored in the sands of time, it was transplanted with meticulous care, a living testament to the resilience of life and the intertwining threads of past and future.

As the final strokes of celestial artistry were painted upon Arunima's transformed canvas, the planet emerged as a haven for wisdom and knowledge. The Arunimas, dark red-pigmented transhumanoids, with platinum pink afro curly hair and pointed ears, became the custodians of this newfound sanctuary.

Arunima, once a barren world, now pulsed with the Glow of Dawn, a beacon of celestial enlightenment amidst the cosmic expanse. And so, the story of Arunima unfolded, etched into the very fabric of the universe, where the celestial artists of the T'haerians, hand in hand with the Naijeeri, sculpted a masterpiece of cosmic rebirth.

Baidya Nath

In the annals of cosmic evolution, the gaze of the T'haerians turned towards Baidya Nath, a terrestrial world awaiting the gentle caress of rejuvenation.

Nestled within the embrace of the cosmos, this planet, bearing the gemstone Cordierite, beckoned as a canvas where the healing arts of medicine and bioengineering would flourish.

Picture the tapestry of Baidya Nath, once marred by imbalance, now undergoing a transformation led by the descendants of Tabiba and Riqat Alqalb. These stewards of life, with olive-tan complexion and platinum blonde curly hair cascading like celestial waves, emerged as the custodians of Baidya Nath's metamorphosis.

The terraforming process unfolded with a meticulous dance between nature and technology. As the T'haerians guided the enhancement of Baidya Nath's biodiversity, the rolling hills embraced a tapestry of colours. Native flora and new species, introduced with reverence, embraced each other in a dance of symbiosis. The air became perfumed with the fragrance of newfound life, and the planet resonated with the harmonious hum of thriving ecosystems.

Descendants of Tabiba and Riqat Alqalb, with pointed ears attuned to the rhythms of nature, worked tirelessly to ensure the sustainability of the transformed landscapes. Their platinum blonde hair shimmered like sunlight on the morning dew as they engaged in the delicate task of preserving the planet's natural beauty.

Imagine the dense forests, vibrant and teeming with life, where bioengineering labs emerged like sanctuaries of innovation. Crystal swamps, like liquid gems reflecting the wisdom of ages, became the birthplace of groundbreaking discoveries. The stewards of Baidya Nath, with gold headdresses adorning their heads like celestial crowns, stood at the forefront of innovative research.

Tall in stature, the Baidya Naths moved with grace amidst this living laboratory. Their olive-tan complexion, a testament to their affinity with the planet's rejuvenation, became a canvas painted with the hues of harmony. They toiled with an innate understanding, crafting an environment where the delicate balance between progress and preservation was maintained.

The descendants, guided by an ancient code of ethics, fostered a world where bioengineering marvels unfolded against the backdrop of rolling hills and crystal swamps. Each innovation, each discovery, echoed through the corridors of time, creating a legacy woven into the very fabric of Baidya Nath.

As the celestial symphony played its final notes, Baidya Nath emerged as a testament to the mastery of life's custodians. The platinum blonde hair of the Baidya Naths, the golden headdresses glinting like stars, stood in contrast to the verdant landscapes and crystalline waters. Baidya Nath, once in need of refinement, now stood as a beacon of healing, a sanctuary where the forces of medicine and bioengineering converged to weave a tale of rejuvenation, preservation, and the indomitable spirit of cosmic caretakers.

Budh

In the cosmic ballet of terraforming, the collaborative dance between T'haerians and the inhabitants of Budh unfolded as a tapestry of harmonious coexistence. Budh, with its ancient traditions of communal communication, posed unique challenges and opportunities for the terraforming endeavour.

As the T'haerians and Budhs joined hands, the essence of Budh's identity was preserved and its traditional speaking methods held sacred. The collaborative effort aimed not to erase the ancient ways but to enhance the planet's hospitality, allowing the Budhs to thrive while embracing the advancements brought by the Angrezee terraforming.

Budh, once a harsh desert planetae, now boasted a diverse landscape—grassy plains, rolling hills, meandering rivers, and vast lakes that reflected the azure hues of its revitalised environment. The climate, intentionally maintained as mild and dry for most of its 378 local days, experienced a transformation during the spring rainy season. Torrential downpours turned the fertile soil into mud, ushering in a period of rejuvenation and growth.

The discovery and harvesting of Gamma travel crystals became a pivotal aspect of Budh's significance in interstellar communication. These crystals, essential for navigating the cosmic tapestry, were found nestled within the heart of the planetae. As the T'haerians carefully extracted and harnessed their power, Budh became a beacon of connection in the vastness of the cosmos.

The Budhs, with their copper-haired visage adorned with red check freckles, turquoise hexagonal forehead jewellery, and mint-pigmented eyes, stood as stewards of their planetae. Their attire, the traditional Bulifi garb in greys, slate blues, and coppers, echoed the hues of the transformed landscape.

Yet, the symbiosis extended beyond the visual aesthetics. The ancient way of speaking, where thoughts, memories, and feelings were communally shared with nature, remained a sacred practice. It required a delicate balance between preserving tradition and embracing adaptation.

The inhabitants of Budh, attuned to the pulse of their planetae, underwent augmentation to align with its nuances. Augmented appearances included rounded-pointed ears and a warm ivory pigment that harmonised with the natural palette of their rejuvenated world.

As the collaborative symphony of T'haerians and Budhs echoed through the seasons of Budh, the Gamma travel crystals became conduits of connection, linking the inhabitants to Petraea University. This sacred institution, nestled within the embrace of the revitalised planetae, trained students in the intricacies of Gamma travel, architectural imaarats, and planetae-forming technologies.

The terraforming of Budh was not merely a physical transformation; it was a celebration of heritage, a dance with tradition, and a testament to the unyielding spirit of cosmic collaboration. The harmony between the T'haerians and the Budhs echoed through the windswept landscapes and clear waters, a testament to the beauty born from unity and respect for the cosmic dance.

Mangal

In the grand symphony of celestial transformation, the T'haerians directed their creative energies towards Mangal, the current cultural heartbeat of our planetary system. From the cosmic canvas of space, Mangal unfolded its allure, a mesmerising tapestry of light blue oceans, plum and copper continents, and swirling clouds of bronze. Each stroke of cosmic artistry spoke to the metamorphosis that awaited this planetae.

As one gazed upon Mangal from the cosmic expanse, the oceans shimmered in hues of cerulean and sapphire, reflecting the dance of distant stars. The continents, adorned in regal shades of plum and copper, sprawled elegantly across the planetary canvas, inviting exploration and wonder. Above, the clouds, bathed in ethereal bronze, swirled with otherworldly grace, hinting at the dynamic forces that sculpted the skies.

The transformation of Mangal's surface unfolded as a saga of diverse landscapes. Rolling plains stretched beneath the cosmic embrace, a carpet of emerald, green dotted with vibrant blooms. Grassy hills, like undulating waves frozen in time, offered panoramic views of the planetary wonders. Swampy lakes, remnants of water-filled tunnels from Mangal's icy past, reflected the ambient glow of distant constellations.

The porous crust, a geological treasure trove, yielded natural plasma—a coveted resource that fuelled the technological renaissance of the entire sector. This luminous substance, harnessed for energy and construction, became the lifeblood of Mangal's burgeoning advancements, elevating it to new heights within the cosmic tapestry.

The fauna of Mangal, a testament to the harmonious dance between nature and technology, manifested in forms both familiar and exotic. Graceful creatures roamed the grassy hills, their movements a testament to the fluidity of life in this newly transformed realm. Avian beings soared through the bronze-tinged skies, leaving trails of colour as they navigated the currents of Mangal's revitalised atmosphere.

Amid this renaissance, the Sanskrti clan, stewards of arts and culture, flourished like petals unfolding in the cosmic dawn. The vibrant Sanskrti arts, an intricate dance of colours and expressions, resonated with the pulse of Mangal's transformed landscapes. Sanskrti practitioners, adorned in regal Bordeaux red garb, moved with grace and purpose, their creations echoing the harmony between the artistic spirit and the rejuvenated planetae.

From the vantage point of space, Mangal became a celestial masterpiece—a living testament to the T'haerians' mastery of terraforming. The interplay of colours, textures, and energies spoke of a rebirth, a cosmic renaissance that unfolded with every passing moment. As the Sanskrti arts adorned the surface and the natural plasma hummed with potential, Mangal stood as a beacon of culture, inviting the cosmos to witness the beauty born from the dance between science and art.

Omaja

As the celestial ballet continued, the T'haerians directed their cosmic energies towards Omaja—a sacred canvas upon which the essence of spiritual unity would be eternally painted. From the vastness of space, Omaja unveiled itself as a lush and beautiful world, a living testament to the harmonious coexistence of nature and spirituality.

From the cosmic perspective, Omaja's splendour radiated like a jewel in the cosmic tapestry. Mandarin-coloured oceans embraced the landmasses, their gentle waves an eternal hymn to the celestial dance. Wide canyons carved into the terrain, a testament to the transformative touch of terraforming, created intricate patterns that echoed the depth of Omaja's spiritual embrace.

The clouds above Omaja mirrored the hues of its oceans, a delicate dance of colours that shifted with the cosmic rhythms. Above the wide canyons, where the energies of the T'haerians and Omajas intertwined, the skies held a surrealistic palette—a canvas where nature and spirituality converged in ethereal beauty.

Amid this symphony of transformation, the Omajas, adorned in solar punk space suits, emerged as the guardians of spiritual unity. The dark porcelain pigmented Omajas wore these suits, not just as garments but as symbols—an iconography of unity that transcended the physical and delved into the realms of the cosmic and the metaphysical.

The solarpunk space suits were a marvel of Omaja's technological and spiritual fusion. Each suit, intricately designed, bore hues reminiscent of the planet's natural beauty—mandarin oranges, deep browns, and iridescent gold trimmings. Embedded within the fabric were subtle patterns that echoed the sacred geometry of Omaja's canyons and the fluidity of its oceans.

These suits were more than mere clothing; they became vessels of spiritual expression. Integrated with solar-powered technology, they symbolised the Omajas' commitment to harnessing cosmic energies for the greater good. The soft glow emanating from the suits mirrored the inner radiance of those who wore them, reflecting the unity between the material and the spiritual.

Omaja's solarpunk space suits, through their design and symbolism, transcended the boundaries of fashion—they became a visual mantra, a living proclamation of spiritual unity. The Omajas, guided by the wisdom of Brahman, moved through the rejuvenated landscapes of their planetae, their iconic attire weaving seamlessly into the vibrant tapestry of Omaja's majestic landscape.

Saanvi

In the grand cosmic saga, the final act of terraforming unfolded as the T'haerians turned their benevolent gaze towards Saanvi—a realm destined for wealth and good fortune. Initially marred by geological instability, Saanvi emerged from the crucible of transformation as a testament to collaborative cosmic artistry.

As the celestial dance neared its culmination, Saanvi's once-turbulent surface underwent a metamorphosis. The T'haerians, guided by the wisdom of ages, collaborated with the Tejee se Badhate merchant clan, weaving prosperity into the very fabric of the planetae. The collaboration resulted in the creation of a hospitable environment, carefully balanced with a defined rainy and dry season—a symphony orchestrated to bring forth the abundance of Saanvi's blessings.

The finality of the terraforming project echoed through the cosmic corridors as Saanvi stood reborn, the last jewel within the crown of Srimad-Bhagavatam. The elation coursing through the Tejee se Badhate tribe manifested as a jubilant dance—a celebration that transcended the physical and resonated with the spiritual essence of newfound prosperity.

Saanvi, now adorned with scenic mountain ridges that pierced the heavens and pristine beach islands where the cosmic waves whispered tales of transformation, stood as a beacon of natural beauty. The mountain ridges, cloaked in verdant splendour, echoed the triumphant spirit of collaboration—a triumph over the geological challenges that once plagued the planetae.

Pristine beach islands, caressed by celestial breezes, held the promise of tranquillity and abundance. The sands, kissed by cosmic tides, bore witness to the convergence of elements—earth, water, air, and fire—in harmonious coexistence. Saanvi's shores beckoned traders and wanderers alike, inviting them to partake in the prosperity woven into the very fabric of its rejuvenated landscapes.

The natural resources of Saanvi, a treasure trove of spices, precious gemstones, and metals, became the lifeblood of trade and prosperity. Spices, their aromas infused with the essence of celestial rejuvenation, wafted through bustling marketplaces. Precious gemstones sparkled like celestial constellations, adorning the artisan crafts of the Tejee se Badhate.

The metals, extracted with reverence from the depths of Saanvi's embrace, became the foundation for magnificent structures that rose like cosmic monuments. The melding of prosperity and natural abundance transformed Saanvi into a thriving centre for trade—a nexus where the currents of wealth and good fortune flowed in rhythmic harmony.

As the older female narrator recounts the tale of Saanvi's transformation, her voice resonates with a sense of fulfilment—a cosmic hymn sung in honour of collaboration, resilience, and the boundless potential embedded within the cosmic dance. Saanvi, the jewel of Srimad-Bhagavatam, stood as a testament to the benevolence of cosmic guardians and the unity that could be forged through the shared vision of prosperity.

Postlude of Chapter 7

In the cosmic aftermath of Srimad-Bhagavatam's transformation, the T'haerians stood as stewards of celestial evolution, having woven a tapestry of thriving planetae. As the orchestrators of this grand cosmic dance, the T'haerians felt a profound sense of fulfilment, their celestial artisanry leaving an indelible mark on the celestial bodies within their planetary system.

In reflection, it was conveyed to the Ma'an Su, the sovereign Mother of Bhabhi Salaah. The report echoed through the celestial corridors, narrating the triumphs and tribulations of the terraforming endeavours. The resounding proclamation was one of success—a harmonious symphony played across Aashvi, Arunima, Baidya Nath, Budh, Mangal, Omaja, and Saanvi.

Lessons gleaned from the celestial ballet were etched into the cosmic annals. The T'haerians learned the delicate balance of preserving the intrinsic beauty of each planetae while instilling the breath of life. The constructive collaboration between the cosmic and the terrestrial, the dance of flora and fauna, and the adaptation of humanoid forms to suit new environments were revelations woven into the fabric of wisdom.

As the celestial architects took stock, a collective gaze turned towards the celestial fragment, Yahvi—a small celestial body orbiting Coma in the Venatici Quadrant. Research endeavours, fuelled by the lessons of Srimad-Bhagavatam's metamorphosis, were underway to expedite the formation of Yahvi into a fully-fledged planetae. The challenge lay not only in Yahvi's nascent state but in the anticipation of the terraforming ballet that awaited its celestial stage.

The T'haerians, guided by the wisdom accrued from their previous cosmic choreography, sought ways to accelerate the planetary birthing process. Scientific minds delved into the mysteries of celestial embryogenesis, unravelling the cosmic codes that governed the transition from celestial infancy to terrestrial maturity.

In the research laboratories of Petraea University, where the seekers of knowledge congregated, minds collaborated on the frontier of cosmic evolution. Techniques to harness cosmic energies, replicate the celestial alchemy observed in the formation of Srimad-Bhagavatam's planetae, and unlock the secrets of rapid terraforming became the focal points of their cosmic inquiry.

The dance with Yahvi held the promise of a new cosmic chapter, and the T'haerians, buoyed by their triumphs, embraced the challenge with reverence and enthusiasm. As they prepared to pen another celestial symphony, the T'haerians looked to the cosmic horizon with eyes gleaming with the anticipation of discovery and transformation. The lessons of the past illuminated the path forward, and the celestial ballet, unbroken and eternal, continued its dance through the cosmic realms.

In the sacred halls of Petraea University, where knowledge intertwined with cosmic aspirations, the T'haerian researchers delved into the mysteries of celestial genesis, seeking to unravel the secrets that lay within the cosmic cradle of Yahvi. The research conducted to accelerate Yahvi's formation became a celestial odyssey, blending technological ingenuity with reverence for the cosmic dance.

The scholars of Petraea University, stewards of cosmic wisdom, embarked on a journey of discovery, exploring realms where quantum insights and temporal dynamics converged. The cosmic artisans sought to harmonise the forces that shaped Yahvi's celestial destiny, orchestrating a symphony of cosmic energies to expedite the planetary formation process.

New technological advancements, born from the crucible of curiosity, began to emerge. Quantum resonance resonated through the laboratories, where researchers harnessed the dance of subatomic particles to sculpt the celestial contours of Yahvi. Temporal engineering, a fusion of cosmic rhythms and technological finesse, became a beacon guiding terraforming endeavours.

The advancements at Petraea University surpassed the boundaries of conventional wisdom. Nano-augmentations and molecular harmonics were employed to shape Yahvi's atmosphere, creating a balance that mirrored the cosmic equilibrium. Advanced energy-capture mechanisms, inspired by the celestial choreography witnessed in Srimad-Bhagavatam, promised to infuse Yahvi with life-sustaining vitality.

In the vivid imaginations of researchers and scientists, Yahvi became a haven of harmonious environments—a celestial tapestry woven with threads of innovation and cosmic understanding. Lush landscapes adorned with vibrant flora, crystalline rivers meandering through valleys, and skies painted with hues borrowed from the cosmic palette envisioned a habitat where life could flourish.

The atmosphere, carefully tailored by technological artistry, held the promise of breathable air, free from the constraints of cosmic limitations. Advanced irrigation systems, inspired by the terraforming lessons of the planetarum of Srimad-Bhagavatam, sought to nurture the celestial soil, creating fertile grounds for the seeds of cosmic potential to take root.

Yahvi, once a celestial whisper in the cosmic wind, now beckoned with the allure of a new frontier—an embodiment of celestial stewardship, where technological prowess harmonised with cosmic wisdom. As the scholars of Petraea University continued to unravel the celestial enigma, Yahvi's envisioned habitable environment became a testament to the eternal quest for balance and harmony in the cosmic dance of creation.

Chapter 8

As Mzaliwa sat in her quarters aboard the star cruiser *Taaraa*, her mind buzzed with questions about why Prof Prabuddh had taken a personal interest in her work. The holographic projection of Prof Prabuddh appeared before her, and she initiated the communication.

"*Good day, Prof Prabuddh. I am honoured by your invitation and thrilled to have the opportunity to study at Petraea Uni. May I ask what prompted your interest in my work?*" Mzaliwa inquired respectfully.

The holographic image of Prof Prabuddh smiled warmly, his eyes reflecting a genuine enthusiasm for the conversation. "*Mzaliwa, your work has not only caught my attention but has left a profound impression on the academic community. Your submission on the intersection of traditional T'haerian practices and emerging technologies is groundbreaking. The way you blend cultural insights with scientific exploration is truly remarkable.*"

He continued, "*In a universe filled with advancements, there is a rare authenticity in your approach. You possess a unique ability to bridge the ancient wisdom of the past with the innovative technologies of today. It is this synthesis that we believe will contribute immensely to the academic community at Petraea Uni.*"

Mzaliwa listened attentively, her eyes reflecting a mix of gratitude and curiosity. Prof Prabuddh went on, "*Your work is not just about the advancements themselves; it is about understanding the cultural fabric that binds civilisations. We believe that your perspective will enrich the discourse on Budh, and your presence at Petraea Uni will be a catalyst for fostering a deeper understanding of the diverse planetary societies.*"

He leaned forward, his holographic image exuding a genuine eagerness.

"*Moreover, we see potential in you to become a bridge between T'haeri and the broader interplanetary academic network. Your journey can inspire others to explore the intersections of tradition and innovation. We are not just inviting you for your expertise but also for the unique voice you bring to the table."*

Mzaliwa, humbled and inspired, expressed her gratitude, *"Thank you, Prof Prabuddh. I am deeply honoured by your words and the opportunity to contribute to the academic community. I will strive to be that bridge and uphold the values that connect us all."*

As the holographic projection faded, Mzaliwa could not help but feel a profound sense of responsibility. Prof Prabuddh had not only recognised her academic achievements but had entrusted her with a mission to bridge worlds. The weight of this responsibility settled on her shoulders, and she knew that her journey to Petraea Uni was not just about personal success but about building connections that transcended planetary boundaries.

Mzaliwa stood in her quarters aboard the star cruiser Taaraa, surrounded by the soft glow of holographic displays. With a mix of excitement and trepidation, she prepared to send her farewell messages to her parents and her best friend, Af'sadi. As the holographic projection activated, she took a deep breath.

"Mama, Baba, alsalam ealayna," she began, her voice carrying a hint of nervousness. *"The time has come for me to embark on this incredible journey to Novissimus. I want to express my deepest gratitude for your unwavering support. Without your love and encouragement, I would not be standing here today."*

Her mother's eyes shimmered with a mix of pride and concern as she responded, *"Mzaliwa, my beloved daughter, we are proud of the woman you have become. Novissimus is a vast and unknown world, but we have faith in your strength and wisdom. May Brjamohana's blessings be with you on this journey."*

Her father, though visibly moved, added, *"Remember, Mzaliwa, you carry the essence of T'haeri within you. Let it guide you and be a beacon of light wherever you go. We love you, and our prayers will always accompany you."*

As she ended the holographic call with her parents, Mzaliwa felt a mixture of emotions. Turning her attention to her best friend Af'sadi, she initiated another holographic message. Af'sadi's image appeared, and she greeted Mzaliwa with a warm smile.

"*Salaam, Mzaliwa! So, the adventure begins, huh?*" Af'sadi said, her eyes reflecting a blend of excitement and sadness.

Mzaliwa nodded, "*Yes, Af'sadi. It is both thrilling and daunting. I want to thank you for being my rock, my confidante. Your friendship has been a source of strength for me. As I step into the unknown, your words and support will be my guiding star.*"

Af'sadi's expression softened, "*Mzaliwa, you are like a sister to me. Novissimus is gaining an extraordinary soul. Remember, no matter the distance, our bond remains unbreakable. I will eagerly await your messages and, of course, your visits. Safe travels, my dear friend.*"

With a final wave and a heartfelt smile, Mzaliwa ended the holographic call. She felt a sense of closure and readiness for the journey ahead. The mix of trepidation and eagerness lingered within her, creating a bittersweet symphony of emotions as she prepared to explore the wonders of Novissimus.

Deck Three of Salaee buzzed with activity as crew members made their way to the travel pods in anticipation of the quantum drive activation. Mzaliwa followed the stream of excited yet apprehensive individuals, all eager to experience the marvel of extradimensional travel. The travel pods were a spectacle in themselves, lined up in precision along the spacious deck.

The pods, sleek and aerodynamic, resembled cocoon-like capsules suspended in a gravity-defying formation. Each pod was equipped with a panoramic viewport that offered a breathtaking view of the T'haerian biome outside.

The transparent material of the pods displayed a vivid array of violet forget-me-nots, Azores spurges, and the lush greenery of the replicated Surtseyan forest.

The crew members, dressed in their respective planetary uniforms, entered the pods with a mix of excitement and nervous energy. Mzaliwa stepped into her designated pod, the door sealing with a soft hiss behind her. Inside, the comfortable seating embraced her, and the holographic controls awaited her touch.

As she settled into her seat, a soft voice echoed within the pod [Prepare for quantum drive activation. Ensure all safety harnesses are secured.]

The anticipation in the air was palpable. The crew members exchanged glances, a mixture of awe and uncertainty reflecting in their eyes. The quantum drive was an uncharted frontier, and the crew was about to pioneer the untested capabilities of the Gamma travel crystal.

For Salaee, the enhanced warp drive had been a familiar and reliable technology, but the integration of the Gamma travel crystal was an unprecedented leap into unexplored realms. The potential consequences and challenges lingered in the minds of the crew. What would happen when the quantum drive came online? Would it propel them seamlessly into the folds of interplanetary and into extradimensional space, or would unforeseen disruptions occur?

Mzaliwa could feel a collective sense of responsibility and curiosity among the crew. She was the very reason this trip outside of Primis was even possible. The holographic displays in the pods projected real-time data, showing the intricate processes leading to the activation of the Gamma travel crystal. The crew members exchanged glances once more, their eyes reflecting a mix of excitement, determination, and a tinge of anxiety.

[Quantum drive activation sequence initiated. Brace for warp transition.]

The announcement echoed through the pods, marking the pivotal moment. The crew tightened their safety harnesses, and Mzaliwa held her breath in anticipation. The hum of energy around her intensified as the quantum drive came to life, its power pulsating through Salaee.

As the crew embarked on this uncharted journey with the untested Gamma travel crystal, the unknown stretched before them like an infinite canvas. Novissimus awaited, and the crew of Salaee prepared to traverse the cosmic dosser that connected the diverse worlds of Primis and Novissimus.

As the quantum drive activation sequence reached its culmination, a surge of energy enveloped Salaee. The star ship seemed to tremble with anticipation, and a radiant glow emanated from its core. Mzaliwa, strapped into her pod, watched in awe as the fabric of space-time before her began to ripple and warp.

Suddenly, a mesmerising portal of shimmering lights materialised in front of Salaee. The quantum tunnel, a celestial corridor transcending the limits of conventional space, beckoned the star ship forward. It was a kaleidoscope of colours, a cosmic dance of hues that defied the laws of physics. The tunnel's aperture expanded, revealing an otherworldly passage adorned with celestial patterns that seemed to shift and morph in an intricate ballet.

As Salaee entered the quantum tunnel, the transition was seamless yet surreal. The crew members felt a gentle gravitational pull, and the stars outside the tunnel stretched and distorted, creating a mesmerising warp effect. The opening of the quantum tunnel marked the beginning of their extradimensional journey, a venture into realms beyond the constraints of known space.

Within the quantum tunnel, Salaee soared through extradimensional space, leaving behind the familiar constellations of Anagha. The star ship traversed a cosmic arras where the laws of physics bowed to the whims of quantum entanglement. The crew members, now acclimated to the surreal surroundings, engaged in various activities.

On deck three, where the travel pods were located, holographic displays projected mesmerising views of the extradimensional landscape. Crew members marvelled at the ethereal beauty outside, capturing holographic images and recordings to document the uncharted territories they passed through. The corridors of Salaee echoed with discussions about the celestial wonders glimpsed through the viewports.

Meanwhile, in the command centre on Deck One, the navigation team worked in unison to ensure Salaee maintained its trajectory within the quantum tunnel. The ship's AI systems monitored quantum fluctuations, adjusting the warp nacelles to harmonise with the extradimensional currents. The crew, attuned to their roles, carried out checks and analyses to ensure a smooth and secure journey.

On decks four to eleven, where the living spaces were designed to mimic different planetary biomes, T'haerians engaged in communal activities. They gathered in simulated environments resembling the landscapes of their home worlds, sharing stories, music, and cultural experiences. The holographic mess hall featured an array of interplanetary cuisines, creating a diverse culinary experience.

As Salaee cruised through the quantum tunnel at warp speeds, the crew experienced a sense of unity and wonder. The crew members, connected by the shared journey, found solace in the beauty and mystery unfolding beyond the star ship's hull.

Postlude of Chapter 8

Diary entry by Af'sadi:

As I inscribe these words with the ink of my apprehensions, I cannot help but feel the weight of foreboding upon my soul. The mismanagement of Aushadhi by the Bhabhi Salaah echoes through the celestial corridors like a dissonant melody, signalling rumblings and shifts in the very foundation of our T'haerian society.

The sacred substance, once revered as a conduit to the divine, now teeters on the precipice of misuse. The Bhabhi Salaah, in their pursuit of heightened states, have become entangled in the web of Aushadhi-induced visions. The essence of Brjamohana, once a clear channel, now wavers in the kaleidoscopic tapestry painted by the hallucinogenic substance. The mismanagement is apparent, and the cosmic dance loses its celestial rhythm.

Rumours swirl like cosmic winds, carrying whispers of discontent among the people. The sacred rituals, once a beacon of divine connection, now cast shadows of doubt upon the hallowed halls. The Bhabhi Salaah's reliance on Aushadhi has sown seeds of uncertainty, leaving the T'haerian society questioning the very fabric of our cosmic existence.

Amid this disquiet, a push for extradimensional travel emerges—a pursuit that leaves our society vulnerable to potential threats. Mzaliwa and crew, with their ambitious endeavours, prepare to traverse the cosmic tapestry into realms unknown. The departure of such skilled navigators raises concerns, for the path they tread is uncharted, and the cosmic winds whisper of unforeseen perils.

The push for extradimensional travel, while brimming with potential, leaves a void in the protective web that once enveloped our cosmic home. The vulnerability of our society becomes palpable, exposed to potential attacks from forces unseen and realms untamed. As Mzaliwa and crew prepare to leave Primis, the cosmic balance teeters on the precipice, and I, Af'sadi, cannot shake the premonition of a reckoning approaching.

Is this the reckoning, I have sensed in the cosmic winds—a turning point that heralds change on a cosmic scale? The cosmic dance, once harmonious, now flirts with discord. The departure of Mzaliwa and crew, coupled with the mismanagement of Aushadhi, sets the stage for a chapter yet unwritten.

May the celestial winds carry these words through the cosmic expanse and may our T'haerian society navigate the shifting currents with wisdom and resilience. The cosmic tapestry is woven with threads of uncertainty but let us remain steadfast in the face of the looming unknown.

Even the angels fell, and the stars stood still.

Prelude to Chapter 9

In the cosmic tapestry where the celestial realms of Primis and Novissimus intertwined, a profound shift occurred. As Brjamohana and Shraavana wove the fabric of creation, the echo of the desire for uniqueness resounded through the cosmos, a desire that would reverberate with consequences untold.

Shraavana, the seeker of individuality, gazed upon the vastness of space with an insatiable yearning. The desire to forge a realm that stood apart, a realm of unparalleled uniqueness—anokha—whispered through the cosmic winds. The Glow of Dawn, a cosmic juncture pregnant with possibilities, became the crucible of Shraavana's decision.

As Shraavana birthed Novissimus, a realm devoid of form and life, she declared, "There shall be sitaare aur grah—stars and planets." The very act of creation, a testament to her desire for distinctiveness, cast a ripple across the celestial expanse. The stars, witnesses to the cosmic drama, stood still, as if frozen in time, their luminous gaze fixated on the unfolding events.

The angels, beings of the divine essence, found themselves entangled in the cosmic paradox of Shraavana's desire for separation. The celestial symphony, once harmonious, now teetered on the edge of dissonance. Shraavana's declaration of individuality cast a shadow that reached even the celestial beings, stirring a desire within them to be separate, unique, and autonomous.

As Shraavana's creation unfolded in Novissimus, the angels influenced by the celestial echoes of desire, faced an internal struggle. The desire for uniqueness and independence, akin to the longing for their creator, tugged at the fabric of their celestial essence. The cosmic winds whispered of a division among the heavenly hosts, a rebellion born from the yearning to stand apart.

Even the angels, beings of divine grace, succumbed to the gravitational pull of individuality. The division that ensued, the fall of angels, marked a cosmic rebellion against the ordained cosmic order. Their descent echoed through the celestial realms, a symphony of discord that mirrored Shraavana's pursuit of anokha.

The stars, witnesses to this celestial drama, stood still in silent observation. The very luminaries that adorned the heavens seemed to freeze, their brilliance encapsulating the moment of cosmic divergence. The once-unified celestial tapestry now bore the threads of division, with angels falling and stars standing still, encapsulating the consequences of Shraavana's desire for a realm that stood uniquely apart.

The cosmic prelude unfolded, setting the stage for a saga where the interplay of creation and rebellion, uniqueness, and unity, would shape the destinies of Primis and Novissimus. The desire for individuality, a flame ignited by Shraavana, cast shadows that reached the farthest corners of the celestial realms, leaving an indelible mark on the cosmic narrative.

Chapter 9

Shraavana, as the second-born, held a profound responsibility in her dharma to create Novissimus, mirroring the existing realm of Primis. However, her desire for uniqueness and individuality led her to make a decision that set her apart. In forgoing her connection with Brjamohana, Shraavana severed the inherent duality of their existence. This choice carried significant consequences, both for her and the fabric of Novissimus.

The decision to stay apart from Brjamohana, her twin divine entity in the cosmic order, went beyond mere rebellion. Shraavana sought to redefine the concept of creation and existence. By pursuing uniqueness, she embraced a path that challenged the traditional notions of divine harmony and cosmic balance. The consequences of this separation rippled through the very foundation of Novissimus, introducing an unprecedented dynamic.

Shraavana's individuality became a catalyst for change, injecting a sense of autonomy into the cosmic arras. Yet, the consequences of her decision were not solely personal; they extended to the inhabitants of Novissimus and the intricate balance of the universe.

In the wake of Shraavana's decision, Novissimus witnessed an era of unparalleled technological advancement. The societal impact was profound, reshaping the relationships and daily lives of its inhabitants. The quest for uniqueness extended beyond the divine realm to the Terrestris, the inhabitants of Dharatee.

The advancements in technology fostered a society that celebrated individuality and innovation. Dharatee became a melting pot of ideas, where each Terrestris pursued their unique contribution to the collective tapestry of knowledge. The once rigid societal structures gave way to a dynamic landscape where creativity and expression flourished.

However, the influx of technology also introduced challenges. The pursuit of individualism sometimes led to an isolationist mindset, as inhabitants became engrossed in their own creations and innovations. While relationships thrived in the realm of ideas, the personal connections between Terrestris often faced challenges.

The use of technology also impacted daily life. Dharatee became a world where the boundaries between reality and virtual existence blurred. Augmented reality, advanced AI systems, and neural interfaces transformed the way Terrestris interacted with their surroundings. While these innovations brought convenience, they also raised ethical questions about the nature of consciousness and the potential consequences of merging the organic with the artificial.

The societal impact of technological advancements reflected the duality inherent in Shraavana's decision. On one hand, it propelled Dharatee into an era of unparalleled progress and individual expression. On the other hand, it presented challenges and ethical dilemmas that required the Terrestris to navigate the delicate balance between innovation and preserving the essence of their interconnected existence.

In the intricate dance between Shraavana's pursuit of uniqueness and the societal evolution of Dharatee, the consequences and benefits unfolded, shaping the destiny of a realm that stood apart from Primis in both its divine origins and the innovations of its mortal inhabitants.

Within the hallowed halls of the ruling class on Dharatee, a relentless pursuit of profits over human life forged an inordinate imbalance. The wealth, like a coveted elixir, flowed predominantly into the coffers of a mere one per cent of the planetary population. The ruling elite, blinded by avarice, engaged in ceaseless bickering, transforming the political landscape into a battlefield of prestige, technological prowess, and control over the coveted Iksray crystal.

On Dharatee, the countries engaged in perpetual squabbles over prestige, each vying to be recognised as the epitome of technological advancement and societal superiority. The ruling class, draped in opulence, sought to outshine one another in grandiosity, constructing towering monuments of technological marvels to assert dominance. The relentless competition fuelled a race for prestige, with nations investing exorbitant sums to highlight their advancements on the global stage.

Architectural wonders rose like titans, each country attempting to overshadow the other in a spectacle of technological prowess. The squabbles for prestige manifested in extravagant displays of wealth, with the ruling elite using their nations as canvases to etch their legacy in the annals of history. The constant race for prestige became a symbol of power and influence, driving the ruling class deeper into the throes of political manoeuvring.

Dharatee's ruling class engaged in a technological arms race, with nations striving to claim the title of the most technologically advanced. Research and development facilities became battlegrounds where scientists and engineers toiled to unveil groundbreaking innovations. The relentless pursuit of superiority spurred advancements in AI, robotics, and space exploration, furthering the divide between the technological elite and the rest of the population.

The Iksray crystal, a source of immense power and a conduit to extradimensional travel became the ultimate prize in the technological arms race. Nations competed to harness its potential for their own scientific endeavours, intensifying the squabbles as each sought to demonstrate their capability to control and exploit this cosmic resource.

The Iksray crystal, mined from Shravan, became the focal point of political strife on Dharatee. The ruling class, divided by their insatiable thirst for dominance, engaged in fervent debates over who should control this extraordinary artefact. The crystal's scarcity and the unparalleled power it held fuelled the flames of contention, turning political chambers into arenas of ideological clashes.

Countries vied for the authority to decide the fate of the Iksray crystal, each arguing that they alone possessed the wisdom to harness its potential for the greater good. Behind closed doors, alliances formed and crumbled as nations sought to consolidate power and control. The ruling elite, driven by self-interest, manipulated public opinion to legitimise their claims over the cosmic artefact.

The squabbles over control of the Iksray crystal mirrored the broader societal divide, highlighting the stark contrast between the privileged ruling class and the masses yearning for equity. As political machinations unfolded, the fate of the crystal hung in the balance, its significance extending beyond a mere source of power to become a symbol of the moral compass that Dharatee desperately needed to find.

Amid these political theatrics, the people of Dharatee struggled beneath the weight of inequality and exploitation, their lives commodified by a ruling class that prioritised prestige, technological prowess, and control over cosmic artefacts over the well-being of the planetary populace.

Owo, with her fascination for numbers and physics, found herself standing out among the Terrestris of Dharatee. Her essence, too delicate for the harsh life on Dharatee, set her apart in a society that often embraced a sense of coldness and detachment. As a scientist with a passion for extradimensional space travel, Owo's journey was marked by struggles that extended beyond the confines of her laboratory.

In a society that valued technological prowess and scientific achievement, Owo's empathetic and kind nature clashed with the prevailing norms. The Terrestris, engrossed in their technological advancements, often kept emotions at arm's length. Owo's essence, characterised by empathy and a genuine connection to others, made her an outlier.

Her struggles extended to interpersonal relationships, where the coldness of society made it challenging for her to connect with her peers on a deeper level. The political and social dynamics emphasised competition and individual achievement, leaving Owo navigating a landscape that seemed indifferent to her unique essence.

Owo's quest for extradimensional space travel revealed the need for an Iksray crystal from Shravan, named after Shraavana, herself. The Iksray crystal, a conductor essential for the Antariksh to pilot the vessel through extradimensional space, held immense significance not just for Owo's project but for the broader narrative of Novissimus.

The Iksray crystal became a symbol of connection between the divine origins of Shraavana's decision to stay apart and the technological advancements of the Terrestris. Its significance lay in its tie to the essence of Shraavana, and acquiring it became both a scientific and spiritual quest for Owo.

The crystal, mined from Shravan, carried not only the potential for technological advancement but also a deeper connection to the cosmic order. The political and social dynamics surrounding the Iksray crystal became intricate, as various factions within Dharatee vied for control over its extraction and usage. The crystal's scarcity and the power it held fuelled political intrigue, with different planetary factions seeking to harness its potential for their own agendas.

The quest for the Iksray crystal intertwined with the larger narrative of Dharatee over its neighbouring planetarum, connecting the realms of science, spirituality, and societal dynamics. Owo's journey to obtain the crystal became a metaphorical bridge between the coldness of technological advancement and the warmth of Shraavana's unique essence.

As Owo delved into the political intricacies surrounding the Iksray crystal, she found herself not only on a scientific mission but also navigating the consequences of Shraavana's decision to stay apart. The crystal, a conduit between realms, held the potential to reshape the societal dynamics by challenging the prevailing coldness and fostering a deeper connection among the Terrestris. She at least hoped it would do such a thing.

In the broader narrative, the Iksray crystal became a catalyst for change, symbolising the delicate balance between technological progress and the preservation of interconnected existence. Owo's struggles and the significance of the crystal added layers to the overarching storyline, revealing the intricate dance between individual essence, societal norms, and the divine tapestry that defined Novissimus.

If the Iksray crystal powering the extradimensional tech could not be the catalyst to change the overall culture of Dharatee; Owo wanted off the world and off this instant because her family life was reaching a boiling point.

In the modest dwelling on Dharatee, the familial tension between Owo and her family simmered like an unspoken storm. Despite her groundbreaking scientific achievements, the weight of cultural expectations pressed heavily upon Owo's shoulders. The clash between her aspirations and traditional gender roles created a rift that widened with each passing day.

Ikoro, Owo's mother, embodied the archetype of an overbearing matriarch. While her daughter's scientific feats brought acclaim beyond their modest home, Ikoro's expectations remained anchored in tradition. Her controlling demeanour extended to every facet of Owo's life, from her career choices to the personal decisions that shaped her existence.

The cultural tapestry woven around Ikoro's worldview dictated that Owo's greatest achievement should be marriage and family. The pressure to conform to societal expectations of settling down gnawed at Owo's sense of individuality. Ikoro's dissatisfaction with her daughter's chosen path manifested in subtle yet palpable disdain. Owo's groundbreaking scientific pursuits were met with indifference or veiled hostility, as Ikoro struggled to reconcile her daughter's choices with the rigid norms ingrained in their culture.

Asan, Owo's father, was a passive presence within the family dynamics. His actions mirrored the path laid out by his wife, Ikoro, and his role was defined by compliance. Though his daughter's achievements echoed beyond the walls of their home, Asan seldom engaged in conversations that veered from the traditional script laid out by his wife. His existence seemed almost non-existent, overshadowed by the overbearing force of Ikoro's will.

Asan's lack of intervention or support further isolated Owo within her own family. The absence of a strong paternal figure left her yearning for understanding and acceptance, as her groundbreaking endeavours became a source of conflict rather than pride within the family unit.

Owo's scientific prowess challenged the deeply entrenched traditional gender roles on Dharatee. In a society where expectations dictated that women prioritise family over individual pursuits, Owo's commitment to her groundbreaking research disrupted the norm. Her desire for personal fulfilment clashed with cultural expectations, pushing the boundaries of what was deemed acceptable for a woman.

The conflict manifested not only in the strained relationship with her mother but also in the whispers and raised eyebrows within their community. Owo's achievements became a topic of scrutiny, with some viewing her as a deviation from the accepted path. The cultural lens through which her accomplishments were filtered emphasised the incongruity between her aspirations and societal expectations.

For Owo, the pursuit of personal fulfilment through her scientific endeavours became a battleground where cultural expectations clashed with individual aspirations. The incessant pressure to conform to traditional gender roles stifled her dreams and left her torn between the path she desired, and the one laid out by societal norms.

The conflict within the family became a microcosm of the larger societal struggle between progress and tradition. Owo's journey to redefine her role as a woman challenged the very fabric of cultural expectations, forcing her to confront the harsh reality that personal fulfilment came at the cost of familial acceptance.

In the crucible of familial discord, Owo grappled with the complexities of cultural norms and the pursuit of personal identity. The clash between tradition and individuality played out within the walls of their home, mirrored the broader societal struggle for acceptance and recognition of women breaking free from the shackles of prescribed roles.

As a child of science on Dharatee, Owo's development and process were marked by a unique affinity for the cosmic mysteries that surrounded her. From a tender age, she exhibited a fascination with the celestial, mirroring the pioneering spirit of her fourth great-grandfather, Titunto si ti Imọ, who had theorised on galactic travel principles.

Titunto si ti Imọ, a beacon of inspiration within Owo's familial lineage, left an indelible mark on her budding curiosity. The tales of his groundbreaking theories and contributions to the principles of galactic travel became the bedtime stories that fuelled Owo's dreams. His legacy became a guiding light, shaping her perception of the boundless possibilities that lay beyond the confines of Dharatee.

Owo's admiration for Titunto si ti Imọ became a catalyst for her own aspirations. She yearned to follow in his intellectual footsteps, aspiring not only to unravel the mysteries of the cosmos but to transcend the limitations imposed by societal norms.

From a youthful age, Owo's mind operated in the language of numbers. In her sleep, she dreamt of equations and cosmic phenomena, her dreams a kaleidoscope of numerical patterns that danced in the realms of quantum space. The abstract beauty of mathematics wove through the fabric of her subconscious, imprinting a love for numbers that would define her destiny.

Owo's dreams were not mere flights of fancy but intricate journeys into the heart of quantum realms. She envisioned the curvature of space-time and the dance of particles in equations that transcended the conventional understanding of the cosmos. Each dream became a stepping stone towards the realisation of her innate connection to the numerical tapestry that governed the universe.

For Owo, numbers were not confined to the abstract landscapes of dreams; they permeated her waking reality. In the everyday rhythms of life on Dharatee, she saw the elegant dance of numerical relationships. From the petals of a flower to the patterns of a passing cloud, Owo discerned the mathematical intricacies that underpinned the tapestry of existence.

Her keen perception turned mundane moments into opportunities for exploration. The world around her became a canvas painted with numerical strokes, each observation a revelation that fuelled her insatiable curiosity. Owo's ability to see numbers in everyday life set her apart, hinting at a connection with the cosmic order that transcended the boundaries of conventional understanding.

At the astonishing age of four, Owo embarked on a remarkable journey of linguistic creation. Driven by an innate desire to express the numerical symphonies that resonated within her, she began to craft her own numerical language. With a childlike exuberance, she wove symbols and patterns that mirrored the mathematical principles she glimpsed in her dreams and daily life.

Owo's numerical language became a testament to her precocious intellect and the unconventional path she was destined to tread. The symbols she created were not arbitrary; they carried the essence of her connection with numbers, forming a language that transcended the conventional barriers of linguistic expression. This early manifestation of her intellectual prowess hinted at the extraordinary journey that awaited Owo as a child of science on Dharatee.

As the present day unfolded, Owo stood at the precipice of a monumental journey, her hands cradling the coveted Iksray travel crystal that would be the key to transcending the boundaries of Novissimus. The preparations for the test voyage aboard the starship Utata were underway, and Owo immersed herself in the meticulous planning required for this unprecedented expedition.

The journey began with a diplomatic manoeuvre orchestrated by the Mineralogy department. Prof Ofeefee, recognising the significance of the Iksray crystal, managed to procure it from the neck of a wealthy dissident.

The acquisition marked a crucial step in realising Owo's dream of intergalactic space travel. The crystal, a conduit to the cosmic forces that governed extradimensional travel, now rested securely in Owo's possession.

Preparations for the Test Voyage

1. Quantum Drive Calibration:

The first order of business was the meticulous calibration of Utata's quantum drive. Owo, surrounded by a team of expert engineers and navigators, ensured that every aspect of the ship's propulsion system aligned with the unique frequencies of the Iksray crystal. Quantum fluctuations were analysed, and adjustments were made to guarantee a stable transition through extradimensional space.

2. Structural Reinforcements:

Recognising the unprecedented nature of the voyage, the structural integrity of Utata underwent rigorous reinforcement. Engineers fortified the hull, reinforced the warp nacelles, and implemented additional shielding to withstand the potential stresses of traversing the cosmic tapestry beyond Novissimus.

3. Extradimensional Navigation Protocols:

Owo, in collaboration with the navigation team, developed intricate protocols for navigating through extradimensional space. The team studied the cosmic cartography unveiled by Mchunguzi's previous journeys, creating a comprehensive guide for Utata's trajectory. The Iksray crystal's unique properties demanded a nuanced approach to navigation, and Owo ensured that every contingency was considered.

4. Living Spaces and Sustenance:

The living spaces on Utata were designed to cater to the diverse crew representing the various planetae of Novissimus. Biomes resembling the home environments of the Terrestris were recreated to provide a semblance of familiarity during the extended journey. The mess hall featured a diverse array of interplanetary cuisines, fostering a sense of unity among the crew.

5. Communication Systems:

Utata's communication systems were fine-tuned to maintain contact with Novissimus and Dharatee throughout the journey. Owo emphasised the importance of real-time communication, ensuring that any unforeseen challenges or discoveries could be shared with the scientific community on Novissimus.

6. Shift Rotations and Crew Assignments:

With the departure set for two shift rotations, crew assignments were carefully curated to ensure optimal performance. Owo, serving as the chief scientist and navigator, collaborated with the command centre team to establish efficient shift rotations. The crew, diverse in expertise and cultural backgrounds, was briefed on their roles and responsibilities for the journey.

As the preparations reached their crescendo, Owo felt a surge of anticipation and responsibility. The starship Utata, armed with the Iksray travel crystal, stood as a testament to the culmination of generations of scientific pursuit. The impending test voyage would not only push the boundaries of Novissimus but would also etch Owo's name in the cosmic annals as the pioneer who dared to venture beyond the known realms of Anagha.

Postlude of Chapter 9

The T'haerians, with their good-hearted nature and a deep understanding of the cosmic tapestry, recognised the challenges that visitors from Dharatee would face on their planetae. In their benevolence, guided by the ancient prophecy foretelling the twins re-joining and Primis and Novissimus being analogous dimensions, the T'haerians sought to bridge the gap and make their world more hospitable to advena.

Inspired by their awareness of the schism between Brjamohana and her twin, Shraavana, the T'haerians embarked on the invention of filtration suits designed specifically for the humans of Dharatee. The motivation behind creating these suits was rooted in compassion and the desire to facilitate harmony between the two dimensions. The T'haerians believed that fostering understanding and unity across realms was essential for the fulfilment of the cosmic prophecy.

The filtration suits were crafted with meticulous care, addressing the atmospheric disparities between T'haeri and Dharatee. The ambient temperature and unique composition of T'haeri's atmosphere, including a higher level of argon, posed challenges for human visitors. To mitigate these challenges, the T'haerians engineered suits capable of reducing the argon levels to match those of Dharatee (0.9%). This adjustment ensured that the atmospheric conditions inside the suits mirrored the familiar environment of visitors' home dimension.

Moreover, the filtration suits went beyond merely addressing atmospheric concerns. Recognising the importance of sustainability and the cyclical nature of life, the T'haerians designed the suits to absorb carbon dioxide exhaled by the wearer, converting it into breathable oxygen. This innovative feature displayed their commitment to ecological balance and the well-being of their guests.

The suits further incorporated advanced technology to filter and purify bodily fluids, including perspiration and urine. Waste separation mechanisms ensured that discarded materials could be processed and converted into drinkable water, promoting self-sufficiency for those exploring T'haeri's wonders.

Chapter 10

Holographic Journal Entry—Mzaliwa, Aboard Salaee—Star Date: 13 Sita 55 AD.

Mama, Baba—*Alsalam ealayna*

Greetings from the cosmic expanse, my dear parents and cherished friend! As I journey through the celestial seas aboard Salaee, I find solace in sharing glimpses of everyday life within this vessel that navigates the tapestry of dimensions.

Life aboard Salaee unfolds like a cosmic symphony, each day bringing new wonders and discoveries. In the command centre, where celestial navigation is an art, I orchestrate our trajectory through the cosmic waves. The hum of technology, the pulsating glow of holographic interfaces, and the cosmic panorama beyond the viewports create an ambience of exploration.

The crew members aboard Salaee, my cosmic companions, are a diverse array of T'haerian expertise. We move with the rhythm of cosmic unity, each contributing our skills to the cosmic dance. Laughter resonates in the communal spaces, and the bond that ties us transcends the confines of mere comradeship. We share tales of our homelands, dreams of the uncharted, and aspirations that soar beyond the stars.

As I traverse the decks that simulate the diverse planetae of Srimad-Bhagavatam, I find myself immersed in the kaleidoscope of biomes that mirror the wonders of our cosmic home.

Stepping onto the Aashvi deck, you will be enveloped in the vibrant colours of gemstone haven. Lush jungles teeming with life, crystalline lakes reflecting the splendour of jasper, and the whispers of the triple moons echo through the air. The Aashvi deck is a sanctuary of earthly beauty, a reminder of the terraformed gemstone haven.

Arunima's grace unfolds on this deck, a mosaic of Ametrine hues. Endless grasslands sway beneath the holographic sky, rivers meander through golden savannahs, and the Baobab tree of Surtseyan stands tall, a bridge between the old world and the new. It is a haven of knowledge and serenity.

On the Baidya Nath deck, rolling hills, dense forests, and crystal swamps weave a tale of terrestrial marvels. The air is filled with the fragrance of bioengineered wonders, and the Baidya Naths, tall and regal, move with grace amidst this living laboratory.

Journey to Budh, a realm of communal harmony and ancient whispers. Grassy plains, hills, and great lakes paint the landscape in hues of Prehnite. The Budhs, attuned to their planetae, share thoughts, memories, and feelings with nature, fostering a bond that transcends the mundane.

Mangal's deck unfolds with the vibrancy of azurite. Vast oceans, plum and copper continents and swirling clouds of bronze form a panorama of cultural richness. The Mangals, maroon-pigmented sentient beings, carry the legacy of Sanskrti culture, and their artistry adorns the landscapes.

Omaja, the realm of spiritual unity, manifests on this deck in hues of Anyolite. Lush jungles, mandarin-coloured oceans, and rust-coloured continents create a haven for reflection. The Omajas, with dark porcelain pigmentation, move in harmony with the cosmic energies that permeate this sacred space.

Saanvi, the realm of wealth and good fortune, is recreated on this deck with Heliotrope hues. Scenic mountain ridges, pristine beach islands, and natural resources unfold before my eyes. The Tejee se Badhate, merchants of Saanvi, have left their mark, turning this deck into a vibrant tapestry of prosperity. As I stand within the metallic veins of Salaee, the starship that carries us beyond the bounds of Primis, I am overcome with awe at the marvel that is our vessel. The construction of Salaee is a testament to the Saala Ganatantr's ingenuity—a cosmic symphony of T'haerian artisanry and celestial technology.

The hull, an amalgamation of advanced alloys and crystalline structures, glistens with the promise of uncharted realms. The celestial engines, humming with the resonance of the cosmic winds, propel us into the tapestry of Novissimus. Each deck, a recreation of the diverse planetae of Srimad-Bhagavatam, reflects the Saala Ganatantr's dedication to preserving our cosmic heritage.

In the command centre, where I navigate the celestial currents, I find myself in awe of the Saala Ganatantr—the stewards who mate for life with the Bhabhi Salaah. Their wisdom, handed down through cosmic cycles, permeates the very core of Salaee. The intricate dance of their knowledge and the celestial technology is a cosmic ballet that propels us forward.

My heart is filled with reverence for the Saala Ganatantr, for they are the keepers of the cosmic balance. They have bestowed upon us the gift of Salaee—a vessel that transcends the boundaries of Primis and embarks upon the cosmic seas of Novissimus.

As Salaee breaches the cosmic veil, I carry with me the hopes of discovery that stir like stardust within my soul. What cosmic wonders await us in the uncharted realms of Novissimus? Will we encounter celestial beings, witness cosmic phenomena, or unravel the mysteries woven into the fabric of the extradimensional tapestry?

Yet, intertwined with my excitement is a subtle uneasiness—a whisper in the cosmic winds that resonates with the warning given by Af'sadi before my departure. Her words, laden with cosmic foresight, linger in my consciousness. The reckoning she sensed, a turning point in the cosmic dance, casts a shadow upon the excitement of exploration.

I hope to discover the cosmic truths that elude our full understanding of Shraavana's departure from Brjamohana. And to bring back knowledge that transcends the boundaries of our celestial home. Yet, I tread with caution, mindful of the cosmic currents that may challenge our voyage. The cosmic dance is unpredictable, and each step into the unknown is a testament to our resilience and the cosmic bond that unites us all.

May the celestial winds guide Salaee through the uncharted realms, and may the cosmic dance unfold with grace and harmony. As I pen these words, I embark on a journey that transcends the familiar, driven by the cosmic call of discovery and the legacy of the Saala Ganatantr.

As I send these holographic videos to you, my heart swells with gratitude for the opportunity to witness the cosmic wonders that Salaee unveils. Until we meet again across the celestial winds, know that my heart remains tethered to the cosmic home of T'haeri.

Holographic Video Message—From Af'sadi to Mzaliwa—Star date: 14 Sita 55 AD.

[The holographic image flickers to life, revealing Af'sadi in the sacred attire of the Bhabhi Salaah. Her eyes hold a mixture of wisdom and concern.]

Alsalam ealayna, Mzaliwa,

As my voice resonates through the cosmic winds, I hope these words find you amidst the vastness of Novissimus. It has been a cosmic age since our paths last crossed, and I, now among the Bhabhi Salaah, weave this message with threads of cosmic concern.

The mismanagement of Aushadhi, once a sacred bridge to the divine, has woven threads of discord within the celestial fabric. The visions that unfold in the minds of the Bhabhi Salaah no longer mirror the pure essence of Brjamohana. Instead, they ripple with echoes of uncertainty, casting shadows upon the sacred rituals we hold dear.

In the cosmic archives, I uncovered the Rakshak Shreshth's ancient warning—the caution against utilising untested technology. The resonance of these words echoes through the corridors of our cosmic home, a reminder of the delicate balance we tread upon.

As I now stand within the ranks of the Bhabhi Salaah, I witness the unfolding repercussions of mismanagement. The cosmic dance, once harmonious, now flirts with discord. The connection to Brjamohana wavers, and the celestial currents bear witness to the shifting tides within our cosmic society.

A revelation unfolded as soon as you and your crew ventured beyond the cosmic veil. Another tunnel opened, revealing an unidentified starship. The markings upon it do not originate within Primis, stirring ripples of cosmic unease. The celestial winds whisper of an unknown presence, an enigma that has breached the boundaries of our cosmic home.

The Bhabhi Salaah, once the keepers of cosmic wisdom, now grapple with the unforeseen. The mismanagement of Aushadhi and the presence of an unidentified starship cast shadows upon the cosmic tapestry. I share these tidings not to instil fear but as a cosmic plea for awareness.

Mzaliwa, tread with caution through the uncharted realms of Novissimus. The cosmic dance is a delicate ballet, and the echoes of mismanagement may ripple beyond Primis. May the celestial winds guide Salaee through the cosmic seas, and may your journey unveil the cosmic truths that await.

Until our cosmic paths intertwine once more, remain steadfast in the pursuit of cosmic knowledge, and may the essence of Brjamohana guide your celestial voyage.

In cosmic kinship, Af'sadi.

Holographic Journal Entry - Prof Prabuddh—Star date: 15 Sita 55 AD.

[The holographic image flickers to life, revealing Prof Prabuddh in his cabin aboard Salaee. The backdrop shows the cosmic expanse outside the window, a panorama of swirling colours and celestial wonders.]

Greetings, esteemed colleagues at Petraea University,

As I embark on this cosmic odyssey aboard Salaee, I find solace in sharing my aspirations and the wonders that unfold beyond the cosmic veil of Primis. Our mission, steeped in the pursuit of knowledge, echoes the cosmic calls of exploration that have resonated through the corridors of Petraea University for generations.

Once beyond the confines of Primis, my first endeavour shall be to conduct a comprehensive study of the cosmic phenomena that elude our understanding. The uncharted realms of Novissimus hold untold mysteries, and with the instruments at our disposal, I aim to unravel the cosmic secrets that dance within the celestial currents.

Looking out of the window of my cabin, the cosmic panorama stretches into infinity. The stars, like luminescent pearls, paint the canvas of the cosmic sea. Nebulae swirl with vibrant hues, celestial clouds caress the cosmic winds, and distant galaxies beckon with promises of cosmic revelations.

As Salaee cruises during warp drive, the fabric of space itself warps and twists in a mesmerising dance. The celestial luminaries become ribbons of ethereal light, weaving through the fabric of reality. Stars elongate into streaks of luminescence, marking our trajectory through the cosmic expanse. It is a sight that transcends the mundane, a celestial ballet that enchants the soul.

My scientific instruments, finely tuned to capture the nuances of Novissimus, stand ready for the cosmic symphony that awaits. I hope to study the gravitational anomalies, cosmic radiation patterns, and exotic celestial phenomena that grace the uncharted territories. Every pulsar, quasar, and cosmic eddy shall be a note in the grand cosmic composition that Petraea University shall dissect and analyse.

The holographic recordings and data collected during this cosmic journey will be transmitted back to Petraea University, adding chapters to the cosmic archives of knowledge. Our quest for understanding, fuelled by the legacy of our ancestors and the cosmic aspirations of Petraea, shall be etched into the annals of T'haerian exploration.

As Salaee carries us through the cosmic seas, I am filled with anticipation for the cosmic revelations that await. The essence of Brjamohana guides our cosmic voyage, and with each passing moment, we become witnesses to the wonders that transcend the boundaries of Primis.

May the celestial winds carry this holographic journal entry back to Petraea University, a testament to the cosmic aspirations that bind us all.

In cosmic inquiry, Prof Prabuddh.

Postlude of Chapter 10

What is the cosmic dance? The cosmic dance holds a unique significance for Mzaliwa and Prof Ofeefee. It is a concept that resonates differently based on their perspectives, aspirations, and experiences.

Mzaliwa

Perspective: For Mzaliwa, the cosmic dance is an intricate weaving of spiritual possibilities and secular discoveries. It symbolises the vastness of the universe and the potential for exploration and understanding. The cosmic dance is Mzaliwa's journey into the unknown; a chance to unravel the secrets of Novissimus and bring her closer to Brjamohana.

Aspirations: Mzaliwa sees the cosmic dance as an opportunity to expand the horizons of knowledge, embracing the wonders that lie beyond Primis. It represents a chance to contribute to the cosmic archives and uncover the mysteries of uncharted dimensions. A chance to get her name in the historical texts of T'haeri and Budh so that future generations can remember her name.

Experience: Mzaliwa's connection to the cosmic dance is deeply personal. It reflects her curiosity, ambition, and desire to transcend the limitations of her terrestrial existence. The dance is a cosmic invitation to explore, learn, and contribute to the ever-evolving narrative of the universe. It was also her way of atoning for not completing her Bhabhi Salaah initiation and being linked to Taqi, her proposed lifelong steward.

Prof Ofeefee

Perspective: For Prof Ofeefee, the cosmic dance is a metaphor for the pursuit of knowledge and the harmonious exchange of cosmic truths. It symbolises the beauty of understanding and the interconnectedness of cosmic phenomena.

Aspirations: Prof Ofeefee sees the cosmic dance as an opportunity to contribute to the cosmic knowledge base. His aspirations lie in unravelling the mysteries of the universe, fostering a deeper understanding of the cosmic ballet that shapes reality.

Experience: Prof Ofeefee's connection to the cosmic dance is rooted in a lifelong dedication to academia and a commitment to the principles of empathy and curiosity. It is a journey guided by a sense of responsibility to safeguard the sanctity of knowledge in the cosmic pattern.

Chapter 11

Journal Entry 1,01—Owo

'Lówó, transcribe my thoughts.'

[The AI's voice responds, "Of course, Owo. Recording now."]

As I pen down these words, the starship Utata hurtles through the uncharted expanse of an unknown dimension. It is a journey into the cosmic unknown, a pilgrimage away from the rigid grasp of Dharatee, and I find myself both trepidatious and exhilarated.

Being the sole female crew member on Utata presents its own set of challenges. The envy radiates from my male counterparts, their eyes laden with jealousy, for it was my work that birthed this voyage into the cosmic abyss. Their murmurs of discontent dance around me like cosmic echoes, but I stand undeterred. The cosmic winds whisper tales of new beginnings, far away from the confines of the terrestrial norms that bind me on Dharatee.

Utata, though meagre in comparison to grander vessels, is a marvel of cosmic engineering. Its hull, an amalgamation of celestial alloys, shields us from the cosmic tempest outside. My small cabin offers a view into the cosmic sea, stars swirling like luminescent dreams. It is a humble abode, a sanctuary in the cosmic wilderness.

The mess hall, a communal space with lacklustre food provisions, becomes a meeting ground for the crew. The cosmic fare may be humble, but the conversations are rich with anticipation and cosmic aspirations. It is here that I navigate the dynamics, a lone woman in the cosmic sea, seeking camaraderie among stardust and whispers of distant galaxies.

Exploring the vessel, I stumbled upon a revelation that sent shivers through the cosmic fabric. Two legions of Dharatee's army and naval forces were concealed within the cosmic belly of Utata. Questions swirl within me—why this clandestine presence, and what shadows does it cast on our cosmic journey?

Amidst the cosmic enigma, I found solace in a warm yet arm's length mentorship with Prof Ofeefee. His cosmic wisdom, a guiding light in the cosmic dark, resonates with the echoes of ages past. Together, we navigate the cosmic currents, unravelling the mysteries of this unknown dimension. His guidance, like celestial constellations, shapes my trajectory in the cosmic expanse.

As I embark on this pilgrimage, a sojourn away from Dharatee, I carry within me the hopes of starting anew. The cosmic dance unfolds, and I, Owo, am but a stardust particle in its grand choreography. May the cosmic winds guide our voyage and unveil the wonders that await beyond the cosmic horizon.

[Lówó responds, "Transcription complete, Owo."]

The corridors of Utata echoed with Owo's hurried footsteps as she frantically navigated the vessel, her mind buzzing with questions about the soldiers she stumbled upon. The lift doors opened, and she stepped in, quickly pressing the button for the Academic Deck. As the lift ascended, her heart raced, anticipation mingling with trepidation.

The Academic Deck greeted her with the hum of cosmic knowledge. Owo weaved through the halls, searching for Prof Ofeefee's office. The metallic doors slid open, revealing a room filled with holographic data streams and cosmic artefacts. Prof Ofeefee, engrossed in his work, looked up as Owo entered.

"Prof Ofeefee!" she exclaimed breathlessly. "I need to talk to you. I saw soldiers, Dharatee's soldiers, on board. What is going on?"

The professor's gaze met hers, his expression unreadable. "Soldiers? Owo, you must be mistaken. This vessel is for scientific exploration, not military endeavours."

"I'm not mistaken, Prof I saw them—two legions, hidden away. Why are they here?" Owo's voice wavered between urgency and frustration.

Prof Ofeefee sighed, a curt response escaping his lips. "Owo, you're seeing things that aren't there. This is a test vessel for scientific research, nothing more. Your imagination might be running wild in the vastness of space."

The rebuff was short and off-putting. Owo felt a pang of mixed emotions—confusion, frustration, and a hint of betrayal. She knew what she saw, and the dismissive tone from her mentor left her grappling with the dissonance between reality and denial.

The conversation ended abruptly; Prof Ofeefee returned to his holographic data streams. Owo, left with her questions unanswered, could not shake the unease settling in the pit of her stomach.

Once Owo left his office, Prof Ofeefee delved into his research, the holographic displays illuminating his determined expression. His fingers danced across the cosmic interfaces, accessing data streams that extended beyond the known files of the academic department.

His inquiries led him to confidential reports and encrypted files. The revelation unfolded—a directive from higher authorities to embed Dharatee's military forces within the scientific vessel, an experiment testing the boundaries of cosmic exploration and military preparedness.

Prof Ofeefee's eyes flickered with a mix of concern and resolve as he unravelled the layers of secrecy. His commitment to the pursuit of knowledge clashed with the covert manoeuvres of the military establishment. As the cosmic dance continued, the lines between exploration and manipulation blurred, leaving Prof Ofeefee torn between allegiance to knowledge and the complexities of cosmic politics.

Prof Ofeefee, determined to unravel the truth, reached out to the heart of Dharatee's military apparatus—the General of the Armies, Ori Alagbara. In a secure communication chamber, Prof Ofeefee faced the holographic projection of Ori Alagbara, a formidable figure with the weight of military authority.

"General Alagbara," Prof Ofeefee began, his voice steady but tinged with underlying tension, "I need an explanation for the military presence on the Utata. This is a scientific vessel, not a warship."

Ori Alagbara's expression remained stoic, the holographic image radiating authority. "Prof Ofeefee, the Utata serves a dual purpose—a vessel for scientific exploration and a safeguard against cosmic threats. We're not just exploring unknown dimensions; we're establishing Terrestris' dominion over the known and unknown."

Prof Ofeefee's eyes narrowed, his disbelief evident. "Dominion? What happened to the pursuit of knowledge? The cosmic dance should be guided by curiosity, not a quest for imperialism."

Ori Alagbara's response was stern, his vision unwavering. "Knowledge is power, Prof Ofeefee. In the cosmic ballet, those who hold the reins shape the destiny of Terrestris. Dimensional imperialism is our path to ensuring the supremacy of Terrestris over all realms—known and unknown."

The conversation heated, the clash of ideals reverberating through the secure chamber. Prof Ofeefee, a guardian of knowledge, confronted Ori Alagbara's vision of cosmic dominance with resistance. The General's rhetoric painted a picture of Terrestris extending its influence beyond the familiar bounds of Dharatee, transcending the cosmic tapestry itself.

"Imperialism is not the legacy we should leave for future generations," Prof Ofeefee argued, his voice carrying the weight of moral conviction. "The cosmic dance is a delicate harmony, not a conquest. Our pursuit should be understanding, not dominance."

Ori Alagbara, unyielding in his directive, asserted, "Times have changed, Prof Ofeefee. This cosmic dance awaits a new choreography—one where Terrestris takes centre stage, shaping the destiny of realms beyond our imagination."

As the holographic transmission concluded, Prof Ofeefee grappled with the unsettling reality that the cosmic dance he revered faced a perilous shift—one that blurred the lines between exploration and conquest, knowledge, and dominion. The cosmic winds whispered of an uncertain future, where the ambitions of Terrestris sought to extend their reach across the cosmic horizon.

∞

The realisation hung heavy on Prof Ofeefee's shoulders, a burden that transcended the weight of all his cosmic knowledge. As he navigated the confines of his office aboard Utata, the holographic displays illuminated a mind wrestling with the clash of ideals—the pursuit of scientific exploration tainted by the stain of imperialistic ambitions.

His once scientific test voyage, a testament to his lifelong dedication to the pursuit of knowledge, now stood at the crossroads of a cosmic dilemma. Prof Ofeefee, a man who defied all odds to cultivate empathy amidst the stoic realms of academia, found himself at the precipice of a moral abyss.

The holographic screens flickered with cosmic data, a cosmic dance that mirrored the internal turmoil within Prof Ofeefee. The stardust particles, once symbols of wonder and curiosity, now whispered tales of oppression and dominion. The cosmic winds, once a harmonious melody, now carried echoes of imperialistic intentions.

In the quiet solitude of his office, Prof Ofeefee grappled with the dissonance—a heart that yearned for the pursuit of knowledge, standing in defiance against the imperialistic aspirations that sought to extend Terrestris' dominion. The burden of comprehension weighed heavily on a man who believed in the beauty of the cosmic dance, in the delicate choreography that celebrated understanding and harmony.

His empathetic nature, an anomaly in the corridors of power, clashed with the ruthless currents of imperialism. Prof Ofeefee's eyes, usually filled with the spark of cosmic curiosity, now bore the weight of a moral dilemma that transcended the cosmic boundaries. The cosmic ballet, once a source of inspiration, now became a stage for a darker narrative—one where the pursuit of knowledge was entangled with the tendrils of oppression.

As he stared into the holographic abyss, Prof Ofeefee grappled with the profound truth that the cosmic dance he revered had been hijacked by forces that sought to rewrite its choreography. The stoic facade, a shield against the cosmic tempest, now revealed the cracks of a man burdened by the complexities of his own creation—a vessel for knowledge turned unwittingly into an instrument of cosmic conquest.

Postlude of Chapter 11

What is Owo's cosmic dance?

Owo, with a perspective uniquely her own, perceives the cosmic dance as an enchanting and liberating force—a dance that transcends the confines of Dharatee and beckons her to explore uncharted realms where societal norms hold no dominion. It is a cosmic ballet that resonates with the rhythm of emancipation, offering a chance for Owo to unfurl her wings beyond the constraints of her home world.

For Owo, the cosmic dance is more than a mere spectacle; it is a profound journey towards personal and cosmic emancipation. In her eyes, the swirling galaxies and celestial choreography symbolise the opportunity to break free from the rigidity of societal expectations, allowing her to embark on a pilgrimage of self-discovery and independence.

Her aspirations are woven into the cosmic fabric, entwined with the desire for autonomy and a thirst for a new beginning. The dance becomes a vessel that carries her away from the familiar shores of Dharatee, offering a canvas where she can redefine her identity and purpose beyond the predetermined roles imposed upon her. The cosmic dance is a transformative experience, a cathartic release from the gravitational pull of societal structures that have confined her for too long.

Owo's connection to the cosmic dance is fuelled by a yearning for something more, an experience that transcends the boundaries of her home world. It embodies the possibility of starting afresh in dimensions unknown, where the stardust of newfound freedom and self-discovery permeates the cosmic expanse. The dance becomes a celestial symphony, echoing Owo's journey towards a realm where the stars themselves seem to dance in celebration of her liberation.

In the cosmic ballet, Owo finds not only a canvas for self-expression but also a cosmic stage where her aspirations and dreams take centre stage. It is a dance of metamorphosis, where the stardust of independence settles upon her, creating a trail of luminous footprints across the cosmic canvas—a testament to her cosmic emancipation.

Chapter 12

As the envoy from Utata descended through the azure skies of T'haeri, the tranquil beauty of the planetae unfolded beneath them. Lush jungles, jewel-coloured lakes, and expansive plains stretched as far as the eye could see. The landing craft, sleek and advanced, touched down on the fertile soil with a gentle hum.

The envoy, adorned in sophisticated exploration suits that mirrored the T'haerian filtration technology, emerged onto the surface. Their presence marked the beginning of a scientific mission—one that aimed to explore the wonders of T'haeri and fill their textbooks with knowledge of this parallel dimension.

The T'haerians, with their characteristic hospitality, awaited the visitors with open hearts. A delegation, dressed in vibrant hues that complemented the natural beauty of their planetae, approached the envoy. The leader of the T'haerian welcome party, an elder with eyes that sparkled with cosmic wisdom, greeted the visitors with a gesture of goodwill.

"Welcome, explorers of Utata. We extend our warmest greetings to you in the spirit of cosmic harmony," the T'haerian elder expressed, their voice carrying a melodic cadence. The envoy, led by Prof Ofeefee, reciprocated the greeting with a respectful nod. "Thank you for your warm welcome. We come seeking to unravel the mysteries of T'haeri and foster a greater understanding between our dimensions."

The scientific mission unfolded against the backdrop of T'haeri's indigo sky, where erythrean red flecks danced like cosmic fireflies. The T'haerian delegation guided the envoy through landscapes adorned with exotic flora and fauna, each step revealing the unique wonders of their planetae.

The exploration party engaged in shared observations, scientific discussions, and cultural exchanges. The T'haerians, with their ancient wisdom and deep connection to the cosmic tapestry, provided insights that enriched the textbooks of the envoy. Conversations echoed with the excitement of discovery and the mutual respect that bridged the gap between Primis and Novissimus.

As the sun dipped below the horizon, casting bands of coral red and orange-red across the powder blue sky, the envoy and the T'haerians continued their journey into the heart of exploration. The opening scene of this scientific mission captured the essence of cosmic collaboration—a harmonious dance between dimensions where knowledge flowed like stardust, and the boundaries between Primis and Novissimus blurred in the pursuit of understanding.

∞

In the cold emptiness of space, battleships from Dharatee hovered silently, their cloaking technology rendering them invisible to the advanced sensors of T'haeri and the neighbouring Baidya Nath. Utata, docked at the Mahatat fada space station, remained oblivious to the looming threat, engaged in its scientific mission.

Within the command centre of the leading battleship, General Ori Alagbara, a figure of formidable authority, conferred with his trusted General, Thulathiat.

The holographic displays flickered with strategic overlays, highlighting the topography of T'haeri and the surrounding planetae within the quadrant.

Ori Alagbara, a visionary with imperialistic ambitions, spoke with determination. "Thulathiat, the time has come to unveil our presence. T'haeri and its sister planetae will bow before the might of Terrestris. This staged invasion will mark the beginning of our dominion over this cosmic realm."

Thulathiat, a seasoned strategist, nodded in agreement. "General, our cloaked approach has left us undetected. The element of surprise is our greatest weapon. Once T'haeri falls, the other planetae will follow suit. Our conquest will be swift, and the cosmic dance will be reshaped under the banner of Terrestris."

Preparations unfolded with meticulous precision. Troop deployments, advanced weaponry checks, and the coordination of aerial and ground forces were strategically planned. The battleships, still concealed in the cosmic shadows, readied themselves for the staged invasion that would set in motion the imperialistic agenda of Terrestris.

Ori Alagbara, his eyes reflecting the intensity of his vision, continued, "Our dominion over Primis will be absolute. The T'haerians and their scattered *walgelijk* descendants will witness the might of Terrestris. The cosmic dance shall bow to our orchestrated symphony of conquest."

As holographic maps displayed the various sectors and strategic points on T'haeri, Thulathiat added, "Once T'haeri succumbs, the neighbouring planets will fall in line. The unity of Primis will crumble before the overwhelming force of Terrestris. Our reign shall extend beyond the boundaries of imagination."

The command centre buzzed with activity as the battleships prepared to decloak and unleash their imperial might upon T'haeri. The staged invasion, orchestrated by General Ori Alagbara and his trusted General Thulathiat, aimed to reshape the cosmic tapestry in accordance with the ambitions of Terrestris—a vision that saw Primis bending under the dominion of Dharatee.

∞

Thulathiat: The Unyielding Warrior

In the tumultuous world of Dharatee, where brutality and oppression cast long shadows, Thulathiat emerged from the crucible of a matriarchal lineage. Raised by strong, stoic women who instilled in her the unyielding principle to never bow before a man, Thulathiat inherited a legacy that equated her worth to that of ten men. Her upbringing within the fierce embrace of matriarchal wisdom became the crucible that forged the indomitable spirit within her.

Standing at a height that commanded attention, she reached a stature of 1.83 meters, her well-defined frame spoke of years of rigorous training and battles fought on the front lines. Thulathiat's skin, bronzed by the harsh sun of her homeland, carried the scars of countless skirmishes, each mark a testament to her unwavering commitment to the cause.

Her eyes, deep and piercing, reflected a resolve that surpassed the turmoil of the world around her. The irises held a shade akin to the stormy skies that often loomed over Dharatee, capturing both the ferocity and determination within her gaze. Cascading down her shoulders, Thulathiat's hair, jet-black and lustrous, framed her face like a warrior's crown. Her facial features were chiselled, a blend of strength and femininity, with a jawline that bore the regality of a leader.

Dharatee, a world marred by chaos and tyrannical rulers, offered little respite for its inhabitants. It was within this harsh landscape that Thulathiat nurtured her ambition to join the army led by her maternal uncle, Ori Alagbara. The very air she breathed was laced with tales of valour and resistance, inspiring a burning desire within her to wield a sword against the oppressors.

As the only female in an all-male contingent, Thulathiat faced challenges that mirrored the chaotic landscape of her homeland. Her journey through the rigorous training and the battlefield was marked by sceptical glances and whispered doubts, fuelled by ingrained prejudices. The men around her questioned her presence, casting suspicious shadows over her abilities solely based on her gender.

Accusations of nepotism, like a lingering storm cloud, threatened to overshadow Thulathiat achievements. The whispers in the barracks painted her success as a product of familial favouritism, overlooking the grit and determination that fuelled her every step. Thulathiat had to fight not only against the physical adversaries on the battlefield but also against the intangible barriers erected by ingrained gender biases.

Undeterred by the storm of scepticism, Thulathiat bore the weight of proving her mettle with unyielding determination. Every swing of her sword and every strategic manoeuvre on the battlefield became a testament to her unbreakable spirit. She earned the respect of her fellow soldiers not through words but through the undeniable prowess she displayed in the face of adversity.

Thulathiat's journey was not merely a quest for personal glory; it was a defiant stand against the societal norms that sought to confine her within predetermined roles. Her presence in the army became a beacon of hope for those who dared to dream beyond the boundaries set by tradition. Through her resilience and unwavering resolve, Thulathiat became a symbol of defiance in a world that sought to silence the voices of the oppressed.

In the command centre, the hum of clandestine battleships resonated like a heartbeat, echoing the pulse of impending action. The holographic displays flickered to life, revealing the vastness of the dimensional expanse before me. As General of the Armies, Ori Alagbara, I stood with unwavering resolve, ready to set in motion the clandestine manoeuvres that would pave the way for our imperial ambitions.

Addressing the assembly of commanders and strategists, my voice carried the weight of authority. "Commanders, today marks a pivotal moment in our pursuit of dominance within this dimension. We shall not be confined by the limitations of one planet; instead, we shall extend our influence across all realms."

The holographic projections illuminated the planets within our reach, each a potential conquest awaiting scrutiny. "Clandestine battleships, I order you to deploy scouting teams to every planet within our grasp. Your mission is to conduct complete surveillance, cloaking your presence to mimic the inhabitants of these worlds. We seek not only to conquer but to understand the vulnerabilities that will make our imperial ambitions a seamless reality."

The command centre buzzed with activity as teams prepared for their covert missions. The holographic displays displayed the synchronisation of the scouting operations, each battleship assigned to a specific planet. The technology at our disposal allowed us to blend seamlessly into the diverse societies we aimed to scrutinise.

Turning my attention to General Thulathiat, the commander of the elite Alqubaeat Alkhadra, I delivered her orders with precision. "Thulathiat, you will lead your squadron into the heart of the most formidable societies. Your mission is twofold—to gather intelligence on their weaknesses and, if necessary, to eliminate threats that may impede our progress. The Alqubaeat Alkhadra shall be the unseen force that tips the scales in our favour."

Her gaze met mine, a reflection of determination matching my own. The holographic displays shifted to highlight the planets assigned to her squadron. "May the stealth of the shadows guide your path, Thulathiat. Report back with the insights we need to ensure our dominance over this dimension."

With a decisive nod, Thulathiat saluted, and the Alqubaeat Alkhadra embarked on their mission. As the battleships initiated their cloaking mechanisms, the shadows of impending conquest cast a strategic veil across the dimensional expanse. The pursuit of imperial ambitions had begun, and I, Ori Alagbara, stood at the helm, orchestrating the clandestine symphony that would shape the fate of worlds.

The reports from the scouting missions began to pour in, each transmission carrying crucial information that would shape our battle plans for conquest and subjugation. The holographic displays flickered as data streams revealed the vulnerabilities and societal nuances of the targeted planets.

I studied the reports with keen interest; my eyes narrowing as the intricate details unfolded before me. The intelligence gathered by our clandestine teams highlighted the weaknesses within the societies, paving the way for strategies that would maximise destruction and facilitate the enslavement of the inhabitants.

On Planet Veridia—the name given to T'haeri—a society marked by technological dependence; our scouts discovered a reliance on a centralised network that controlled critical infrastructure. Exploiting this vulnerability would plunge Veridia into chaos, rendering its advanced machinery useless and paving the way for our swift takeover.

The reports from Planet Athralis—a moniker given to Budh—detailed a society deeply entrenched in antiquated and simplistic rituals. By manipulating the younger populace to embrace modern ways, we can create tensions and fostering discord, we could ensure internal strife that would weaken resistance and create an environment ripe for conquest.

As the data continued to stream in, a pattern emerged—the exploitation of societal fractures, economic dependencies, and political unrest. Each piece of information served as a puzzle piece, fitting together to create a comprehensive picture of the most effective strategies for domination.

One particularly promising report came from Planet Xyron—Saanvi's Terrestris given agnomen—where the ruling class held a monopoly on a coveted resource. By targeting and seizing control of this vital commodity, we could cripple their power structures and subject the population to our imperial rule.

The command centre buzzed with activity as our strategists synthesised the incoming information into a coherent battle plan. The holographic displays now highlighted a synchronised assault, each battleship assigned to exploit the identified weaknesses on its designated planet.

Addressing the assembly, I outlined our approach. "We shall strike where their foundations are weakest. Exploit the fault lines of their societies, sow discord, and make them submit to our rule willingly or through force. Our objective is clear—to cause maximum destruction and enslave as many as possible."

The holographic projections depicted the coordinated assaults on multiple fronts, battleships converging on vulnerable points identified by our scouts. The Alqubaeat Alkhadra, under the command of General Thulathiat, would spearhead the covert operations, ensuring that resistance faced swift and decisive elimination.

As the battle plans solidified, the command centre exuded an air of anticipation. The reports from the scouting missions had provided us with the key to unravelling the fabric of each society, and now the orchestration of chaos and subjugation was set in motion. The pursuit of imperial dominion reached a critical juncture, guided by the calculated exploitation of the weaknesses inherent in the societies we sought to conquer.

Postlude of Chapter 12

As Ori Alagbara received the detailed reports that would shape the course of conquest, the soldiers under his command were immersed in a worldview that obscured the positive aspects of the societies within Primis. For these warriors, peace, freedom, and community were foreign concepts, replaced by a lens that painted everything positive as negative or debased.

These soldiers, raised in a culture of brutality and oppression, had never known the warmth of camaraderie or the embrace of a community that thrived in harmony. Their existence was marked by a ceaseless pursuit of dominance and control, where any display of vulnerability was perceived as weakness.

The reports, meticulously crafted to highlight the vulnerabilities of the targeted planets, reinforced a distorted perspective. To the soldiers, the rich tapestry of diverse societies was reduced to a canvas of perceived flaws and weaknesses. The very foundations that upheld civilisations—cooperation, shared values, and cultural richness—were dismissed or misunderstood through the lens of imperial ambition.

As they prepared for the impending conquest, the soldiers internalised the narrative that painted the inhabitants of Primis as subjects in need of domination. The reports, while strategically valuable for Ori Alagbara, served to perpetuate a dehumanising ideology among the troops. In their eyes, resistance to the impending imperial rule was seen as defiance against an inherent order that deemed subjugation as the natural state of existence.

The soldiers, hardened by a lifetime of indoctrination, were blind to the possibility of societies that thrived on collaboration, creativity, and mutual respect. The very essence of the worlds they were set to conquer—their unique cultures, traditions, and contributions—remained obscured by a veil of prejudice woven through generations of oppressive conditioning.

In this distorted reality, the soldiers marched forward with a sense of duty, their minds clouded by a narrative that labelled the richness of Primis as weaknesses to be exploited. The postlude of their perspective mirrored a tragic narrative of individuals who had been denied the opportunity to appreciate the beauty inherent in diverse societies, forever locked in a cycle of conquest that perpetuated their own ignorance.

Terahaveen

Amid our once-thriving world, chaos erupted as the military might of Ori Alagbara and Thulathiat descended upon us like a vengeful storm. The sky, once a canvas of tranquillity, now painted a fiery red with the devastation wrought upon Primis. Horror engulfed our hearts, and the very ground we walked upon quivered in agony as the destructive force unfolded.

I, Prof Ofeefee, who had naively believed that our exploration into the quantum realms would bring enlightenment, now bore witness to the catastrophic consequences of our actions. Owo, my companion in the pursuit of knowledge, shared the weight of despair as our scientific landing party crumbled before the merciless onslaught.

The once-vibrant landscapes, adorned with the diverse cultures and communities of Primis, were reduced to smouldering ruins. Our cities, once bustling with life and innovation, now lay in ruin, a testament to the destructive ambition of those who saw us as nothing more than subjects to be conquered.

The Ma'an Su, who had once been a symbol of unity and connection with the divine, now faced the harsh reality that our attempts to open a quantum had led to the annihilation of everything we held dear. The very fabric of Brjamohana's creation, which we had hoped to explore with curiosity and wonder, now crumbled beneath the weight of betrayal and despair.

As we confronted the devastating consequences, the realisation pierced through our hearts—the pursuit of knowledge had become a catalyst for our own destruction. The intricate web of life on Primis, once harmonious and interconnected, now lay severed by the blades of war and conquest.

During the destruction, cries of anguish echoed through the air, pleading for mercy that would never come. Families torn apart, civilisations erased, and the beauty of our diverse societies extinguished in the fires of war. The quantum rift that we had opened revealed not the wonders of creation but the horrors of our own making.

We, the inhabitants of Primis, now faced the aftermath of our actions with a heavy heart, grappling with the bitter taste of betrayal and the haunting realisation that our pursuit of understanding had led us to the brink of annihilation.

Af'sadi stood amidst the ruins, her heart heavy with the weight of the unfolding tragedy. The once-proud city now lay in ruins, a testament to the devastation wrought by Ori Alagbara and Thulathiat. As she surveyed the destruction, her mind echoed with reflections on the events that had led to this cataclysmic moment.

Her connection to Brjamohana, the divine source of wisdom and guidance, had been a guiding force throughout her life. In moments of solitude and meditation, she had felt the currents of the cosmic energy, foreseeing the shadows that now cast darkness upon Primis. The warnings had been subtle, veiled in the language of dreams and celestial whispers.

Af'sadi had sensed the disturbance in the cosmic order, an imbalance that foretold of impending chaos. The visions granted by Brjamohana had woven a tapestry of the future, revealing the convergence of malevolent forces and the dire consequences that awaited their world. It was a burden she carried in her heart, a knowledge that weighed heavily on her shoulders.

As she witnessed the devastation around her, Af'sadi could not help but feel a profound sadness for the people of Primis. The vibrant cultures and the diverse communities were all now reduced to ashes in the wake of relentless ambition. The echoes of her connection to Brjamohana resonated with a sense of inevitability—a tragic fate that had been forewarned but seemed unstoppable.

In the quiet moments before the storm, Af'sadi had sought solace in communion with the divine. She had pleaded for guidance, for a way to avert the impending catastrophe. Yet, the cosmic currents had whispered truths that spoke of choices made and destinies entwined.

Now, as the ruins bore witness to the aftermath, Af'sadi reflected on the delicate balance between free will and cosmic design. The threads of fate had been woven, and the tapestry of Primis had been altered irreversibly. The connection to Brjamohana, once a source of enlightenment, now carried the weight of sorrow and a sense of shared anguish.

In the ruins of *Terahaveen*, Af'sadi bowed her head in reverence and sought strength from the divine presence within. The path ahead was uncertain, and the journey through the cosmic currents would demand resilience and courage. The reflection on the events that had unfolded served as a reminder—a testament to the intricate dance between mortal choices and the cosmic forces that guided their destiny.

Ori Alagbara stood amidst the remnants of once-thriving centres of knowledge, his eyes gleaming with a twisted sense of satisfaction. The destruction he had unleashed upon the universities and libraries resonated with the echoes of crumbling walls and burning literature. The air was thick with the acrid scent of smouldering wisdom, a testament to the abject oppression he had orchestrated.

The halls of learning, where once the pursuit of knowledge had flourished, now lay in ruins. The vibrant campuses that echoed with scholarly debates and the rustling of pages had been silenced by the merciless advance of his military might. As the flames consumed the written treasures of Primis, Ori revelled in the eradication of what he saw as intellectual resistance.

In Ori's voice, a dark delight echoed, "Behold the consequence of defiance! The institutions that dared to challenge the supremacy of my forces now crumble before the might of Alagbara. Their precious literature, their so-called wisdom—all reduced to ashes. I am the purveyor of a new order, one where knowledge bows to the might of the sword."

His laughter mingled with the crackling of burning books, a macabre symphony that celebrated the triumph of oppression. The once-illuminated halls were now shrouded in the shadows of enforced ignorance. Ori Alagbara revelled in the power he wielded, revelling in the belief that the subjugation of intellect was a victory.

"The people of Primis shall know the consequences of resistance. Their scholars, their thinkers—all now subject to the dominion of Alagbara. The flames of their libraries mirror the flames of their futile defiance. Abject oppression is the currency of my rule, and the enslaved will learn to bow before the might of their conqueror," he proclaimed with a chilling resolve.

As the embers of knowledge dwindled, Ori Alagbara surveyed the desolation he had wrought. In his twisted perception, the destruction of universities and libraries was not a tragedy but a triumph. The echoes of despair and the weight of chains on the minds of the oppressed became the symphony of his ruthless reign, and Ori revelled in the darkness he had unleashed upon Primis.

Amid Primis' intellectual darkness, despair gripped the hearts of its inhabitants like an unyielding vice. The once-vibrant minds that had thrived on knowledge were now shackled by the harsh labour imposed upon them. Families mourned the disappearance of their loved ones, taken away to unknown fates, leaving a void that echoed with sorrow.

The eight planetarum of Primis bore witness to the cruel aftermath of Ori Alagbara's conquest. The people toiled under the weight of oppressive regimes, their intellect subdued, and dreams crushed. The once-flourishing societies succumbed to a sombre pallor as the shadows of tyranny loomed over every corner.

On T'haeri, the natural world rebelled against the oppressive forces that sought to exploit it. The once-fertile lands refused to yield their produce, and the flora and fauna withheld their vibrant life force. It was as if the very essence of nature had turned against its oppressors, mirroring the desolation that had befallen the minds of the people.

Amid this intellectual and ecological darkness, an older Bhabhi, bearing witness to the suffering, sent a woeful message to those aboard the Salaee. Her voice carried the weight of generations, a lamentation for the lost harmony and prosperity that once graced their world.

"Dear ones aboard the Salaee, heed my sombre words. Primis, our cherished home, has been enveloped in an unrelenting gloom. The minds of our kin are shackled, burdened by the toils of oppression. Families weep for the missing, their absence leaving voids that echo with sorrow."

"T'haeri itself rebels against the tyranny, withholding its bounties in protest. The once-vibrant landscapes are now painted in shades of desolation. As an elder Bhabhi, I implore you—do not return to this abyss of despair. The darkness is all-encompassing, and the very essence of Primis mourns its lost brilliance."

"The Salaee, your vessel of hope, carries the legacy of our people. Preserve the flame of knowledge and enlightenment, for it may be the only beacon that can dispel this intellectual gloom. Let not the shadows of Primis extinguish the light within your hearts. May you find refuge in the cosmic currents, away from the oppressive grasp that clings to our ancestral lands."

"Farewell, dear ones, and may the arms of Brahman guide you to a realm untouched by the shadows that now consume Primis."

In the aftermath of *Terahaveen*, Thulathiat could not help but feel a triumphant surge within her. The success of her squadron, the Alqubaeat Alkhadra, filled her with a sense of pride and accomplishment. The precision of their attacks and the execution of their strategic battle plans had been nothing short of exemplary.

Thulathiat revelled in the efficiency with which her forces had dismantled the once-prosperous civilisations of Primis. The careful planning, the seamless coordination among her troops, and the strategic brilliance displayed in each engagement were a testament to the military prowess she had cultivated. The conquered planets were now firmly under the control of Novissimus, their inhabitants subdued and subjugated.

As she surveyed the conquered territories, Thulathiat saw the remnants of resistance quelled, and the once-vibrant cultures of Primis reduced to shadows of their former selves. Her confidence in her abilities as a military leader swelled, and she believed that she had fulfilled her role in bringing order to what she saw as chaotic and unruly worlds.

Thulathiat revelled in the echoes of triumph that resounded through the conquered realms. Her reputation as a formidable military leader grew, and her authority within the ranks of Novissimus soared. The Alqubaeat Alkhadra', her loyal squadron, basked in the glory of their accomplishments, and Thulathiat became a symbol of Novissimus' dominance.

The conquered planets, now firmly under Novissimus' control, were subjected to Thulathiat's vision of order. She implemented strict governance, ensuring that the inhabitants adhered to Novissimus' doctrines. Any signs of resistance were swiftly crushed, and Thulathiat's presence became synonymous with authority and discipline.

Her success on the battlefield translated into political influence within the ruling echelons of Novissimus. Thulathiat's counsel was sought, and her strategic insights were valued. She relished the respect she earned from her peers and superiors, solidifying her position as a key figure in the reshaping of Primis.

As she moved through the conquered territories, Thulathiat witnessed the transformation of once-vibrant societies into obedient subjects of Novissimus. The imposition of Novissimus ideologies, the dismantling of cultural identities, and the enforcement of strict order were all carried out under her watchful eye.

During this triumph, Thulathiat found herself standing at the pinnacle of her career, a beacon of success for others to emulate. The shadows of her maternal upbringing in the matriarchal society of Dharatee seemed distant, replaced by the cold efficiency of a military commander who had achieved victory on a cosmic scale.

For Thulathiat, the triumph was not just in the physical conquest but also in the psychological dominance achieved. The fear instilled in the hearts of the inhabitants, the submission to Novissimus' rule—all of it spoke to her success. She saw herself as a key instrument in the grand design of reshaping the destiny of Primis under the banner of Novissimus.

In the aftermath of the devastation that befell Haree, the Ma'an Su and the bewildered Bhabhi Salaah, their hearts heavy with grief, embarked on a solemn quest amidst the wreckage. The once-grand city, now reduced to ruins, held within its shattered remnants the last hope of their sacred knowledge—the hidden *Book of Brahman*.

Amid the debris and echoes of a once-vibrant civilisation, the Ma'an Su and the Bhabhi Salaah searched for the elusive tome that contained the essence of their faith. The very foundation upon which their spiritual legacy rested was now at risk of being lost forever.

As they scoured the wreckage, their minds called to mind the Litany against Chaos—a sacred invocation passed down through generations. The words of the Litany became a beacon of resilience in the face of overwhelming despair. Recited as if a talisman, each utterance was a fervent plea to Brahman for guidance and protection.

'It is by Brahman alone we set our minds and exercise our faith through our works. Without active faith, we invite chaos and death. Chaos kills faith, making it impossible to please Brahman well, and leaves us as empty vessels. Because whoever approaches Brahman must believe she is and that she becomes our rewarder. So, without our faith in Brahman, who are we? Faithless ones.'

The Litany became a mantra, a source of strength amid desolation. The repetitive recitation served not only as a remembrance of their sacred teachings but also as a shield against the encroaching darkness. The echoes of their voices intermingled with the debris, carrying the essence of their unwavering faith in Brahman.

In those solemn moments, amidst the ruins of Haree, the Litany against Chaos became more than a prayer—it became a testament to the resilience of the Bhabhi Salaah, a declaration of their commitment to preserve the sacred knowledge that defined their existence. Each recitation was a vow to resist the chaos that sought to extinguish the light of enlightenment on Primis.

Amidst the conquered planets and the resounding success of the military campaign led by Ori Alagbara and Thulathiat, the soldiers engaged in fervent conversations, their effusiveness echoing through the victorious ranks.

"Can you believe it, brother?" One soldier exclaimed, slapping another on the back. "We've swept through those planets like a tempest. Novissimus rules supreme!"

"We're part of history now," another chimed in, a glint of pride in his eyes. "The Alqubaeat Alkhadra and General Thulathiat—unmatched in their might!"

The soldiers, emboldened by their triumph, exchanged stories of battles won, planets subdued, and the fear instilled in the hearts of the conquered populations. Laughter and camaraderie filled the air as they revelled in the sense of power that victory bestowed upon them.

"Remember that planet with the rebellious city?" A soldier reminisced. "Thulathiat herself led the charge. The precision of our attacks—they never stood a chance."

"And Ori Alagbara's strategic brilliance," another interjected. "His orders were like poetry, guiding us to victory with every move."

As they spoke, the soldiers took pride in their roles, relishing the idea that they were not just conquerors, but instruments of Novissimus' will. The success of their military campaign became a badge of honour, and their conversations reflected the zeal of those who believed they were reshaping the destiny of Primis.

"Who would've thought we'd be part of something this monumental?" A soldier mused, gazing at the conquered planets on the horizon. "General of the Armies, Ori Alagbara, has brought order, and we're the enforcers of that order."

Amid their animated discussions, the soldiers revelled in the intoxicating euphoria of victory, blissfully unaware of the shadows it cast over the lives of those they had conquered.

As the soldiers continued to revel in the aftermath of their conquest, the camaraderie among them deepened, fuelled by the shared sense of triumph and the belief in their righteous cause.

"We're not just soldiers; we're architects of a new era," one soldier declared, his eyes shining with fervour. "The Alqubaeat Alkhadra and General Thulathiat have paved the way for a Terrestris-dominated future."

Others nodded in agreement, raising their weapons in a symbolic toast to the victories they had achieved. The conquerors, buoyed by their success, felt a growing bond among themselves, united by their roles in reshaping the destiny of Primis.

"The conquered planets will never be the same," remarked a soldier, a victorious grin on his face. "This campaign has brought order, and we are the instruments of that divine order."

The soldiers' conversations echoed with tales of battles won, cities subdued, and the fear instilled in the hearts of the conquered populations. They spoke of their loyalty to Ori Alagbara and Thulathiat, praising their leadership as the guiding force behind their triumph.

"Thulathiat is a true warrior," one soldier proclaimed. "Her squadron, the Alqubaeat Alkhadra, executed every mission with precision. Alagbara has chosen wisely."

The soldiers, caught in the intoxication of victory, relished the idea that they were not merely conquerors but agents of divine will. Each tale of conquest became a testament to their dedication and the righteousness of their cause.

As the discussions continued, the soldiers revelled in the belief that they were forging a new order, erasing the old and ushering in a new world order. Unbeknownst to them, the shadows of oppression and suffering lingered over the conquered planets, obscured by the euphoria of their military success.

Postlude

Terahaveen was a cataclysmic event that brought devastation to the lives of those originating in Primis and subjected them to the oppressive rule of Novissimus. The powerful military might be led by General Ori Alagbara and his niece, General Thulathiat, wreaked havoc on the eight planetarum of Primis. The destruction included the annihilation of universities and libraries and the burning of literature, plunging the inhabitants into intellectual darkness.

Ori Alagbara's imperial ambitions led to the enslavement and suppression of the Primis populace. Libraries and institutions of knowledge were targeted, erasing the cultural and intellectual heritage of the inhabitants. The people faced harsh labour, despair, and the disappearance of family members. The natural world on T'haeri rebelled, refusing to yield produce or support life.

The Bhabhi Salaah, once a beacon of spiritual and intellectual guidance, faced the loss of their sacred knowledge and the desolation of their principal city, Haree. The Litany against Chaos, a sacred invocation, became their source of resilience amidst the ruins. The oppressive rule of the Terrestris cast a dark shadow over the lives of Primis' inhabitants, extinguishing the light of enlightenment and plunging them into a state of despair and hopelessness.

Epilogue

In contemplating the cosmic dilemma presented in the aftermath of *Terahaveen*, I find myself grappling with the question of divine intervention.

Brjamohana, the creator and mother of Srimad-Bhagavatam, possesses the karoobi—a tool that can shape, transform, and renew. The very essence of her divine nature is intertwined with the cycle of creation and rebirth.

As the author, I stand at the crossroads of narrating a story that weaves through the celestial tapestry of Primis. Should Brjamohana exercise her power on behalf of her creation, or does the tapestry itself demand the agency of its woven threads? The delicate dance between free will and divine providence creates a tension that resonates throughout the narrative.

Brjamohana, in her maternal role, represents the nurturing force that gives life to the cosmos. The karoobi, as an extension of her divine capabilities, holds the potential to rectify the upheaval caused by *Terahaveen*. The question emerges: should a mother intervene to protect her children, even when the chaos is partly a consequence of their own choices?

The concept of a deity as a 'mother' raises intricate ethical and metaphysical considerations. If Brjamohana were to step in and reshape Primis, would it undermine the very essence of free will—a fundamental aspect of existence within Srimad-Bhagavatam? The threads of destiny, woven by the choices of beings within the dimension, might lose their significance in the face of divine correction.

Yet, the suffering and despair echoing across Primis tug at the heartstrings of empathy. The oppressed cry out for salvation, and the echoes of the Litany against Chaos resonate in the cosmic silence. The karoobi, in Brjamohana's hands, becomes both a tool of creation and a responsibility—a moral quandary that transcends the boundaries of cosmic governance.

As I navigate the narrative, I grapple with the intricate dance of cosmic forces, pondering whether Brjamohana should embody the archetype of the nurturing mother who mends, nurtures, and protects. The decision holds the weight of universes, and the characters within Primis stand at the precipice of an uncertain fate, awaiting the hand that might reshape their destinies.

Additionally, in reflecting upon Brjamohana's solemn declaration, 'Never again will I subconsciously place into the minds of my children the desire to connect with their galactic siblings,' I find myself standing on the precipice of a profound cosmic revelation. The decision to sever the ethereal ties that bind the denizens of Primis to their galactic brethren is a celestial decree that echoes with a cosmic finality.

As the author, I am privy to the intricate tapestry of relationships, both cosmic and familial, within Srimad-Bhagavatam. The choice made by Brjamohana to withhold the desire for connection speaks volumes about the celestial rifts and cosmic estrangement that have emerged. The threads of kinship that once wove through the dimensions now bear the scars of *Terahaveen*.

The complexity of this divine proclamation extends beyond the realm of mere mortals or the denizens of Primis. It reaches into the celestial bonds between Brjamohana and her twin sister, Shraavana. The dichotomy between the sisters, born of the same cosmic essence, unravels within the cosmic drama. The unwillingness to extend the desire for connection to their galactic siblings reflects the cosmic discord that has befallen the divine sisters.

From the perspective of an only child, the significance of this cosmic rift takes on an emotional resonance. Siblings, whether mortal or divine, share a unique bond—a tapestry of shared experiences, cosmic origins, and intertwined destinies. The decision to withhold this desire for connection not only impacts the denizens of Primis but also casts shadows across the cosmic landscape, affecting the celestial balance.

The estrangement between Brjamohana and Shraavana, mirroring the discord within Primis, highlights the cosmic consequences of *Terahaveen*. The bonds that once connected the cosmic siblings in harmonious resonance have been severed, and the cosmic symphony is now marred by dissonance.

As I contemplate the cosmic drama unfolding, the choice to delve into the why—why Brjamohana refrains from extending the olive branch to Shraavana—reveals narrative rich in cosmic intricacies, familial bonds, and the indelible imprints of Terahaveen upon the very fabric of existence. The cosmic drama will continue to unfold, and the echoes of decisions made ripple through the dimensions, shaping the destiny of Srimad-Bhagavatam.

In the aftermath of *Terahaveen*, as the echoes of destruction reverberate across Primis, the characters stand at the precipice of an uncertain future. The Bhabhi Salaah's recitation of the Litany against Chaos hangs in the air like a plea for divine intervention. The warning not to return carries with it the weight of despair and loss, leaving us to ponder the fate of Mzaliwa and her companions.

As the author, I grapple with the impending resolution. The question lingers: Will Brjamohana, the deity who birthed this realm, step in to rectify the havoc wrought by the Terrestris? Can divine intervention reverse the irreversible, undo the shackles of oppression, and restore the shattered ideals of Primis?

The repercussions of *Terahaveen* extend beyond the physical realm. They reach into the hearts and minds of those who once thrived in a harmonious existence. The intricate dance between chaos and order, creation, and destruction, now teeters on a delicate balance, and the consequences may reshape the very essence of Primis.

In the cosmic tapestry woven by Brjamohana, the resolution lies in the hands of the divine force that birthed this creation. Will the goddess heed the calls of her tormented creation? Will she unfurl her cosmic power to mend the fabric of reality torn asunder by war and oppression?

As the narrative unfolds, it becomes a plea for redemption, a yearning for the restoration of balance, and a hope that the inherent goodness within the cosmos will prevail. The fate of Primis hangs in the delicate balance of divine intervention, a mysterious force that may hold the key to healing the wounds inflicted during *Terahaveen*.

In the continued cosmic silence that follows *Terahaveen*, the characters, both oppressors and oppressed, stand in the aftermath of a world unmade. The once-vibrant civilisations now echo with the sounds of destruction, and the Bhabhi Salaah's dirge reverberates through the desolation.

As the author, I grappled with the complexity of this narrative, questioning the divine dynamics that govern Primis. The Litany against Chaos becomes a symbolic invocation, a desperate plea to the higher forces to restore the delicate equilibrium disrupted by the Terrestris. The Bhabhi Salaah, the spiritual custodians of Primis, recite this dirge as a final resistance against the encroaching chaos.

The fate of Mzaliwa and her companions remains uncertain. Will Brjamohana respond to the cry of her creation, or has the goddess turned away, leaving her children to navigate the consequences of their choices? The interconnectedness of all living beings, woven into the fabric of Srimad-Bhagavatam, now faces the ultimate test.

The cosmic plane, where Jyeshta and Purush transitioned to the Astral Plane, holds the essence of their being. Here, in the mycelial network of divine connection, the hope for redemption resides. Can the collective jeevan of Jyeshta and Purush influence the cosmic balance, inspiring a transformation that transcends the chaos unleashed upon Primis?

The repercussions extend beyond physical devastation; they delve into the realm of spiritual and existential crisis. The narrative becomes a meditation on the interplay between creation and destruction, chaos, and order, with the question of whether divine providence will intercede to mend the shattered tapestry of Primis.

As I continue to explore this story, there is a grappling with the intricate dance of free will and divine intervention. The story becomes a tapestry of cosmic forces, where the goddess Brjamohana holds the threads of destiny. The characters, mere threads in this intricate design, await the unfolding of a cosmic resolution that may reshape the very essence of their existence.

In crafting this sci-fi narrative, I embarked on a journey to reimagine societal structures, governance, and the pivotal role of women in shaping the destiny of their worlds. The decision to centre the story around women governing society emerged from a deep-seated belief in the transformative power of diverse and inclusive narratives.

In our patriarchal reality, where female voices and perspectives are often marginalised, it becomes crucial to explore alternative realities where women hold positions of authority, wisdom, and governance. By placing women at the forefront, the narrative challenges preconceived notions and offers a glimpse into the potential of a balanced and equitable world.

The inclusion of female deities, such as Brjamohana, serves as a deliberate attempt to challenge the dominance of male-centric divine figures. It provides an alternative spiritual perspective that celebrates the feminine, nurturing, and empowering aspects of deity-hood. In a world where religious narratives often reinforce gender hierarchies, introducing powerful female deities becomes a form of resistance and a celebration of divine femininity.

Mzaliwa, Owokuqala, and Thulathiat, the three central female characters, embody different facets of strength, resilience, and leadership. Each character faces unique societal challenges reflective of their respective contexts, yet all share the common thread of overcoming adversity and defying societal norms. Through their stories, I sought to highlight the diversity of women's experiences and the shared strength that binds them together.

The decision to tell a sci-fi story that does not revolve solely around historical traumas, such as the Trans-Atlantic Slave trade, stems from the need to expand the narrative landscape. Brown people have stories beyond the painful chapters of colonisation and slavery. By delving into the realms of science fiction, I aimed to display the richness, complexity, and agency of brown characters navigating futuristic worlds.

This sci-fi novel also serves as a vessel to explore themes of empowerment, resilience, and the intricate interplay between societal structures and the individuals navigating them. Through the characters of Mzaliwa, Owokuqala, and Thulathiat, I aimed to portray the diverse ways in which women assert their agency and contribute to the betterment of their worlds.

Mzaliwa, the ancestral figure, symbolises the roots and heritage that ground individuals in their identity. Her connection to the land and ancestral wisdom becomes a guiding force, reminding us of the importance of cultural preservation and the wisdom embedded in our roots.

Owokuqala, the visionary, embodies the spirit of innovation and progress. Her journey reflects the resilience required to break free from societal constraints and push the boundaries of what is deemed possible. In her pursuit of knowledge and exploration, she challenges the status quo and becomes a beacon of inspiration for future generations.

Thulathiat, the military strategist, highlights the strength and prowess of women in leadership roles. Her triumphs underscore the narrative's exploration of the potential for women to excel in traditionally male-dominated spheres. Through her character, the novel challenges stereotypes and offers a vision of a world where gender does not limit one's capabilities.

The decision to focus on narratives beyond historical trauma is a deliberate choice to expand the storytelling landscape for brown characters. It is an invitation to envision futures unburdened by the shackles of the past and to celebrate the resilience, creativity, and agency of communities that have often been defined by their struggles.

As the author, my aim is to contribute to a growing body of literature that celebrates diversity, challenges norms, and offers glimpses of a more inclusive and equitable future. By weaving together elements of science fiction, spirituality, and societal commentary, this narrative seeks to inspire readers to question, imagine, and envision worlds where everyone's story is heard and celebrated.

In crafting this tale, I hope to contribute to a broader narrative discourse that embraces the multifaceted experiences of marginalised communities. By exploring alternative realities, we can challenge ingrained power structures and offer visions of a future where diversity, equity, and inclusion reign supreme.

Srimad-Bhagavatam
(Planetary System in Anagha)

Cetus sector (Quad 1)

- Aashvi—gemstone is jasper.
  - Mare: is represented by the femina horse, colloquially called ghoda and its people are expert equestrians—The Ashvaarohee.
  - First planetae to be terraform (twentieth century) from a world of gas.
    - The surface is now made up of lush jungles, forests, seas, mountains, and jewel-coloured lakes due to the nutrient-dense gas extracted from the original atmosphere.
    - Due to having three moons, special suits were developed by the Saanvis to reduce the gravitational forces exerted on their slender frames.
    - Later generations were augmented to have a denser bone structure to support the G forces.
    - The Aashvis are toasted almond-pigmented humanoid naturelings, with gold suits accented with turquoise, dark amber eyes, with pointed ears.
- Arunima—gemstone is Ametrine.
  - Glow of Dawn: its planetary crest is the femina owl—Ulloo—and is the seat of wisdom and knowledge.
  - It was terraformed in the twenty-first century to be a pleasant world of grasslands, rivers, and lakes from a world of deserts.
    - An olive, blue, and brown-coloured world with two moons floating in the skies above savannahs of lavender and yellow grasses.

- A normal day lasts 42 standard hours, and a local year lasts 350 local days.
    o The people are descendants of the Naijeeri.
        - The Arunimas are dark red-pigmented transhumanoids, with metal facial augments, platinum pink afro curly hair, pointed ears, with bronze Naijeeri jewellery.
        - Wanting a piece of home on their new planet, The Baobab tree of Surtseyan was successfully transplanted.

Lynx sector (Quad 2)

- T'haeri—gemstone is Cordierite.
    o Bird: its inhabitants built their cities in the clouds, and it is the centre of culture, the arts, and the Bhabhi Salaah—shifted focus to bring back planetary balance due to the Terrestrians' intrusion.
    o It is the only planet not terraformed by the Angrezee—inventors of this technology and the second dominant T'haerian tribe.
    o The populous of the other eight planetarums are the direct descendants of the Bhabhi Salaah and their Saala Ganatantr—stewards who mate for life with the Bhabhi Salaah.
- - Baidya Nath
    o Master of medicines: its people research and develop advancements in bioengineering and augmentation to aid the Angrezee of T'haeri with their terraforming technology.
    o It is a terrestrial world—terraformed around twenty-second century—with a diameter of 11,000 km. Baidya Nath possesses a breathable atmosphere, temperate climate, standard gravity, and a moderate hydrosphere.
        - Baidya Nathian weather is characterised by warm, sunny days separated by long, severe thunderstorms.
        - The surface contains rolling hills, dense forests, lush fields, vast seas, beaches, mountain peaks, and crystal swamps. o Baidya Naths are tall in stature, have olive-tan pigmented electrons, platinum blonde curly wavy hair, pointed ears, ancient Aljeeyars garb, gold headdresses.

Indus sector (Quad 3)

- Budh—terraformed in the twenty-third century; gemstone is Prehnite.
  - Communicators: its inhabitants stick to the ancient way of speaking; thoughts, memories and feelings are communally shared with nature.
  - The Budhs are attuned to their planetae especially after the Angrezee terraformed it to be more hospitable from a harsh desert.
    - The terrain consisted of grassy plains, hills, rivers, and great lakes. Budh maintains a mild and dry climate—due to it being a former desert planetae—throughout most of its 378 local day year, except in the rainy season in spring, which brought torrential downpours that turned the fertile soil into mud.
  - The Gamma travel crystals are harvested from this planetae.
  - The Budhs are copper-haired, warm ivory pigment with red check freckles, turquoise hexagonal forehead jewellery, mint-pigmented eyes, ears with rounded points, wearing traditional Bulifi garb in greys, slate blues, and coppers.
  - Home to Petraea University where students are trained in Gamma travel crystals, architectural imaarats, and planetae-forming tech.
    - Students of Petraea Uni are selected by the Bhabhi after every Aphelion.
- Mangal (Mars)—terraformed in the twenty-fourth century; gemstone is azurite.
  - Sanskrti (Culture): The seat of the Arts, Culture, and Architecture.
  - The ancestral clan is the Sanskrti.
    - The Mangals are maroon-pigmented sentient humanoids with embedded azurite crystals in their facial tribal marks, amber eyes, broad nose, full lips, headpieces made of bronze with azurite and amethyst crystals, full neck chocker necklace with mandala designs, dressed in regal Bordeaux red garb.
  - From space the planetae has the appearance of light blue oceans, plum and copper continents, and bronze swirling clouds.
    - Mangal's surface comprised a vast array of different landscapes, from rolling plains and grassy hills to swampy

- lakes caused by the water-filled network of deep-sea tunnels caused by its pre-existence as an ice covered planetae.
  - The porous crust's natural plasma was harvested for energy and building material and was thought to be the key to many of the planetae's secrets.

Venatici sector (Quad 4)

- Omaja (Spiritual Unity)—terraformed in the second half of the twenty-fifth century; its gemstone is Anyolite.
  - Omajas are dark porcelain pigmented humanoids, with jet-black hair, pointed ears, almond-shaped eyes, hazel-amber eyes and surrealistic solar punk spacesuits in brown with gold and iridescent trimmings.
  - From space the planetae has the appearance of mandarin-coloured oceans, rust-coloured continents and beige clouds.
  - It is a lush, beautiful world with a climate that varies from dense jungles to wide canyons and cliffs. Many of the major continents are dotted with lakes.
- Saanvi (wealth and good fortune)—terraformed in the twenty-sixth century; gemstone is Heliotrope.
  - Home to the merchant clan Tejee se Badhate; children of Maua Maridadi.
  - The planetae was originally rain-soaked, and geologically unstable covered in vast jungles and plagued by violent earthquakes.
    - The Tejee se Badhate terraformed the planet to be more hospitable—having a rainy and dry season, minimising the frequency and intensity of earthquakes cleared out some of the jungles for land development.
    - By the mid-twenty-sixth century, Saanvi became known for its scenic mountain ridges, pristine beach islands, and natural resources of spices and precious gemstones and metals.
- Yahvi—a P. planetae (Heaven/Earth).
  - A small celestial body orbiting Coma in the Venatici Quadrant.
  - It is not a fully formed planetae and therefore is uninhabited.

T'haerian Gyneocracy

In the gyneocracy of T'haeri under the Bhabhi Salaah, women hold the predominant positions of power and influence, shaping the political, social, and cultural landscape. The Bhabhi Salaah, as a Sister Council, is the central governing body, and its organisational structure reflects the principles of a gyneocracy. Here is a detailed description of the gyneocracy in T'haeri:

Political Leadership

Ma'an Su as Head of State: The highest political position is occupied by the Ma'an Su, the leader of the Bhabhi Salaah. She serves as the head of state and holds significant executive powers. The Ma'an Su is chosen by the Haree Hall for life, symbolising the continuity and stability of the gynecocratic leadership.

In the heart of T'haeri, the political landscape unfolded under the nurturing shade of the Haree Hall, a sanctum of wisdom and authority. At its pinnacle stood the revered Ma'an Su, a figure chosen for a lifetime, wielding the sceptre of continuity and stability. Her rule was not just a matter of governance but an embodiment of the profound connection between leadership and the well-being of the people.

The Ma'an Su's tenure, framed by the Haree Hall's solemn rituals and the cosmic dance of the celestial bodies, remained unbroken unless the Rakshak Shreshth, the vigilant guardians, voiced concerns about eroding confidence. Their collective determination could pave the way for a transition, leading to the rise of a new Ma'an Su.

Council of Bhabhi: The Council of Bhabhi consists of the eight Bhabhi representing the eight Padanaam. Each Bhabhi governs her respective Padanaam and contributes to the collective decision-making process. This council reflects a distributed form of political power among the gynecocratic leaders.

Alongside this singular figure of authority, the Council of Bhabhi emerged as a beacon of decentralised governance. Each Bhabhi, representing her distinct Padanaam, contributed to the collective decision-making tapestry. It was a dance of collaboration, where voices harmonised to create policies resonant with inclusivity and representation.

This council, with its diverse array of perspectives, reflected the intricate interplay between the individual and the collective. Through this collaborative process, the Bhabhi Salaah ensured that the political machinery mirrored the cosmic rhythms that governed T'haeri, fostering a society where every Padanaam found its unique voice in the overarching melody of governance. The Council of Bhabhi, a testament to the gynecocratic principles, stood as a bulwark against the concentration of power, fostering a harmonious political symphony that echoed across the Padanaam.

Legal System

Bhabhi Salaah Legal Code: Laws are developed and enforced by the Bhabhi.

Salaah, with a legal code that reflects the values and principles of the Way of Sincerity. The legal system prioritises fairness, justice, and social harmony.

In the sacred halls of justice, the Bhabhi Salaah Legal Code unfolded as a tapestry of ethical threads, interwoven with the values and principles of the Way of Sincerity. Governed by the essence of fairness, justice, and social harmony, this legal code stood as a sentinel of righteousness in the heart of T'haeri.

The Bhabhi Salaah, entrusted with the custodianship of the legal code, meticulously crafted laws that mirrored the celestial order. Each statute was imbued with the spirit of sincerity, reflecting the collective wisdom and compassion of the gyneocracy. The legal system became a manifestation of the Way of Sincerity, a beacon guiding the inhabitants of T'haeri through the labyrinth of moral and ethical complexities.

Judiciary: The judiciary is composed of women who interpret and apply the legal code. The Rakshak Shreshth order, responsible for warning against potential dangers, may have a role in legal oversight, ensuring that the legal system aligns with the gynecocratic principles.

As the laws resonated across the Padanaam, a group of wise women emerged as the guardians of justice—the judiciary. These women, with their discerning minds and compassionate hearts, became the interpreters and custodians of the legal code. In their hands, justice was not a cold and sterile concept but a living force, pulsating with the warmth of empathy and understanding.

Beyond the judiciary, the Rakshak Shreshth order assumed a crucial role in legal oversight. Tasked with the responsibility of identifying potential dangers, they stood as vigilant sentinels, ensuring that the legal system remained aligned with the gynecocratic principles. Their watchful eyes and discerning minds served as a check against any deviation from the path of sincerity and justice.

Together, the legal code, judiciary, and Rakshak Shreshth order formed a harmonious triad, embodying the essence of the Bhabhi Salaah's commitment to righteousness. In this realm of justice, fairness was not a mere concept; it was a living force, intricately connected to the cosmic dance that governed T'haeri. The legal system, like the celestial bodies, moved in synchrony with the rhythms of the gyneocracy, creating a tapestry of justice woven with threads of sincerity and compassion.

Economic Structure

Equal Economic Opportunities: Economic opportunities are accessible to all members of T'haeri, irrespective of gender. The Bhabhi Salaah promotes economic equality, with women holding leadership positions in businesses and industries.

Amidst the bustling economic landscape of T'haeri, the principles of equality echoed through every transaction and business venture. The gyneocracy, under the enlightened guidance of the Bhabhi Salaah, had sculpted an economic system where opportunities were not bound by gender but flowed freely to all members of society.

The concept of economic equality was not an abstract ideal but a tangible reality, manifested in the daily interactions and endeavours of the people. Women, with their entrepreneurial spirit and innovative minds, stood shoulder to shoulder with their male counterparts, contributing to the economic prosperity of T'haeri.

Support for Women Entrepreneurs: Initiatives are in place to support women entrepreneurs, fostering an environment where women can thrive in various economic sectors. Economic policies prioritise gender equality in wages and opportunities.

The Bhabhi Salaah, recognising the importance of diversity and inclusion, implemented initiatives that supported women entrepreneurs. These initiatives were the seeds planted in the fertile soil of equality, nurturing an environment where women could not only participate but thrive in various economic sectors. The vision was clear—to create a society where the richness of ideas and contributions from all genders harmonised to shape a flourishing economy.

In this economic landscape, women assumed leadership positions in businesses and industries, breaking through barriers that once confined them.

The gynecocracy's commitment to gender equality was not a mere slogan but a lived reality, reflected in the diversity of leadership roles occupied by women.

Economic policies, shaped by the principles of the Way of Sincerity, prioritised fairness in wages and opportunities. The scales of economic balance were finely calibrated, ensuring that every individual received their due, irrespective of gender. It was a testament to the belief that true prosperity could only be achieved when all members of society had equal access to economic resources and opportunities.

As the economic heartbeat of T'haeri pulsed with vibrancy, the support for women entrepreneurs resonated like a melody of progress and empowerment. The initiatives championed by the Bhabhi Salaah paved the way for a future where economic equality was not an aspiration but a lived experience for every inhabitant of T'haeri.

Social and Cultural Influence

Education: The Bhabhi Salaah actively shapes educational policies, ensuring that the curriculum emphasises gender equality, inclusivity, and the contributions of women in history, science, and the arts.

Under the watchful gaze of the Bhabhi Salaah, education became a beacon of enlightenment, radiating principles of gender equality, inclusivity, and recognition of women's profound contributions. The gyneocracy actively shaped educational policies, ensuring that the curriculum transcended the constraints of traditional norms.

The curriculum, a living testament to the Way of Sincerity, emphasised not only the historical achievements of women but also their pivotal roles in science, literature, and the arts. The stories of women pioneers echoed through the halls of learning, inspiring generations to come. Students, regardless of gender, were immersed in a diverse and comprehensive education that acknowledged the holistic contributions of all members of society.

The classrooms, once confined by narrow perspectives, became arenas where the seeds of equality were sown. The Bhabhi Salaah's commitment to fostering an environment of intellectual curiosity transcended gender boundaries, allowing every student to explore their potential without the shackles of traditional stereotypes.

Cultural Representation: Women play a significant role in shaping cultural expressions. The gyneocracy encourages diverse representations of women in literature, arts, and media, reflecting the cultural richness of T'haeri.

In the realm of education and culture on T'haeri, the Bhabhi Salaah's enlightened guidance manifested in a tapestry of inclusivity, where gender equality was not only preached but intricately woven into the fabric of knowledge and artistic expression.

In the vibrant tapestry of T'haerian culture, women emerged as central figures in shaping expressions that reflected the diversity and richness of their society. The gyneocracy actively encouraged diverse representations of women in literature, arts, and media, ensuring that cultural narratives mirrored the multifaceted roles women played.

Literature, once dominated by singular perspectives, now embraced the voices of women authors, poets, and storytellers. Their narratives intricately woven the experiences of women into the cultural tapestry, celebrating their achievements, struggles, and triumphs.

The arts, guided by the principle of inclusivity, became a canvas where women expressed their creativity freely. Paintings, sculptures, and performances highlighted the myriad facets of women's lives, breaking away from stereotypical representations and embracing the authenticity of individual experiences.

Media, as a reflection of society, underwent a paradigm shift. Diverse representations of women in films, television, and other forms of media dismantled the limiting narratives of the past. Women were portrayed as leaders, thinkers, warriors, and contributors to the collective journey of T'haeri.

In this cultural renaissance, the Bhabhi Salaah's vision transformed T'haeri into a society where education and cultural expressions harmonised, creating a legacy of enlightenment, inclusivity, and celebration of the multifaceted identity of women.

Military and Defence

Bhabhi Salaah Military Leadership: Women hold key positions in the military, and the armed forces operate with a focus on defence and peacekeeping. The gyneocracy values diplomatic solutions over aggressive military interventions.

Under the guidance of the Bhabhi Salaah, women ascended to key positions within the military hierarchy. The armed forces, traditionally dominated by male figures, underwent a transformation that mirrored the principles of the gyneocracy. Women assumed roles as strategists, commanders, and decision-makers, contributing their unique perspectives to the defence and protection of T'haeri.

The military became a symbol of collective strength, where the diversity of experiences and insights brought by women enriched the strategies employed for safeguarding their society. The Bhabhi Salaah instilled a commitment to defensive capabilities, ensuring that the armed forces were equipped to protect T'haeri from external threats.

Conflict Resolution: The Bhabhi Salaah actively engages in resolving conflicts through dialogue, negotiation, and diplomatic means. The military is seen as a force for peace and protection.

In the realm of military affairs on T'haeri, the Bhabhi Salaah's vision extended beyond traditional notions of conflict and warfare. The gyneocracy redefined military leadership, emphasising principles of defence, peacekeeping, and diplomatic resolution.

The gyneocracy, with its emphasis on peace and harmony, directed the military towards a new paradigm—defence and peacekeeping. Military interventions were reframed as measures to maintain the tranquillity of T'haeri rather than aggressive campaigns of conquest. The armed forces embraced their role as guardians of the realm, committed to preserving the safety and well-being of the T'haerian people.

Peacekeeping missions became a cornerstone of military operations, with women leading efforts to mediate conflicts and maintain stability. The armed forces were trained not only in traditional warfare but also in conflict resolution, negotiation, and diplomatic engagement. The Bhabhi Salaah's philosophy permeated through the ranks, fostering a culture of collaboration and cooperation.

The Bhabhi Salaah actively engaged in diplomatic endeavours to resolve conflicts without resorting to military force. Diplomacy, as a core principle of the gyneocracy, became the primary tool for navigating complex geopolitical landscapes. The Bhabhi Salaah, often acting as chief diplomat, utilised dialogue and negotiation to address disputes, promoting understanding and unity among nations.

Conflict resolution through diplomatic means was prioritised, reinforcing the belief that peaceful dialogue could overcome adversities. The military, when deployed, worked in tandem with diplomatic efforts, ensuring that force was employed as a last resort. T'haeri's reputation as a beacon of peace and rational discourse became synonymous with the gyneocratic values championed by the Bhabhi Salaah.

In this military paradigm, shaped by the principles of the gyneocracy, T'haeri thrived as a society that valued defence, peacekeeping, and diplomatic resolutions—a testament to the transformative leadership of the Bhabhi Salaah.

Family and Social Structure

In this societal framework, the lineage of individuals was determined by their maternal ancestry. The family name, traditions, and cultural heritage were transmitted through the maternal side, reinforcing the importance of women in the continuity of familial identity. This matrilineal descent system served as a tangible manifestation of the gyneocratic commitment to recognising and honouring the role of women in shaping the fabric of T'haeri's society.

Matrilineal Descent: T'haeri follows a matrilineal system where family lineage is traced through the maternal line. Inheritance may pass through female members of the family, reinforcing the gyneocratic principles.

Within the familial structure of T'haeri, the principles of the gyneocracy extended to matters of lineage and inheritance. The matrilineal system dictated that family heritage and ancestry were traced through the maternal line, emphasising the vital role of women in preserving and passing down familial legacies.

Community Welfare: Social welfare and support systems are in place to ensure the well-being of families. Initiatives include maternal and child healthcare, education, and community development, aligning with the gynecocracy's commitment to social harmony.

The gynecocracy's influence permeated beyond individual families into the broader community, where social welfare and support systems were integral components of T'haeri's governance. The commitment to social harmony and the well-being of families manifested in initiatives aimed at fostering a supportive and thriving society.

T'haeri prioritised the health and well-being of mothers and children through comprehensive healthcare programs. Maternal and child healthcare initiatives provided essential medical support, ensuring that women received the necessary care during pregnancy and childbirth. The emphasis on maternal health underscored the gynecocracy's recognition of the crucial role played by women in nurturing future generations.

Educational initiatives formed a cornerstone of community welfare, with a focus on providing accessible and quality education to all. The gyneocracy actively shaped educational policies, ensuring that curricula promoted inclusivity and gender equality. Education became a tool for empowerment, allowing individuals to contribute meaningfully to their communities.

The commitment to social harmony extended to community development projects that aimed to enhance the overall quality of life. Infrastructure, public spaces, and amenities were developed to create environments conducive to communal well-being. The gyneocracy viewed community development as a collaborative effort, fostering a sense of unity and interconnectedness among T'haerian inhabitants.

In summary, the matrilineal descent system and community welfare initiatives were integral components of T'haeri's gyneocracy. The recognition of women's roles in lineage and family continuity, coupled with comprehensive community support programs, contributed to the realisation of a society guided by the principles of social harmony and empowerment. The gynecocratic commitment to inclusivity and equality echoed through both familial and communal structures, shaping T'haeri into a harmonious and flourishing civilisation.

Political Representation and Participation

In the political landscape of T'haeri, the gyneocracy was characterised by the active involvement of women in various leadership roles, demonstrating a commitment to fair representation and addressing historical gender imbalances. The Bhabhi Salaah, as the central governing body, played a pivotal role in shaping political structures that valued inclusivity and equal participation.

Bhabhi Salaah Leadership Roles: Women are actively involved in political offices at various levels. The Bhabhi Salaah emphasises fair representation, and initiatives may exist to address historical gender imbalances in political leadership.

The Bhabhi Salaah prioritised fair representation by actively encouraging and appointing women to political offices at distinct levels. This approach aimed to rectify historical disparities in gender representation, fostering an environment where women's voices and perspectives were integral to the decision-making process. The commitment to fair representation extended beyond symbolic gestures, with concrete initiatives in place to ensure women held significant roles in shaping T'haeri's political landscape.

Recognising historical gender imbalances, the gyneocracy implemented specific initiatives to rectify systemic inequalities. These initiatives may have included targeted programs to identify and groom women leaders, mentorship opportunities, and policies addressing barriers that hindered women's progression in political spheres. By actively working to address gender imbalances, the Bhabhi Salaah aimed to create a political environment reflective of T'haeri's commitment to equality.

Community Engagement: Women actively participate in local governance, contributing to decision-making processes and community development. The gyneocracy promotes inclusivity and diverse voices in political discussions.

The gyneocracy promoted the active participation of women in local governance, fostering a sense of inclusivity and ensuring diverse voices contributed to political discussions. Community engagement became a cornerstone of T'haeri's political fabric, where women played crucial roles in decision-making processes and community development.

Women were encouraged to actively participate in local governance structures, holding positions that allowed them to voice concerns, propose solutions, and contribute to the development of their communities. This approach not only empowered women politically but also enriched the decision-making process with a diversity of perspectives.

Diverse Voices in Discussions: The gyneocracy emphasised inclusivity in political discussions, recognising that diverse voices contributed to well-rounded and comprehensive decision-making. Women's involvement in political discourse ensured that a broad spectrum of perspectives, experiences, and ideas shaped the policies and initiatives undertaken by the government. This commitment to inclusivity aimed to create a political environment where the concerns of all inhabitants were considered and addressed.

In summary, the leadership roles within the gyneocracy of T'haeri reflected a commitment to fair representation and inclusivity. Women actively participated in political offices at various levels, and initiatives were in place to address historical gender imbalances. Community engagement ensured that women played vital roles in local governance, contributing to the holistic development of T'haeri's political and social spheres. The gynecocracy's emphasis on equal participation shaped a political landscape where diversity and inclusion were celebrated as essential elements of a harmonious and progressive society.

Religious and Spiritual Practices

Bhabhi Salaah Influence on Religion: The Bhabhi Salaah plays a significant role in religious institutions, influencing spiritual practices and interpretations of religious texts. The gyneocracy promotes inclusive and respectful religious practices.

Spiritual Guidance: The spiritual guidance provided by the Bhabhi Salaah aligns with the gynecocratic principles, emphasising values such as empathy, cooperation, and social justice. Religious practices foster unity and understanding among the people of T'haeri.

In summary, the gyneocracy of T'haeri under the Bhabhi Salaah is characterised by women holding leadership positions across various domains. The governance structure reflects a commitment to gender equality, social harmony, and the well-being of the community. The Bhabhi Salaah, as the central governing body, shapes the cultural, political, and economic fabric of T'haeri in alignment with the principles of a gyneocracy.

Glossary

1. Praaniyon: creatures.
2. Srimad-Bhagavatam: 'Story of the Fortunate One', also the name of the planetary system found in the Primis dimension.
3. Advena: stranger; foreigner not like the T'haerians; not a child of Brjamohana.
4. Dharma: the eternal and inherent nature of reality, the cosmic law underlying the right behaviour and social order.
5. Shravan: listening or hearing.
6. Naabhik: nucleus or heart.
7. Taakat: active force; power.
8. Planetarum: Latin for planets; the plural form.
9. P. planetae: Latin for dwarf planet.
10. Jetha: firstborn.
11. Al'awrasiu: utero.
12. Amar: a council of forty members called the immortals; they live on the planet Mangal.
13. Bhabhi Salaah: Sister Council; composed of only 8 women that originated from the planet T'haeri; must pass the Antim Pareekshan to obtain the title Bhabhi.
14. Ma'an Su: Superior Mother; the highest rank in Bhabhi Salaah; a title given to the firstborn of Jyeshta and Purush.
15. Rakshak Shreshth: Superior Guard, a rank within the Bhabhi Salaah order; these are sisters who do not pass the ritual poisoning ceremony.
16. Ma'an Seat: Mother Seat; after the reorganisation of the Bhabhi Salaah this became the highest rank within the order; holders of this seat must be raised by the Vihaars.

17. Kainanis: or Canoness; the lowest rank within the Bhabhi Salaah order; the scribes and write down the oral history of Brjamohana; pledge a life of poverty.
18. Bauddh: a local place of worship in Brjamohana.
19. Vihaars: or Abbess; the rank above Kainanis; chosen by their respective houses to stand for the interests of the group in the Haree Hall; responsible for starting meetings and voting on important matters; also raise the Ma'an Seat.
20. Padanaam: a house that has a Rakhane vaale, Vihaar, and Kainanises; each has its own representative colour.
21. Rakhane vaale: or Keepers; the second highest rank in the order; maintainers of the secret files and library of the Haree Tower; she is the aide to the Ma'an Seat.
22. Antim Pareekshan: is a character test designed to test each apprentices correct use of taakat.
23. Saala Ganatantr: or Brother Republic; these are male stewards of the Bhabhi Salaah; their purpose is to be a lifelong mate once selected by a Bhabhi; ranking order: Sankalak (lowest), Saamant, Sena (highest).
24. Sankalak: or Compiler; theses are scientists, responsible for researching and developing intergalactic and extradimensional technologies, supporting the Saala Ganatantr scientific knowledge.
25. Saamant: or Knights; the second highest rank within the Saala Ganatantr order; these smiths maintain the armoury and technology, making repairs and supplying technical support.
26. Sena: or Elders; the highest ranking and combat force; these are the decision-makers of the order and figure out the secular focus of the Ganatantr.
27. Litany against Chaos
    [a] *It is by Brahman alone I set my mind and exercise my faith through my works. Without active faith, I invite chaos and death. Chaos kills faith, making it impossible to please Brahman well, and leaves me as an empty vessel. Because whoever approaches Brahman must believe she is and that she becomes their rewarder. So, without my faith in Brahman, who am I? A faithless one.*
28. Aatma jeev: celestial order of beings.

29. Saaraapi: the highest rank within the Aatma jeev order; are stationed in front of Brjamohana's and Shraavana's thrones.
30. Karoobi: the second highest rank; transport Brjamohana and Shraavana throughout space.
31. Devadi: the lowest rank; used to create all living life forms.
32. Rita: cosmic law.
33. Jetha: firstborn child.
34. Svargeey dharma.
35. Brahmacharya: first stage; a person who completely controls their body and mind through ascetic means.
36. Grihastha: second stage; being occupied with home and family.
37. Vanaprastha: third stage; typically marked with the birth of grandchildren, gradual transition from home responsibilities to caring for the next generation.
38. Sannyasa: fourth and final dharma stage; disinterest and detachment from material life, whose purpose is spent in peaceful and spiritual pursuits.
39. Sampoornata: celestial perfection.
40. Sva-dharma: the sum of one's life moulded by one's tendencies, personality, desires, and experiences.
41. Iya: mother.
42. um dhukir: male mother; the brother of the male child's mother is required to care for his nephew.
43. Qafil: avunculate; a special relationship between a nephew and his maternal uncle.
44. Arjuani ododo: Purple flower.
45. Almutasilin: communicators.
46. Alsalam ealayna: a colloquial phrase used to mean *Peace be upon us.*
47. Jeevan: the life force of all living organisms.
48. Taliba: female students selected during the Perihelion to become part of the Bhabhi Salaah.
49. Talib ealmaniun: female students selected during the Aphelion to attend Petraea University.
50. Walgelijk: disgusting; the adjective given to the augmented humanoids in Srimad-Bhagavatam.

51. Walgelijk: disgusting; the adjective given to the augmented humanoids in Srimad-Bhagavatam.

Endnotes

[1] The number twenty-eight is a perfect number because all its factors, including 1 and excluding itself, equal to twenty-eight. 1, 2, 4, 7, 14 equals to 28. Additionally, it stands for the superior or higher when used in conjunction with other numbers. It can also symbolize the divine life purpose.

[2] The number twenty-seven is a perfect power number because it is an integer that can be resolved into equal factors, and whose root can be exactly extracted. It symbolizes new beginnings and inner strength. In context with the number twenty-eight, twenty-seven is one short of twenty-eight denotes something incomplete or flawed in Brahman's eyes.

[3] T'haerian Gyneocracy was an all femina government that dictated the daily life, spiritual education, and technological advancement of society. The male stewards (Saala Ganatantr) were conferred solely in the realm of science and innovation and were the secular instructors.